ARYA MATTHEWS

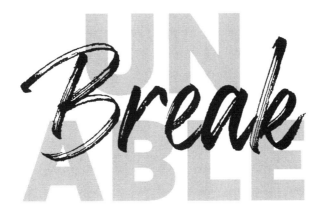

RELUCTANT HEARTBREAKERS & SWEET TROUBLEMAKERS

INKED
KEYBOARD
PUBLISHING

unBREAKable
Reluctant Heartbreakers & Sweet Troublemakers vol. 2

Published by Inked Keyboard Publishing.

hello@inkedkeyboard.com

ISBN 978-1-7332386-5-6 (ebook)
ISBN 978-1-7332386-7-0 (paperback)

Book, cover, and additional graphic design by Varvara Jones @ Inked Keyboard Publishing.

This is a work of fiction. Characters, names, events, and dialogue are products of the creator(s)'s vision and are not to be perceived as real. Any likeness or similarity to existing persons, products, or events is purely accidental.

Fearlessness

Inspiration

Freedom

Inner Strength

Loyalty

The Thunder Master

CJ

A good song sets the crowd on fire.

As long as the band members have what it takes.

Judging by this lit audience, my band has what it takes. Project Viper has been number one on every alternative rock chart for close to two years now. Although, the ratings are not why I pick up a guitar and surrender my life to the hysterical audiences hungry for music and my body. It's the bite of the strings, the pressure of the in-ear monitor, and the oppressive heat of the venue air swirling with fog. Sometimes, when the colored beams hit me just right, I think, "That's not green. That's E flat on the A string, sixth fret." It's also the posters in the hands of the girls on the very front row. They may be behind chest-high metal dividers and surveyed by former-military-turned-private-security hulks, but that doesn't stop the sweet darlings from waving their confessions with all their might. Such innocent devotion. It fills my heart with the kind of sympathetic sadness for their desperate youth that keeps me writing songs.

Hanging out at the edge of the stage, behind the bright orange grip tape, I'm suspended in the best place in the world. Really, this is the feeling I wait for at every show. I have to chase it, a surfer with the wave, but I always catch it. The stadium ahead of me chants the lyrics from our last song of the set, *All Your Broken Promises*, while Marshall's relentless but smooth baritone and Graham's drumbeats pour over me from the massive speakers in the back. The bass line caresses my skin, the familiar temptress, drawing my eyes to Alexandra, our new Thunder Master. This festival is her first show with us. She's on fire, same as me, same as every one of the rest of my bandmates. Alexandra's body is attuned to every beat, surrendered to the flow of music as her fingers spark dark magic that brings the bass guitar to life. She'll never be the same again.

The thought slaps a huge grin onto my face. I've wanted Alexandra to taste this buzz since the day she started with us. It's worse than any drug. It's better, too. I need her to love this so she'll stay.

As soon as Marshall offers to share the mic with her during the last chorus, I know she's hooked. Alexandra may have a soft spot for him, but with her eyes closed, hands on that bright red axe of hers, she's done for. I see the real spell possessing her heart, and it's not my best friend. She's head over heels with our element—the stage.

Our rhythm guitarist Shane and I saunter toward the center of the stage from opposite sides and sandwich our bassist and singer as the song comes to a close. The last two measures are perfect to wrap the set, four quarter-length chords and a long, crackling A. We use no pyrotechnics tonight, but the effect on the audience is the same—hands in the air, whistles, cheers, and chants for more. I would've happily played an encore, but we're on a strict schedule with other bands waiting their turn. A lot of them already hate us for our popularity.

"Well, that was awesome," I say, holding a button on my earpiece to limit the output to my team only.

Alexandra whirls around to face me, long, black hair sailing through the air. Her chest heaves with exhilarated breaths, but there's no way her elation can match mine. I've been Project Viper's bassist for six years before she arrived. And it's not that I hated it—

"That totally didn't blow!" Zach jumps on my back from behind, clamping his long arms around me.

I let my guitar hang on its strap and grab his legs under his knees. He wants a piggyback ride? Fine. The fans will love it, and this isn't the first time I carried him off the stage like this. Still I yell, "You want to break my back? A little warning or something."

"That would ruin all the fun." Zach jumps off me as soon as we're backstage. "*Matryoshka*! You did it!" He swoops Alexandra into a suffocating hug.

Our stylist stuffs a black towel into my hands, and I wipe the sweat off my forehead. Cheers and sobs cling to my back, the best reward I could ever ask for. These waves of approval and demand used to be what I needed the most at first. The crowds, the attention, the awards—proof I'm not as worthless as everyone set me out to be. Then I learned that music is the air I need to breathe.

I always suspected that, so when my path crossed with that of the other guys, I knew we were meant to be a band. Everyone had a spark, a zing that made Project Viper a no-brainer. Marshall's got one heck of a voice and overabundant charisma. Graham's gifted with the steadiest hands made to hold drumsticks. Zach's one of those Asian whiz kids with piano embedded into his DNA, and Shane... Shane has rhythm, a hatred for being left behind, and the most mulish kind of perseverance the rest of us wish we had. He also absolutely refused to be the bassist when we were divvying up the band roles. That's how I ended up with the bass, not with the only thing in my life I can truly call my girlfriend—the guitar. I had to choose between being picky or having a band with my favorite people. I chose the band and took up the bass.

We high five everyone we can.

"Six Vipers? It works." Marshall drapes his towel over his neck.

"You didn't think it would," I say to him.

"Yes, yes. Go ahead. Rub it in. I'm the pessimist and the unbeliever. But you already knew that—" His voice catches as he glances at Alexandra, who seems to be in a bit of a trance while she poses for a photo with a bunch of teens lucky enough to get a backstage pass. Her huge smile barely covers up the shock splashed all over her face. I remember it. Our first full arena left me flapping in disbelief, fish-out-of-water style, as well.

As the chaos simmers down, we get dinner and watch the other bands from one of the VIP balcony booths—it's only good manners to stay and support your fellow artists.

"You crazy son of a bass." Shane drops in a chair next to me, a heap of salad nearly toppling off his aluminum bowl. "You pulled it off. *We* pulled it off." He glances over his shoulder at Alexandra.

"I know." I stick a spoonful of cilantro rice into my mouth and wait for the relief that comes after accomplishing something long in coming and arduous.

All I feel is exhaustion. It's the nerves. We were all too wound up prior to this gig, and now there's nothing but the lingering did-we-really-do-it kind of tension. Six months ago, I declared I wouldn't play bass anymore and that we needed to find someone else. The guys knew for a long time how I felt, and they had mercy on my sorry skin. The way Alexandra joined the band, though, was a bit…unconventional. She was literally handed to us by our recording label. *You want to have a new bassist? This is your one and only choice.* Of course it wasn't, but we went along with it. Or most of us went along with it, anyway. Marshall was not a fan of Alexandra at all at first, but she grew on him. A lot. On all of us.

Alexandra makes her way to a seat in the row ahead of me.

"Fiona's fending off everyone who wants to talk to me for a couple of minutes." She drops into a padded blue chair, exhales, and stares at the ceiling. "This isn't real."

Both Shane and I chuckle.

"Soak it in," I say.

Her gaze settles on me, calm and…dark. A worry that I was wrong about Alexandra falling in love with show business places its sticky claw on my shoulder.

"You okay?" I ask.

"Thank you. For giving me this chance." She presses her lips tight and fans her face with her hands.

Too cute.

I set my food on a seat next to me and climb over to sit next to Alexandra and hug her. Shane clears his throat and gives me a look that might as well be saying, *Marshall's gonna have an aneurism.* That's fine with me because in the book of my relationships, Alexandra occupies the line that belongs to the little sister. She's my fierce bass successor and the girl who gave me back my dream. I owe her forever, and I will protect her forever, but I will never love or want her *that* way. Alexandra is Marshall's heart's agony, and she loves him. I will never disrupt their Happily Ever After. Not after what it took us all to get there. But that won't stop me from being there for her.

Sitting with Alexandra this close to me finally brings the relief I've been waiting for. From now on she will play bass, I'll wield the guitar, weave melodies that haunt me in my sleep, and put an end to the unrest that's been festering in my chest for months and months.

Nothing to Fix

Fiona

2 weeks later

Silence is my favorite.

I work as a manager's assistant for one of the largest bands in the world, and I love music, but silence is beautiful. It allows me to hear the intimate slither my pencil lead creates as it slides on paper. I also love the *shick-shick-shick* of the eraser and the gummy bits it leaves behind. Blowing away the mess and starting over is so satisfactory. There are no mistakes I can't fix when I work with pencils. Nothing is permanent.

This morning my workload is minimal. My boss, Kiera, is out of the office, and I'm left behind to answer phones and emails. Later I'll head out to a fundraiser, but for now, I'm relishing this lull in the insanity. There has been plenty. Project Viper, the music superstars we're in charge of, have been in the media non-stop for the last two weeks. When an all-dude band says they're going to add a girl to their ranks, public attention skyrockets. This is the first day since the announcement that I'm able to do something for myself. Even at home, I've been monitoring emails and sending out press releases, and not drawing. Which, of course, made it so that I want to draw all the more, and the stories in my head won't keep quiet. They're only louder when I have no time to jot them down.

There's one, itsy-bitsy *but* in the mix. Along with the joy of having time to work on my comics, I once again have the skin-crawling pleasure of waiting to hear from my agent. My project, *Dimensions of Darkness*, has been on submission with the publishers for the last four months. I know I should be patient. I'm a debut artist and have minimal following, but I believe in my art, and my story is solid. If not, I wouldn't have an agent. But ugh.

I look out at the window and tap the pencil against my open palm.

What if no one acquires my story about a night-vision-impaired former detective hunting supernaturals in their natural habitat, the darkness?

I shake my head to chase the doubts away. I shouldn't let myself fall into the hole of dwelling on the success of my comic book. It leaves me vulnerable and feeling like everyone else around me is already there while I'm still playing in the sandbox. It'll sell. I've been working on the six-volume collection for the last five years. It's been through countless reviews, critiques, beta reads. You name it. Even my brother, Xavier, likes it, and to get him to like a comic book is something extraordinary. We share an affinity for fine arts, but he's incredible when it comes to realistic renderings of pretty much anything while I live in the realm of comic book art.

I push away from the table and walk to a mini fridge in the corner for a bottle of juice. Sharing an office with my boss has a lot of perks—snacks, easily adjustable room conditioning, cushy chairs, and good art on the walls, including a painting of a mist-shrouded lake in the warm orange and brown hues of the fall. That one is Xavier's. After Kiera bought it from him, he stopped saying my job is weird.

I take a sip and smile. He also almost stopped saying I'm wasting my time here.

My phone buzzes in my back pocket. It's time to head to the fundraiser. I hurry through the rest of the juice and shove my drawing supplies and sketchpad into my shoulder bag.

A couple of loud and confident knocks on the door make me jump, then Elise's head pops through the open door. "Ready to go?" She's the Vipers' stylist and Shane's girlfriend of almost five years.

I pick up a folder with schedules and contracts and waivers, reviewed and signed by all necessary parties, from the corner of my desk. "Ready."

"Great. We saved a spot for you in the company van."

"Glamorous," I sing out. Riding in the brand new van is much better than being cramped with all of Elise's gear in her tiny Echo.

Before I lock the office door, I check for messages one last time— no deviations from the plan or last-minute staff substitutions. That's another reason why I had a quiet morning. Now it's the time for the best kind of chaos.

The fundraiser is a local event to support a network of children's hospitals specializing in cancer research and treatment. Project Viper does several events like this every year, and it's not exactly a concert, but tickets are offered to the general public. At special pricing, of course, and only a few. The event will be streamed online, and even though the band will only be doing a short interview, playing a few silly games with the host, and singing one song, the whole support team arrives. A small sound crew, the stylist, the photographer, and me. My job is to make sure no one aggravates the band or ropes them into anything outside of contract obligations, and, in turn, that no one in Project Viper throws a tantrum.

"Are you still nervous?" I ask Alexandra when the band arrives on location, an exhibit hall converted into a filming set. We take one of the smaller conference rooms to get ready for the cameras, and the guys look like they couldn't care less about what's happening. They're bantering and talking about some synthesizer equipment Zach thinks they should try. No nerves. They've done this dozens of times before, but Alexandra's new. She has been in my care since she arrived seven months ago, and I still worry about her.

"Not nervous," Alexandra says with a smile, then adds, "maybe a little. You all keep saying I'm doing great, but I'm terrified of that moment when I'll finally screw up and everyone will see me for the incompetent fool that I am."

"You're not incompetent, and you're not a fool." I rub her shoulders.

"Listen to Fiona." CJ Sanchez joins us.

The way he crosses his arms on his chest accentuates every muscle in his lean, toned body. As always, he's generous with his body spray. The fresh scent always reminds me of warm nights on the beach, but I refuse to succumb to the heady feeling it creates. I've been around these guys for too long to get carried away or to forget my job. I do, however, like the swoop of his bleach-tipped hair today. I might fix it on CJ's latest sketch for my Project Viper collection.

"Everyone doing well today?" I ask him.

CJ nods, two silver earrings in the top of his left ear clinking against each other. It's the most subtle sound, but I catch it and stash it in my mental catalog of interesting details to add to my sketches.

"No fear," I tell Alexandra, whose distant eyes betray the storm of worries raging in her head. "And I've got your back."

"What about my back?" CJ has the gall to *try* and dazzle me with one of the smiles he saves for the girls he dates.

Dating is a very generous description of what CJ does. One or two dinners. Some of them manage to keep his attention for a month, but he's always on the prowl, and I hate it when he uses his tricks on me. He flirts with me out of habit, not because he thinks I'm pretty or special.

I have actually gone out with him once. We were supposed to accompany Marshall and Alexandra to an opera performance, but she got sick that evening, so it ended up being just CJ and me. It couldn't have been considered a date, though. CJ smiled and teased and took me to a fancy restaurant afterward, but he never tried to kiss me or anything. In a sense, I got a lot less than his usual "girlfriends." It broke me a little back then. I'm the manager's assistant. A friend, at best. I'm not sure I'm even that. Either way, I won't let him break me again. No matter how much I may be attracted to him. No matter how much he gets into my head.

"You know I have your back," I say to CJ. "Always. That's the only reason I'm here, Cristian." To solve any and all problems that may stand in your way and watch your pretty, blue eyes throw daggers at me for the use of your full first name.

"I see." CJ grins. "You're in a mood today. I won't participate."

Shame. I love the way his eyebrows come together when he glares.

"Mr. Sanchez won't be part of the show?" The event organizer pops over. "Is something wrong?"

I smile at the already harried man with crooked glasses. "I'm sorry. We were just joking. Everything's good. He'll do everything you need him to do."

The organizer breathes out and rushes away in search of other fires to put out.

"Why are you always such a troublemaker?" CJ takes a step toward me.

Me? I hold his challenging gaze. "Pot, kettle. The Label wants to see some demos by the end of the summer. How's that coming along?"

CJ runs his hand through his hair and glances to the side. "They'll have their demos."

Usually, he's more than eager to talk about music and what he's working on. This reluctance rings alarm bells in my head.

"Hey, Alexandra, I think Elise is ready for you." I nudge Alexandra toward their stylist. After she leaves, I ask CJ, "Anything I can do?"

His smile returns, and it feels grateful. "Probably not, but thanks. I wasn't doubting you earlier. I know you got my back. Our backs. I was trying to get you to smile. You're too dang serious all the time."

"I'm not too serious. And I do smile."

"I'll believe it when I see it," CJ replies, pointing at my mouth.

I swat his hand away. "I'll smile when I want to, not when you tell me to."

He laughs, I want to as well, but I won't on principle.

"I saw it," CJ says.

"Saw what?"

"Your smile. Lurking in the corner. This one." He taps his fingertip next to the right corner of my lips.

I don't know how, but I manage to not lean into that lightning-fast touch. What is wrong with me? The only thing CJ's interested in when it concerns me is to rile me up. "You saw nothing. Now go. Work." I will do the same. Work and not play around with this unapologetic heartbreaker.

CJ starts walking away, but as he does, he says, loud enough for everyone to hear, "You're no fun, but I'll fix it."

"There's nothing to fix," I snap back.

He throws me another one of his blinding smiles, but something tells me he's serious.

I whirl away from him and stomp off to check with the sound

crew, sudden nerves wracking through me. Since when does CJ Sanchez notice how much I smile?

I Don't Mind

CJ

We end up playing some of the cheesiest party games in existence. Zach is blindfolded and entrusted with lipstick to give Alexandra a makeover. Graham and Marshall speed eat small pies, but underneath the fluffy whipped cream is beef-flavored Jell-O. They gag and promise murder with their glares, but they still laugh with the rest of us, and the streaming numbers spike through the roof, along with the donations.

Shane and I go through five rounds of…? You guessed it. Never Have I Ever. All questions have been crafted to only mention the things the two of us have never-ever done. The punishment? Four shots of lime juice followed by a shot of hot sauce for the last question. Shane doubles with laughter when he's presented with the demonic-looking red shot glass. The streaming team and the organizers have been on the floor the whole time. I'm glad they're having fun. My eyes are watering, my mouth's on fire, and I swear there's a pit of lava in my stomach.

"Made you smile," I tell Fiona after it's over and before we do our one song. The organizers had mercy on us and gave me and Shane fifteen minutes to recover our senses. A YouTube gamer entertains the crowd meanwhile.

Fiona's not even trying to stop laughing as she hands me an individually wrapped square of dark chocolate. "Okay, you win."

"I'm never doing that again." I cough, strip open the chocolate, and stuff the whole square into my mouth. The bitter sweetness soothes the raw fire in my throat. I'm so happy I don't have to sing backup anymore. I wouldn't be able to.

"I don't think I could've done that," Alexandra says as the rest of my bandmates join us.

Fiona hands them chocolate as well. "Don't relax too much," she warns. "You're not done here yet."

She's such a dictator. Same as Kiera, our actual manager, but Kiera at least knows when to let us play. Fiona tends to stick to the schedule. Stay alert, be on your best behavior, and don't even think of having fun. Her strict, gray slacks and white shirt drive that image home. However, her clothes can't diminish her confident beauty. Alexandra once told me she thought Fiona was a model when she first met her. Fiona could be. She's the definition of gorgeous—slim and poised, golden-brown skin and hazel eyes that have orange flecks in the irises. Yes, I've noticed them. We've shared many staring matches. And I know she can be fun when she relaxes a little. Why is she so uptight all the time?

I sneak another piece of chocolate from the bag in Fiona's hands. Peeling the chocolate out of its wrapper, I say, "They call Charlie the Social Media Harpy. What should we start calling you? The Viper Tyrant?"

Fiona raises one eyebrow at me. "Hot sauce get to your head?"

Biting on the chocolate, I refuse to give her the pleasure of another staring game. She's goaded me before. She's doing it now. I hope she'll do it again, but ever since we got here, I can't seem to get into the right mindset. I love public stuff like this, for charities or not. Today, though, something is missing.

I rub my face. I could be imagining it. I didn't sleep last night. A line of a lyric kept blasting through my thoughts and wouldn't leave me alone until I got up and put it onto paper. Then music came. Then I had to make a quick demo of it. Then it was morning.

Fiona watches me, and I feel like I've missed a question or something. That's right. I never gave her any kind of a comeback for that hot sauce comment. "You can have this round," I say and turn away. We'll play another time.

Taking a swig from his water bottle, Marshall gives me a curious look. I shrug. So I flirt with Fiona here and there. What we have is all just for fun. I took her out on a date once. She didn't seem impressed.

The organizers get animated at the entrance to the filming set. A small crowd parts and out comes Aiya Mori, the rising queen of pop music. Hips clad in glittering shorts, black tank top with a massive print of a white tiger covering her upper body, Aiya sashays toward us as if she's the ruler of the land and we've been waiting for her all this time. I subdue a chuckle. Get in line, Aiya. You're not the only diva here.

"What a nice surprise." Her voice is light and almost child-like as she clasps her hands in front of her and bounces up and down. "I've been dying to see you guys again."

Alexandra shoots me a curious glance and mouths, "Again?"

Behind me, Fiona mutters, "She hasn't changed one bit."

Before any of us can greet Aiya back, she grabs Alexandra's hands and pulls her away from us. Both Marshall and I reach for our bassist but grasp empty air.

"So the rumors are true. You broke the bros." Aiya presses her cheek to Alexandra's face and looks at us. "Which one is yours then? Hold on. That was the wrong question. Which one can I have?"

Graham walks away. He probably can sense what's coming next and decides to skip on the delicious but unnecessary drama.

Slowly, Alexandra moves her face away and stares Aiya down. Up, that is, because although both of them are quite short, Aiya's playing with her height by means of daring heels. When the pop star finally looks back at Alexandra, my feisty bass princess says, in the flattest tone imaginable, "They're all mine."

Aiya pouts, "Greedy," and squishes Alexandra's cheeks between her palms. "But you're so cute, I forgive you. Just this once."

Alexandra pushes away. I'm surprised she lasted that long. "Who the heck are you?"

I pull Alexandra under my arm and explain, "A female version of Zach." Only less good-natured.

"Project Viper, you're on in five minutes," one of the people on the set calls out.

Alexandra storms away without another glance at Aiya. Marshall goes with her.

"She really is cute." Aiya laughs and ever so casually drapes one arm around my waist. "I can see why you couldn't resist her. But how many times do you want me to beg for one tiny, little single? It'll be good, guys."

Our eyes meet, but her gaze doesn't linger on my face. It travels all over me, without any restraint.

"What do you think?" Aiya asks once more. She has been nagging us for months to work on something together. It would be good for her career to collaborate with a band of our caliber. It probably wouldn't hurt us either, but we've been extra busy.

Oh! I could give her the song I wrote last night. It doesn't fit our usual repertoire, but it could work for her. Maybe it'd get her to leave us alone, although I wouldn't say she bothers me *that* much.

A strong hand pushes me in the back.

"The techs are going to have a heart attack if you don't get your butt to the set right now. You know how they are." Fiona gives me and

Aiya an easy smile, as if suggesting that being ready for the show is a ridiculous thing. She's sure full of tricks.

Aiya folds her arms on her chest. "Don't even start. Everyone's always so hung up about the schedules. Thirty seconds won't ruin everything."

They could, actually, but I say, "Nice to see you, Aiya. I'll be in touch." I may have a song for her, but it still needs work, and I'm not going to give her any hope until I'm sure about every single note.

Fiona nudges me again.

"I'm coming. Coming. Will you relax? She only asked for a collab."

Walking beside me, Zach snorts a laugh. "Aiya may have asked for a collaboration, but that's not what she wants."

Shane waggles his eyebrows. I scowl at them and wave for them to go ahead. It's none of anybody's business what I do or who I do it with. They hurry on, laughing.

"Zach's right," Fiona says, her tone is the kind most people use with children. "Music is the last thing on Aiya's mind. With you, at least."

"I figured." Aiya draping her whole body against me was a pretty clear hint. "I don't mind."

"Of course you don't."

"You think I'm shallow for enjoying someone pretty?"

"CJ, you don't have time for collaborations. Have you seen your schedule for the next four months? No? Let me show you." She sticks her hand into her bag and pulls out an iPad.

I swipe it out of her hands. "I know the schedule, and yet we'll sleep, eat, indulge our hobbies, and do whatever else we want. You're just as territorial as Alexandra, admit it."

"It's not my job to be territorial. My job is to make sure you have no distractions. And trust me, you get plenty distracted. You don't need Aiya right now—"

"I know that. I don't need Aiya at all, but that's not for you to decide." I return the iPad and ignore Fiona's disapproving expression.

I don't *need* anyone.

Chin Up & Keep Sketching

Fiona

Nia throws a handful of scrambled eggs on the floor. You'd think by the age of two and a half she'd be over offering sacrifices to the floor gods. Not so.

"Nia," I say in a strict voice, "are you doing a good thing?"

My niece giggles. "No-o-o."

"That's what I thought. Are you done with your food, then?"

She stuffs a handful into her mouth. Her fork is sitting right there, next to her plate, still untouched, but Nia's too dang cute for me to be upset with her for longer than five seconds. I pick up the fork and offer her a bite. She opens wide and makes loud chewing noises.

My phone rings. It's my boss. I put her on the speaker—she's used to me talking with Nia around. In fact, Kiera's been heaven sent as far as employers go. She allows me quite the flexible hours because of Nia, who I watch until my brother gets home from his graveyard shift and often while he catches up on sleep as well.

"Heads up, I'm still on nanny duty," I warn Kiera as I scoop some eggs with my fork.

"No problem. I just have a quick question for you. We're finalizing the summer tour in Europe for the guys, and I thought it'd be good for you to go with them. You know how we talked about you seeing a few other sides of the business? The tour manager, Rick Valencio, you know him? Well, he said he'll let you be his shadow. What do you think?"

Nia's fingers dig into what remains of her food, and there's that cunning glimmer in her eye. I should probably stop her, but my thoughts are crashing against the rock of Kiera's question.

"Go on tour as the assistant tour manager?" I swallow. I'm not qualified for that.

"Not exactly. Rick already has a guy. Like I said, they're willing to let you shadow them and do a few easy tasks. Really, you'd be with Project Viper in your usual capacity—make sure the band is comfortable and follow them to shows and interviews, but you'll get to learn how tours work in the process— One second. Yes, James. Yes, that's the one."

It's Kiera through and through, talking to multiple people at once.

Nia changes her mind and lets go of her food, and I slide the plate out of her reach. She throws me a scowl, I return it, then allow myself a few seconds to mull over Kiera's offer.

Pros: a summer in Europe, hanging out with Project Viper in their natural habitat, being there for Alexandra should something go haywire, and adding a few more impressive lines to my resume. Tempting. Very tempting.

The cons...?

"How long would we be gone?" I ask Kiera and point a warning finger at Nia who stands on the chair and reaches for her plate across the table. Then Xavier walks into the kitchen. I can't take this phone call in peace, it seems.

I cover the speaker. "It's my boss. Hold on." Leaving Nia to hug and kiss and squeal with him, I weave my way through the toys in the living room to the balcony. It's on the east side of the building, and the early morning sun greets me with its yet tender rays. I lean on the railing and watch the leaves rustle in the light morning breeze. A cat jumps on a railing of the building across the street, stretches, then walks over to the side with a tall potted plant to paw at its leaves.

"June through August, so almost three months. All expenses paid, of course. How does that sound?"

Kiera can't possibly expect me to give her an answer right away. She knows I have obligations.

"How much time do I have to think about it?"

"I need your answer tonight at the latest."

I pinch the bridge of my nose and squeeze my eyes shut. No pressure. Twelve hours should be enough to make a complicated decision, right? Based on my experience, Kiera would say it's more than enough time.

"I'll tell you what. I'm really grateful you created this opportunity for me, but I do need to check with Xavier first." I suppress the resentment that stirs in my chest. Even though now and then I feel chained, Xavier didn't ask me to help him out when his life fell apart. I volunteered. I shouldn't hold my choices against him.

"I'm sure he'll understand and figure something out. I've got to run, sweets. I'll see you in a couple of hours."

Kiera hangs up, and I take a deep breath, which isn't enough oxygen, so I take another. I'm really not looking forward to bringing this up with Xavier. We have a system. He works nights, and I work days and stay home with Nia while he's gone. It's really not that big of a deal. Most of the time he puts her to bed and goes to work, and I feed her breakfast, and I'm there in case she wakes up in the middle of the night. And I almost never go on any dates or girls' nights out because Xavier almost always works weekends…

Resentment keeps trying to rear its ugly head, so I pull out my phone to check if any of my favorite artists posted anything new. A few did. Some vague floral sketches and cat photos, of course, then finally, my pulse kicks up at the sight of a new post from Erik Cho. He's my hero. Not only did I learn some of the hardest drawing tricks from his generous, free tutorials, he's the one who made me fall in love with comic books in the first place.

I admire Erik's quick sketch of a character for his new series he's working on. He even posted a video of his work in progress. I wish my lines were that fluid. I wish for a great many things. Oh, well.

When I return inside, I find Xavier sitting on the living room couch with a glass of milk, dipping Oreos and letting Nia steal nibbles.

"Great. She won't eat normal food, but you'll let her do that?"

"I only have one daughter."

"Yeah, good luck with her later if you keep spoiling her like that."

Xavier grins. "Dad did this with you, and you turned out all right. Who stepped on your toes first thing in the morning?"

My heart climbs up my ribs, begging to be let out. I stuff myself into the corner of our worn, floral couch. It's the one thing we kept after Dad passed away and Mom moved to California to help out our grandparents. The faded yellow hibiscus flowers against the black background carried too many happy memories—movie nights, sick days, mugs of spilled hot chocolate—to get rid of it.

"The guys are going on tour this summer." If I explain it to him in bite-sized chunks, maybe it'll work. Probably won't.

"Ah. It's the Project Viper stuff." Xavier dips another Oreo in milk and eats the whole thing himself.

I get the strongest urge to kick his glass so that it'd spill all over his lap. I hate it when he dismisses the band with that nonchalant *stuff* definition. The guys may be sexy as heck and have young women my age as the majority of their following, but they work their butts off.

"I might be going with them." I think I'd like to.

Xavier sets his glass on the coffee table. "How long is this tour?"

I brace myself. "Three months."

"Three months? What about Nia?"

"I'll help you figure something out. Maybe you could trade shifts with someone for a while or enroll Nia in daycare."

He hates the idea of daycare. I don't love it either, but now and then I wish it was at least an option.

He sighs. "Fiona, I'm being promoted to shift manager. I can't trade shifts. This is a great opportunity for me. For us. I'll be making more money. You could quit that stupid assistant job and stay home with Nia altogether, focus on your art, even go to business school or something. It'll take a few months before that higher income will become the norm for us, though—"

"You know I don't want a business degree." Blood shoots to my head, and I jump from the couch. "How many times do I have to tell you that?"

Nia hugs my legs, curious, her innocent eyes looking up at me.

"Love you, Ladybug." I smile at her, doing my best to project a calm attitude. As soon as Xavier and I started living together, we set up some ground rules. If one of us says no, the other must back it up, and no arguing in front of Nia. "Wanna help me get ready for work?"

"Yes!" She skips to my bedroom, ready to play with my makeup brushes.

"Fiona." Xavier's tone is heavy. "Nia won't be this little forever. She'll go to school eventually—"

"That's three more years!" My voice rises, so I take another calming breath and glance toward my room, see Nia's feet dangling off my bed, and shake my head at myself. "You know I love her—"

"But she's not your daughter?"

It's true, but I won't let him force me to go down this route. "And I love you, but The Label is offering to train me, and—"

23

"We need you."

"What about what I need?"

I really didn't want to say this or see his conflicted face, but sometimes Xavier leaves me no choice. Literally. He has my life all planned and figured out. Nine years older, he forgets I'm almost twenty-three and can decide for myself.

"You need to quit that job before you spend your best years serving someone else's creativity," he says.

This dumb old argument again. "How is anyone supposed to reach their dreams if there are no helpers? And make up your mind, Xav. Do I go to college for a serious degree or do I continue being an artist?"

That seems to corner him, because the only thing he says is, "We need you."

I stare at the ceiling, not knowing what to do. Right now my choices seem to be to crumble under the pressure because this is my favorite brother and my adorable niece and I would do anything for them or to yell at Xavier that it's been long enough, that he can and should start being more self-reliant, and that I'm young and want to see the world.

Of course, my tongue won't turn to utter any of those things to him. He didn't ask to be abandoned with an infant by his wife who decided Xavier's love wasn't worth sticking around for. A guy who gave her an unlimited credit card for splurgy cash was naturally more appealing, but I digress. Xavier never thought he'd end up giving up his promising illustrator career to be a single parent. He never planned to move in with his younger sister so that his daughter could be safe and loved and cared for while he did his best to provide for her.

"I'd better go save my makeup." The words are a croak through my tight throat.

"She's too young to play with that stuff," Xavier grumbles and downs the rest of his milk.

I leave the living room. That has gone about as well as I thought it would.

At the end of the day, after attending a hundred meetings with Kiera while lingering in a sandpaper kind of mood after my *talk* with Xavier, I get yet another email. I almost dismiss it. It's after seven, I'm one foot out of the office, and if it's something urgent, it would have gone to Kiera first. Then I realize it's not my work email. Some days I get absorbed by the sheer amount of different messages and lose track of the sources.

As soon as I open the mail app, my body flushes with hope. An email from my agent. I step back inside, close the door, and lean on it. It could be good news about *Dimensions of Darkness*. Please, please, please. Let it be good news.

```
From: Callie Gataki
<gatakicallie@xyzliterary.com>

To: Fiona Knight
<fknight@deliberatechaosart.com>


Hey, Fiona,


Speech   Bubble   Publishing,   Visual
Expressions,  and  R&F  all  passed  on  your
project.  I'm  sorry,  I  know  it  hurts  a
lot,  but  we  still  have  a  lot  of  options.
I  will  make  it  happen.  Dimensions  of
Darkness  will  hit  the  shelves  yet.  Give
me  a  call  if  you  want  to  chat  about  this,
and  I'll  let  you  know  when  I'm  pitching
DofD  next.  Meanwhile,  chin  up  and  keep
sketching.


- Callie
```

I slide down the door and sit on the smooth carpet tile. Callie said she knows it hurts. She doesn't have a clue. She's got no inkling of understanding, unless she spent countless nights inking image after image, digitally and on paper, redrawing, re-plotting, consuming caffeine by the gallon afterward so that I could function at work, only to keep getting *no* in return.

The laptop bag presses against my thighs. I put my phone on top, but it slides to the floor. I close my eyes and let numbness claim me. It's better than crying.

They always say that finding a publisher is like running a marathon, but it's nothing like that at all. I used to run half-marathons multiple times a year until I moved in with Xavier and Nia, and when I'd start, I'd be full of hope and faith. Somewhere in the middle of it I'd begin getting tired, and about three-fourths of the way I'd want to fall on my face and give up. Eventually I'd see the finish line and get energized again and cross that line, see the time, and feel accomplished.

With publishing, all I ever get is the finish line should be around the corner, but wait, it's not. You have to run another ten miles. Keep the pace, keep the faith, keep sketching. It'll be worth it. And everything is out of my control. I depend on some guy or woman, somewhere out there, to like my stuff and put those stakes with the finish line flag. Which is yet another deception, of course, because afterward, they'll tell me to climb the mountain of being a published author. If I ever get there.

I feel exhausted to the bone.

The door behind me strains. I scramble to my feet to let Kiera in.

"Are you okay?" she asks.

I dab under my eyes—dry. Thank goodness. "Yes. I'm fine. My phone fell." It did.

"Okay." She pats my shoulder and goes to her desk. "So, what do you think about the tour? It'll be good for you. A real eye-opening experience to see what the guys do when they're in full performance mode. It'll give you a different perspective."

The phone, now in my hand, burns my skin, that email, yet another rejection, sitting in its digital guts. Xavier will be mad at me, but I'm not trying to spite him or make him struggle. This tour will boost my career, and I need to get away from my routine of drawing, hoping, and failing. "I'll do it."

It's Enough

CJ

The deck of our Viper Nest is the perfect spot to translate my heart and mind into chords and words.

Everyone else is packing, eating dinner, talking about which equipment to bring with us, which to buy, what will work and what must never, ever, ever be allowed in terms of cables, pedals, amplifiers. But I'm out here, at a sun-soaked table with my guitar and laptop, cleaning up the song I'll give to Aiya.

"That sounds good," Alexandra says behind me when I click the laptop to stop recording.

Her arrival startles me a notch. "Thanks."

Alexandra frowns and comes closer. She offers me a bowl of rice, steamed veggies, and grilled chicken. "Graham's cleaning up. You know how he is, hates dirty dishes and food sitting out for a long time."

I set the guitar aside and take the food. "I keep saying we need to hire a permanent housekeeper, but he complains we already have too little privacy."

Alexandra sits on the bench next to me and rests her head on my shoulder. "Are you okay?"

"Am I okay? You're the one who looks upset."

"I just get this odd feeling that… It's stupid." She leans forward and burrows her face in her arms crossed on the table.

I smooth out her long, shiny hair, remember it's Marshall's favorite thing to do, and hide my hands under the table. "Come on, *Matryoshka*. You can tell me anything. I bet it's not stupid."

She straightens up and straddles the bench, facing me. Her fingers trace the thin gap between the boards. "Ever since the festival, when things went so well…" She air quotes that last *well*.

"It went well. Stop doubting yourself." I take a bite. The food is good. It always is since we have a catering company working in tandem with a nutritionist to prepare most of our meals.

"Fine. Whatever." Alexandra rubs her palms against her knees, a nervous ball of energy. "You've stepped away. Maybe you're just relaxing after bringing me up to par, but it feels as if you're getting ready to move on. You found a replacement, and you'll—"

"You're not a replacement. I'm not moving on."

I open my arms wide, and she takes the hug without hesitation.

Marshall appears in the doorway to the deck. His wild black hair accentuates the glare that's not yet sprouted but is brewing at the sight of me holding Alexandra.

"I suppose I should stop hugging you now that you and Marshall are together," I whisper to Alexandra as I pull away.

She gives me a weak smile, and uses a quiet voice, just for me to hear. "You might've saved my life by bringing me here—"

"But I didn't bring you here." Not in any direct sense. Our recording label president brought Alexandra to the United States.

She glares at me, lips pursed, not appreciative at all of my banter. "You might've saved my life *by deciding to do something different*, but if you leave, I'll never forgive you."

I feign open-mouthed shock, but not all of it is playing around.

Alexandra is a feisty girl; however, she hasn't threatened me with anything yet. And right now she sounds so grave, looks so serious, and still nervous.

"If you leave, then everyone who says I broke you guys will be right." Her whisper is almost inaudible, and before I can respond, she rises from the bench, goes to Marshall, grabs his hand, and disappears inside.

I breathe out and pick up the guitar again, glance at the food in the process, and decide I'm not hungry. Why does Alexandra think I want to leave? She's given me a new lease with the band. I'm finally in the spot I wanted all along, so I'm going to leave?

But she worries about me, and that makes me smile. Sweet Alexandra, the one girl who doesn't see me as a hopeless flirt.

It's been a while since I set foot in an airport. The bustle is exciting and depressing at the same time. Flying means shows, fans, seeing the world (whatever we can catch a glimpse of in between the concerts), misplaced laundry, lost shoes, a lot of crappy food, a lot of great food, new friends, more broken hearts.

Ah, the girls. I love everything about being on tour, but the girls are the best part.

The depressing feeling…? I have no clue where it's coming from other than it's possible I'm preemptively drained. My body remembers the pace and the race to keep up with a smile on my face.

I close my eyes and tune out the surroundings for a second. It'll be fine. I'll get back into the swing of things and party like I used to.

The unease lightens up. I open my eyes and smile. It's all about the mindset. Always.

I surrender my luggage to the airline representative under the watchful eyes of Fiona.

"You pack light," she says, not even trying to hide the sarcasm as she takes in my three loaded suitcases.

"Three months, Fiona. I've got to bring my favorites."

Her lips form a half-smile. "Favorites? Are we talking bags and bags of snacks or lucky underwear?"

"Good morning to you too, Fiona."

"I thought the only thing you need is the girls' adoration."

I lean on the white laminate counter. "Eighty percent of the time. The other twenty percent of the time I require comfy socks and shorts."

"I sure hope you've got more clothes than that." She nods at the suitcases being pulled away from the scales. "I know you think you look great, but don't show up anywhere in just socks and shorts."

"Are you going to pick my words apart all summer?"

"Yours and everyone else's," Fiona says.

I'm looking forward to it. Especially after she smiles wider. It's worth it to let her have fun at my expense.

"I get that you two are enjoying flirting, but can the rest of us get a turn to deal with our stuff?" Graham snipes as he adjusts his loaded duffel hanging over his shoulder.

I step aside, leaving Fiona to take inventory of our bags—she'll be the one hunting them down should any go missing—and catch Alexandra watching me again. This time though, her expression is curious and not worried.

"You're going to have fun, aren't you?" She threads her arm through mine.

I hook my other arm through Marshall's. He sighs as if he hasn't already been enduring my antics for most of his life at this point.

"I can do this, right?" Alexandra asks in a small voice. "The tour? What if people hate me? What if I ruin you guys?"

Exchanging a look that says I hope she hasn't been poring over our band's stats while no one's with her, Marshall and I cage her in a hug sandwich. The reports have been showing a solid decline in our stats, but that's nothing unusual. Things like that happened even before we got Alexandra. Not all songs do well. We're not worried, but she is. She hasn't learned yet that numbers go up and down whether there's a reason or not.

"You'll be fine." Marshall kisses her cheek. "This is a small tour. Consider it practice for when we release the next album."

"Okay." She nods, lifting her chin a little higher.

"Hug time without me?" Zach accuses as he materializes in front of us, fists on his hips.

And just like that, Alexandra wiggles out of our arms and skips to him. She has formed bonds with each of us in no time, the little sister none of us ever had. It warms my heart and makes me all the more excited to show her everything band life entails. Everything good that is, and we'll be there for her when things aren't that great.

The few wispy concerns I had earlier about going on this tour evaporate. This is my tribe, and as long as I have them, I don't need anything else. Not the three suitcases of expensive clothes, not the fancy guitars, not even the fans. As long as I have my brothers and music, it's enough.

It's Just a Song

CJ

Rome, Italy

The tour begins in Rome, but the first day overseas is always a settle-in day. No shows, no interviews. We check into the hotel, adjust to the time difference, and get pumped to work.

Shane and Elise decide to explore nearby streets, but the rest of us stay together. In Zach's hotel suite, we spread out around a coffee table covered in laptops and a large, printed map of our tour. The route is highlighted by a neon green marker. Its shape hurts my eyes. It's insane, zig-zagging several times, looping twice, and refusing to follow logical geographic progression.

"Is this our tour or an escape route for an undercover CIA agent?" I ask.

"You get what you get and you don't complain," Fiona says as she types on her laptop. "Last-minute venue booking, apparently, makes for a lot of interesting itineraries. Plus, the Teen Faves Awards is right in the middle of the tour, so you can thank them for making you loop back."

I can't argue with that, so I pick up my acoustic guitar and start playing. Aiya's song. The melody keeps ringing in my ears, and the more I think about it, the more I believe her silky voice will be perfect to give the music a pinch of salt on top of caramel.

"What are you playing?" Graham asks.

"I don't have a title yet, but I'm thinking of offering this song to Aiya."

Zach's huffs. "She's going to…be excited about that."

"I hope so," I say and turn around when I hear a loud sigh behind my back. Alexandra. "What?"

She shrugs. "I really don't want to do anything with that girl. I have a bad feeling about her."

"Well, don't worry about it. The song's too sappy for Project Viper, and I can tell Aiya that I'll be the only one working with her on it. Something like Aiya Mori with CJ Sanchez in the title."

"You really don't have time for that," Fiona says, glancing over the edge of her laptop screen.

She's probably right, but I don't want the music to go to waste. The longer it sits in the drawer, the less interest I'll have in it. Or it'll keep playing in my head and drive me mad. Aiya, on the other hand, can make it a hit. And for Pete's sake, it's just a song. Nobody needs to get so worked up over it.

Including me.

A Statue on the Roof

Fiona

When we spread out to our rooms for the night, I flop face down onto the pillows on my bed.

CJ.

Always has an itch somewhere. For as long as I've known him, it's one scheme after another, which all culminated in him deciding he wanted to switch from bass guitar to a regular, and while that worked out all right, I'm still waiting for one of his ideas to crash with a bang for all of us.

The biggest problem with it all is that CJ gets away with pretty much everything. A smile, a wink, a compliment or two and he gets what he wants.

Same as Alexandra, I have a bad feeling about Aiya.

My phone buzzes. I grab it off my other pillow, ready for a message from the tour manager, Rick Valencio, but it's Xavier on a video call. We parted on grumpy terms, but it's a relief he's getting over it.

"FiFi!" Nia squeals into the camera after I pick up, although her aim only allows me a partial view of her nose and the bottom of her eyes.

Her enthusiasm tugs at my heart. Two days out of the house, and I miss her.

"Are you home soon?" Nia asks.

"Pretty soon. Are you being good for your dad?"

"Very good. Tell her." She hands off the phone to my brother.

Xavier waves hello. "You are very good, Ladybug. Would you pick up your teddy bears? I think they want a snack."

Nia hurries off his lap, and even though she's off screen, in my mind's eye I can see her picking up her seven teddy bears, one for each rainbow color, and sitting them down in a row, then pulling out her tea set.

"How's Juliette so far?" I may have left Portland for a couple of months, but that doesn't mean I left my brother without help. A friend of mine, the daughter of a photographer who works for The Label, agreed to help us out. Juliette is seventeen, but she's more responsible than some of the forty-year-olds I know, and she's mild-tempered and sweet. Xavier grumbled that Juliette herself needs a babysitter—she's kind of scrawny and petite and looks younger than her age, but she and I agreed on the price, and I left on what Zach has labeled as the *Viper Re-Conquest Tour*.

"Juliette is good," Xavier admits. "Quiet as a mouse, but polite. Nia seems to like her so far. How are you enjoying your freedom?"

"This is work," I remind him. "We're not here to party."

He quirks an eyebrow, doubting me. Older brothers.

"Just be safe, okay?" he says. "Get me a sticker or something."

I smile. "Will do. And don't worry. I'll be back before you know it."

"I know, I know. I'll do my best to not think it's a massive waste of time." He gives me a long look, which is easy to translate into *Prove me wrong.*

"Love you," I say, preparing to hang up. I'm glad he's willing to talk to me, but this is only getting more and more awkward.

"Love you too."

The call ends. I throw my phone aside, grab a sketchbook, and open the window. It's approaching ten in the evening, but there are a few people out and about. Across the street is the United States Embassy. On the other side—another hotel. Around the corner, a bar or a cafe or something. A few greetings and laughter reach me now and then. I sketch out the narrow streets and the outlines of the pedestrians, practicing proper perspective and studying textures of Rome. Scanning the area for juicy details, I find a statue of a nude person, naturally, on top of the roof. Laughing at the absurdity of the statue's location, I sketch it up too, wondering if I could work in something like this in a chase scene or a villain's lair for the next story.

Next story…

A shudder runs down my arms. I rub it off and throw all my focus into getting the right balance between light and shadows of this arch I spotted in one of the buildings, but my mind wanders to things I'd rather not think about.

I still haven't talked to Callie about her latest email. I'm not sure there's anything to talk about. *Dimensions of Darkness* wasn't what the publishers wanted. What is there to discuss?

The lead in my mechanical pencil snaps, leaving a tiny dent in the soft paper. I like newsprint for sketches. It's not all that durable, but its grayness helps me avoid dwelling on perfection. Drawing isn't about getting every stroke right. It's about expression and grabbing the idea by the gills, and… Huh. I think I understand how CJ feels about that song. He's worked hard on it and wants it to see the light of day. Like me, he'll take any venue to hear his music ring and be enjoyed by others, even if it's not his usual style.

My pencil drifts from shading that arch to the smooth lines of CJ's guitar. Guitars are finicky, full of little details that require a larger piece of paper than my A5 sketchbook, so I choose to focus on the soundhole and strings. CJ's guitar has this pearlescent, shiny material around the soundhole. It's a very pretty, cracked texture. Fun to draw.

I think that's what I'll do with my job, if I can while I'm away. Draw for fun. No new *Dimensions of Darkness* chapters, and no worrying about where I'm going. From now on, I'm on a mental vacation. I'll study the architecture, take pictures, and collect inspiration. One of the artists I admire recommends to keep an eye on one's creative bank account because you can't draw inspiration from empty coffers. My coffers aren't exactly dry, but filling them up will be good for me all the same.

Everything I wanted

CJ

At the end of our Rome show, at that moment where we line up to bow, I stand at the edge of the stage, smiling and waving, but something is off. I'm supposed to be full to the brim with endorphins. I should be regretting the show is already over. Any minute now…

We're already leaving.

Jedd takes my Les Paul to be packed away with care until the next concert. Fiona pats each of my bandmates on the shoulder as they pass by her, but I lean away and stumble after Marshall into the green room.

He falls onto an unusually new leather couch and looks at me. "Well? Is it all you hoped and dreamed of? Playing the guitar on stage."

I hoped it'd be…different. More satisfying, more exhilarating, more sizzling. The stage feels the same, and that's where the emptiness must be creeping in from—the disappointment.

I turn away from Marshall. It can't be disappointment. What's there to be disappointed about? The band's still great. Alexandra is happy and taken care of. And I… I didn't lose anything at the very least.

"Of course it's everything I wanted," I say.

Of course it is. I bet it's the exhaustion. I sneeze. There. It looks like I'm developing a cold, and that's why everything feels off.

Marshall exhales. "Good. I wondered if it'd turn out to be the case of the grass is greener—"

Alexandra and Zach enter the room, and I realize why he wouldn't finish that sentence. Alexandra is worried she's ruined our sales, so joking in any way about her joining the band could break her heart.

"You were great," I say to our new bassist, fighting to dispel the feeling of watching my life from the sidelines. What is going on with me? Everything is pretty much perfect.

This is what I wanted. This is what I *want*.

"I thought I'd die." Alexandra paces in the middle of the room, bumping into Shane, twisting around, and finding Zach in her way.

Marshall laughs and pulls her over to sit with him. "Calm down. The adrenaline is still flowing. It'll wear off soon." He gives her a tender kiss.

I turn away to give them some privacy, however useless that may be in a room full of people. Fiona stands in the doorway, eyes trained on me, thoughtful. I have no idea why. I do know, though, that I hate the way my sweat-drenched shirt is sticking to me, so I dig in my bag and grab a clean one.

Alexandra may be sick with the pressure of a show, but I'm calm, my emotions minimal. This makes me sad. The first show of the tour has always been exciting. I swap shirts then stare inside the darkness of my bag. Everything's so strange all of a sudden.

Laughter hauls me out of too much thinking. Marshall is tickling Alexandra. She fights his hands, but he's persistent. The two of them are soulmates a hundred percent.

"Stop rubbing it in how happy you are," I grumble with a smile and zip my bag.

"You had your chance." Marshall throws me a challenging look, reminding me of the not too distant time when everyone thought I had a thing for Alexandra.

"I never had a chance because I never wanted one." I grab my bag and head out of the room. "I'll wait for you outside. It's stifling here."

The van that'll take us back to the hotel is already waiting. I throw my bag in the back and stuff myself in the farthest seat. I wanted air, but sitting in silence feels more appealing. It's a matter of minutes before we're all together again, and I need a moment to breathe.

I never needed time to breathe before.

I press my forehead to the glass. I'm tired. So very, very tired.

The tiredness is hefty, almost the same kind that kept me going in the band's early days. When I was sixteen, loving guitar but playing badly, wanting to make it big. Dying to make everyone see I had the right to exist. That we weren't broken or damaged or worthless just because we had no "normal" parents.

Only this current feeling is duller. I suspect it's waiting to blossom into its full power, and that scares me. What if—

I hate the what-ifs that come before doubts manifest. I thud my head against the seat in front of me, hoping for a decent thwack, but hit softness instead—the seats are padded even in the back. I've devolved to Zach's level of drama. Wow.

The thought makes me chuckle. Just in time since the rest of the band arrives, eager to go back to the hotel.

Middle of the Night in a Beautiful Foreign City

Fiona

The room is hot. Luxurious, with a comfortable bed and stylish decor, definitely a lot nicer than I expected, but hot, and I can't fall asleep. I reach for water, but I'm all out. Room service will take calls from us at any time of the day or night, but a small trip downstairs to drain what little energy is keeping me awake sounds nicer.

I toss the blanket aside and stuff my feet in my shoes. Right, pajamas. I change into a pair of jean shorts and a thin sweatshirt, then grab the key and get out of my room. As soon as I step out, a door a few feet away clicks shut. I glance toward the sound and find CJ, dressed nearly identically to me—dark blue shorts and a hoodie. I smile, but he stands frozen in the spot, eyes wide, a little startled even.

"Breaking the curfew?" I tease him, although there's no such thing.

"Just a bit of insomnia." Stuffing his hands into the front pocket of his hoodie, CJ approaches me.

"Does that happen to you a lot?" I ask.

"Here and there. When I'm stressed." His lips twist into a scowl, and the shadows underneath his eyes darken, revealing his exhaustion. "Never mind me. I'm fine. What about you?"

"Same." I start walking toward the elevators, and he walks along.

"What are you stressed about?" CJ's expression becomes eager. Curious and offering. It seems he's quite interested in hearing about my possible woes.

"All of this is new to me, you know? The tour, being with you guys twenty-four seven, wondering how things are back at home without me."

"Okay. Excitement is good. It'll settle down soon, though, don't worry. And if you need some sleep aides, I'm sure Rick can rustle something up. He's got all the other stuff—antacids, bandages, laxatives—"

"Did anyone ever need *that*?" I can't help laughing.

Pushing the elevator button, CJ bumps my elbow with his. "Do you seriously believe I'll answer that?"

"Relax a little, will you?" I use his favorite question as a weapon against him. He's unusually somber right now. There's not even a hint of a smile in the corners of his lips. I wish he'd smile. I never get tired of watching his eyes light up with promises of sweet trouble when he does.

The elevator doors slide open, and we step inside. CJ leans his back on the elevator wall but remains quiet as I push the ground floor button. Something must be bothering him. I hate to see him this subdued. Of course I do. And not just him either. I worry about all of the Project Viper guys. It's my job, and my concern has nothing to do with the fact that CJ has the kind of smile that causes me to want to watch him forever. There are many other guys who have smiles like that. Many girls as well. It's not as if he's the only person out there who inspires me to draw him. I draw the rest of the Vipers on a regular basis. They're too charismatic and goofy to not to.

"What?" CJ asks, helping me stop my mind from continuing with the tangent and reminding me I'm still staring.

I school my face into a neutral expression. He doesn't need to know what I've been thinking about. His ego will only blow up more. "I didn't realize you wore cheap store-brand clothes. I mean, it's not forbidden or anything. You're usually so…" What can I say that won't reveal how I feel about his looks? "Trendy." Yes, trendy. That's a good word, not that it matters at all what he looks like. At this hour, it's reasonable pajama time. Now I don't have the slightest idea why I brought this up altogether.

CJ grins, and my heart skips a beat. I swear, I swear he knows the power his smile holds.

"This is one of the first things I bought for myself." He pats the side of his black hoodie. "The Tangs issued my first allowance and I…" His eyes meet mine, for a second only before he stares at the ceiling. "One of those things you hang on to. Memories. Symbolism. Reminders."

"I understand."

I want to understand more. Him. His friends. I know they had difficult pasts, but my knowledge is shallow. I've been by their side for two years now. Countless shows, interviews, and meetings. I had run a million errands for these guys, made birthday treats, and brought over feel-better meals. They invite me to a lot of things—parties, game nights, hangouts with their friends. I go sometimes, especially if it's during the workday. That way I can combine work with pleasure. I know that I'm one of the "in" people, but at the same time, I am not. I don't know the depths of the sorrows and trials that made these five, now six, who and what they are. I'm only their manager's assistant. I don't know if I've earned that kind of trust yet.

The doors slide open, but I don't proceed outside. Why are my feet rooted to the spot? It's not until CJ waves for me to go ahead that I am able to move.

We get some bottled water from the snack bar, then CJ walks outside.

I follow him. "Where are you going?"

He shrugs. "I just want some fresh air." He cracks his water open and takes a long drink.

Thirsty as I might have been, I roll my bottle between my palms. The valet, or maybe he's the porter, anyway, the guy in front of the entrance stirs when he sees us. I give him a quick, reassuring wave. He nods in return and resumes doing nothing.

"Want to go on a walk?" CJ asks.

I stare at him. "At this hour? It's almost midnight."

"Not too far. Around the building or something."

All the rules of being in a foreign country race through my mind. Everything about carrying the ID with me to local police harassing foreigners to muggers.

"Let's get Chris or someone." That's what security is for, after all.

"You want to wake him up for a five-minute walk?" CJ's lips purse to the side in a clear sign of you're-no-fun.

He turns to walk away, but I grab his sleeve. "A lot can happen in five minutes."

"Awww. Cute Fiona, worrying about me. I guess that is your job." CJ takes my hand and pulls it through the crook of his arm, presses it against his forearm, and starts walking.

Is that all I am to him? Another person sent by The Label to plague his existence?

I give myself a mental shake. Of course that's all I am. That's all I should care about. I do get paid from the money his music brings in, and for that, I'm grateful, and won't complicate my life with unnecessary regrets.

If I had regrets. I don't regret anything. CJ and his warm hand on mine is making me think nonsense. I step away from him.

"You want us both stabbed in a dark alley?" Still I come along.

"Fiona, look around. It's the embassy street." He spreads his arms wide as we round the corner, drawing my attention to country flags and bright lights. "There are guards everywhere."

There is that. "You're crazy."

"Never said I wasn't." His expression darkens again, and his tone turns distant and cooler than the midnight air.

I really, really, really hate seeing him this way. At any other time, he'd joke, come up with a solid explanation why I was the crazier one of the two of us, and tease me about something. This CJ? He feels off. Something is wrong. Something more than lack of sleep.

"Well, in all fairness, you'd have to be at least a little crazy to do what you do, right?" Maybe banter will bring him back to his usual, never-missing-a-beat self.

Sure enough, CJ shoots me a playful look. "Too late for the compliments. You already condemned me."

I let him have this round. If it makes him feel better, he can tease me. CJ steals a questioning glance at me, his bleached hair bouncing gently.

My hands grow clammy, and I pull them into the inside of my sleeves. It's the middle of the night in beautiful Rome. The air is cool and early summer soft. The sleepy silence reminds me where I should be, in bed. I know my body will regret this tomorrow morning, but I'm walking with one of the sexiest guys I know. We're not talking about work-related stuff, and somehow I've drifted close enough to CJ that our arms are brushing against each other. I can't bring myself to move away. If we're only co-workers and friends, so be it. I'm calling this exposure therapy. The more time I spend with CJ without holding my breath for something more, the sooner I'll get over him.

The Bus

The next afternoon, we board the tour bus.

I've been around and on tour busses before, but the one the Vipers got for this summer tour is truly something. The functionality is standard for what the bus needs to accomplish: a lounge, twelve bunks crammed tight in the back of the bus before one tiny bedroom, a shower and a toilet, and a kitchenette. But all of that is decked out in the grandest way possible. Marble-like flooring and countertops, sleep-inducing white leather couches, two huge TVs with game systems all hooked up already. A breakfast nook with two beautifully padded, spinning chairs faces one of the windows, and I already see myself spending many hours behind that countertop, looking out the window at the passing scenery, sketching and daydreaming.

Or, more likely, night-owling because during the day I'll be working even if I'm on the party bus with international rock stars. The emails, last-minutes fires, and contingencies aren't ever cancelled. Plus, Kiera likes reports on what's happened during every single day. It never ends, but sometimes it pauses.

The last bag gets loaded into the cargo hold, but the band is taking their sweet time exiting the hotel. I wish they would hurry up, but at the same time, I can't blame them. They will be on the road for weeks.

The crew mills around outside, texting or otherwise attached to their phones. I stick my hand into my messenger bag and pull out a sketchbook. The sun hits the corner of the building just so, creating attractive highlights on the glass. I lean against the bus and detach from reality with my pencil lead. I don't have any stumps, the little rolled-up paper sticks, or cotton swabs to blend the pencil, so in my pinky goes. The satisfaction of getting graphite on your hands—nothing beats it.

When the band finally comes out, I've barely started another sketch. I suppress a disappointed sigh. Drawing is soothing and fun and everything in between, and now I feel like someone brought me a cupcake only to snatch it right back. No matter. I'll draw later.

"Ready?" I stick the sketchbook back into my bag as I approach Alexandra.

Eyeing the bus, she shrugs. "I think so."

"You are totally ready." CJ wraps one arm around her and drags her toward the door. "You're going to love it."

I can't help smiling. He's so excited to show her everything. Always has been. He's nice that way, always helpful.

I follow the band and enjoy Alexandra's *oooh*ing and *aaah*ing while Shane goes through every cabinet and drawer, repeating here and there, "Check." When he hits the drawer under one of the couches that houses board games, he checks every box until he breathes out, "No Monopoly. Thank goodness." He gives me a thumbs up.

There was, in fact, a Monopoly in that drawer earlier today, but Rick and I got the band's lists of who needs what days ago, and Shane had only one request, circled several times.

NO MONOPOLY (or I quit)

Rick and I laughed about it but stashed the game in the bottom of the Suitcase of Randomness in the cargo hold.

I throw my bag on my bunk and try not to caress the soft-as-silk sheets that smell of ocean breeze. I've been informed that the mattress is high-grade memory foam, and as tight as the bunks appear, I'm looking forward to trying it. "So, who gets the bedroom?"

"It's mine." Zach squeezes by, falls on the bed, and crosses his hands under his head. Noticing my puzzled look, he goes, "What? You think Marsh and Alexandra should get it just because they're a couple? Or Elise and Shane? No way. I bought the bus with my splurgy cash, so the best spot is mine."

"Splurgy cash?" I sputter. "How much was it? A million or so dollars?"

"Two point ninety-four. Don't judge." He slides the door shut with his foot.

Don't judge? I'm not. I'm…speechless. Two point ninety-four million dollars for a bus. Out of pocket. My car is a lease.

I return to the front lounge and cringe on the inside at how crowded it is. How crowded it's going to be for quite a while. Six Vipers, the driver, Rick, Chris aka the chief of security, Elise, and myself. I shake off the foreboding that creeps up on me. It'll be fine. We'll hang out some, we'll work lots, and there's hope we won't get in each other's faces too much despite the limited space.

"Okay, people and band members." Rick claps his hands together once to get everyone's attention as he stands in the middle of the lounge.

"People and band members?" CJ calls out. "We're *not* people?"

"Not you," Marshall says to him with a smile. Everyone laughs.

Rick clears his throat. "So, the rules."

I already read them. They're the guys' rules, actually, and they all make sense, but Rick must've deemed it worth reminding everyone what's up.

No fans—the bus is the band's haven on the road. Personal toiletries must be kept in the bunks.

Cables and cords must be kept to a minimum to reduce tripping hazard.

Everyone must either use earplugs to sleep or not complain about music being played at night since the guys are prone to writing tunes while others try to sleep.

All food items are communal, but do announce if you're eating the last of something and put it on the provisions list.

Motion sickness meds are in the top drawer under the kitchenette sink, with the driver, and in a cabinet behind the sleeping bunks.

"First aid kits are also in the front and back," Rick concludes and stuffs the list in his slacks pocket. "Now, carry on as you please."

I check my emails and chat with Rick here and there. He wants me to shadow all roles on the tour—everyone from the road crew and sound engineers to production managers and the advance person, the guy who travels ahead of us to make sure all arrangements are a go.

When everyone settles to sleep, I get comfortable at that nook I was eyeing earlier, pop out an LED lamp from the drawer under the counter, and spread out my sketchbook and a few tools.

I have so many notes to take—in ink or pencil, because paper and smudges are my first true love, so many sketches to play with. I'm not going to have any time to work on anything in detail tonight, but I can outline a few things and sprinkle in a few accents to remind myself what caught my attention earlier. Such as CJ with his guitar, not playing, but holding it tight to himself, relishing the feeling of being one with it, I guess. He's been waiting a long time to be the lead guitarist. I outline the curve of his lips, a bit more downturned than usual. CJ seems to take the band more seriously now. I didn't think it was possible. He may be free with the girls, but Project Viper is his whole life. He's the one who started the band.

My phone buzzes. Another email, but this one isn't work. Not The Label's work. My agent. I hesitate to open it. It's been a good day, and I don't want another round of bad news to ruin—

A soft slap of bare feet against the floor pulls my attention away from the darkness that has started gathering in my mind. I flip the page I've been sketching on to a clean one, in a practiced, casual way, so as to not appear like I'm hiding something even though I am, and look up at my visitor. CJ sits on the other chair in front of the nook counter.

"Why are you still awake?" I ask.

"Same as before."

Insomnia.

"Want me to get you something for that?" I close my sketchbook and slide it aside.

"A straight jacket maybe," he mutters, hand covering his mouth as he rests his chin in his palm.

I can't help frowning at his response. Aside from us being on good terms on our own, the thing that's ingrained in my mind since the second month of working with Kiera is Don't Stress Out The Talent. CJ's stressed, and I have to do something about it.

"Are you okay?"

"Yeah." He scans my mechanical pencils and the kneaded gum eraser. "What are you drawing these days?"

Embarrassment, of all things, plants a tight feeling in between my shoulder blades. I should come out and own it, say I'm just sketching his guitar, but somehow, I end up in the vicious headspace of comparing my talent to his. My two-year associate degree in fine arts versus his almost seven years on the stage. Music versus visual arts. It makes zero sense, but I do it anyway.

"Nothing interesting."

I almost groan. What a ridiculous, unhealthy attitude. I don't have to tell him, but I don't have to hide it either.

My attention fixates on the way his hair swoops over his forehead, darkening his eyes, casting a boyish image over him. CJ's not old by any definition—same as me, approaching twenty-three—but there's no shred of the usual flirt in him. Instead of overflowing confidence and charm, there's calmness and a hint of vulnerability. The way he is with me right now, he could ask me anything. I'd blurt it out. But he happened to ask me about my passion when I'm already on the defensive about it. I won't tell him a thing.

A subtle kind of sadness takes over my mood, and I realize I'd love to tell him, to share some of what brings me joy with *him*. But what's the point?

The sadness grows. CJ can never be more than a friend to me. I'm not the kind of girl to catch his interest, and my sadness is ridiculous. It's safer for all involved if nothing ever happened between us.

"Do you like touring?" I ask, hoping to show that I care to talk, just not about me. Besides, I am curious. Project Viper goes on tours because it makes money, but how does CJ feel about it?

"It's good. Most of the time." His smile grows and melts the earlier concerns. "It's fun chaos. If you thought we were crazy before... Well, you'll see it all for yourself."

I smile back.

"A-ha!" He points a finger at my face. "I knew you smiled."

"Of course I do." I start collecting my things off the table. "Will you lay off about the whole smiling thing already?"

"I can't. You're a beautiful, beautiful girl, but all you do is frown and think of work." He spins the chair so that he can sit facing me and rests his side on the counter, leaning close.

"You don't know what I think about..." Instead of getting up or spinning him away from me, I go completely still, every heartbeat loud in my ears.

He... I...

He thinks about me in ways that don't involve scheduling a dry cleaning pickup or delivering fan mail? That I'm beautiful, and that it bothers him that I don't smile enough?

My cheeks warm up. So do the tips of my ears and the very center of my chest. I stare at my hands, afraid of what CJ might see in my eyes if we keep eye contact. No, not afraid. Not afraid at all. Annoyed. It doesn't matter what or even if he thinks about me. It doesn't. Not one bit. The words flow out of his mouth with such ease. He might be a guitarist first, but he's also a singer. And a terrible flirt.

I don't care. I *won't* care.

What is this heavy, insistent feeling tugging my eyes back to him, making me want to keep talking, to seek out another easy joke? CJ is dangerous. It won't take him any effort to enchant me and crush my heart. He probably won't even notice he's done it.

"Fiona?"

I look up. "Mmmm?"

"Want to play a game with me?" he asks.

Bananagrams? Tic tac toe? We could, but that sounds a little boring, and in my attempts to escape the spell he's casting on me, again, I turn to recklessness. "Only the kind that'll give away all your darkest secrets."

He cocks a sexy eyebrow. "You want to know my secrets?"

"It's been a while since I've blabbered something juicy about you guys online." I've never done such a thing.

"We'll have to make it fair. A secret for a secret?" He gets up, opens one of the overhead cabinets, and drops a small bag of chocolate-covered almonds onto the countertop.

How can I resist chocolate and a guy handsome as sin trying to get to know me?

"Are you sure you're ready to bare your soul to me?" I give him a challenging look as I open the almond bag.

53

"Are you trying to chicken me out of this?" CJ returns to his seat.

"Just making sure you won't regret it." I might, depending on what turn this crazy idea will take, but I won't back down.

"How sweet. Bring it on."

I divide the almonds evenly between us and slide his share toward him. "Don't say I didn't warn you. And forget about your usual 'What's your favorite color?' stuff. Real answers only. No bluffing, no evading."

"Fine, but in return for answering, I'll take one of your almonds. You can take one of mine any time you choose to answer my questions. Whoever has most left, wins."

I doubt there will be any left. We're both stubborn enough to spill everything and anything to not lose a game such as this. "What's the winner's prize?"

CJ's mouth spreads into a devilish grin. "A kiss."

My insides twist as my obliging mind presents me with a scene of him leaning for a smooch, but I know he's doing this on purpose. CJ knows I'll either text him an anti-harassment policy (I've done it before) or roll my eyes at him. Jerk. "That's it? A kiss?"

He feigns an offended gasp. "So cold you are. Fine, my prize will be a kiss, though it'll turn me to ice. What do you want? Wait. I have something in mind. But I don't have it with me. I'll have to get it shipped from the US. Will you give me a raincheck?"

"Will it be worth a raincheck?" I am thoroughly intrigued despite my quip.

"Very much so," CJ promises with a confident smile.

"Deal." I had better be ready to turn my soul inside out because he is not getting that kiss. "I'll start. Who's your least favorite in the band?"

CJ drums his fingers against his chin. "Marshall. He's an intolerable show-off, but you know—can't live with him, can't live without him." He takes one of my almonds.

"So that's how you feel about your best friend."

He nods, no remorse on that handsome face whatsoever. "Who's your favorite in the band?"

Dang it. I have to be truthful since I demanded honesty. "Some days, you are." Some days, I kind of hate him. "I love our superficial fights." That much is true.

"Only our fights?"

"Hey, that's two questions in a row from you. It's my turn." I eat one of his almonds. "Why do you hate it when people use your full name, Cristian?"

He shakes his head and slides an almond toward me. "Pass."

Hmmm. I might just have a chance to win this silly game. If I'm honest, though, I'd rather he revealed the trouble with his name. He didn't even hesitate to dodge it.

"You're an artist. What's your wildest dream in terms of that?"

He knows where to dig. I almost take a pass as well, but then I remember the stakes. If he wins, he gets to kiss me. I promised myself I wouldn't let him break me. That kiss could. "I don't think it's any different than what you want with your music. I want to be seen and recognized. I want someone to like my ideas."

CJ nods, then gives me another almond and reaches for my sketchbook.

I snatch it away from him.

His eyebrows rise. "I thought you wanted to be seen."

Not this sketchbook. There are too many Project Viper impressions inside. The only way I'll get him to lay off is to redirect our focus back to him. "What's keeping you up at night?"

He takes one of my almonds and pops it into his mouth, then stares out the window as he chews and fingers the two earrings at the top of his ear. "You had to pick the hardest one, didn't you?"

"You took an almond. You have to answer."

55

CJ sighs. "I've been feeling worn out as of late. The Label expects one more album from us, and usually I'd already have half of it, but all I've been able to do is that one song for Aiya. What if my inspiration is drying up? What is the band going to do?" He gives me a careful look as if checking whether I understand what he's talking about.

Unfortunately, I understand all too well. I spend nights not sleeping, worrying I will never come up with another story. Then something catches my attention, or I hear a song, or I eat a new kind of food, and *knock, knock, knock.* It comes.

"You're not a solo artist," I say. "If you have issues with new words, or melodies, you can and should rely on your bandmates. They can do a thing or two as well."

CJ nods, but the tight corners of his mouth suggest he's not satisfied with my answer. Then again, this isn't a counseling session. If he has a real issue—

Wait a minute.

"Are you going through a creative crisis?" I whisper, grabbing his hand.

As soon as my fingers come in contact with his warm skin, I jerk my hand away. What am I doing?

CJ doesn't seem to notice. His fingers continue messing with the earrings. "Maybe. I don't know. I could be. Probably not. Actually, never mind. Forget I said anything at all. Everything's great. Also, it was my turn to ask questions."

The speed with which he backtracks is nothing short of shocking. From easy admittance to determined denial in less than five seconds. I've been there, flapping between *Everything Is Woe* and *Nothing's Wrong, I'm Just Imagining It.*

"Hey." I wait until he looks at me again and smile when he does. "It's okay. If something bothers you and you don't feel like you can talk about it with the guys, I'm always here for you. You can tell me as much or as little as you want. Sometimes you need someone who's removed from your immediate circle and doesn't have the usual bias."

CJ's eyes search my face. I start thinking he'll give me a polite, "Thanks, I'm good," but he leans closer and, holding my gaze, says, "What kind of secrets would you be willing to guard for me, Fiona? And that's an almond-worthy question, by the way."

I roll my eyes, hiding how much his closeness unnerves me. There's a fascinating, dark hue to his irises, supplied by the emotion and intent I can't understand.

"Do you pass on answering?" CJ reaches for my almonds.

I slap his hand away. "No."

His phone buzzes. "Sorry. Hold on." He pulls it out of the pocket of his sleep trunks, and both of his eyebrows shoot up at the message.

"Is everything okay?" I ask.

He shows me his screen.

```
Aiya: Hey, handsome. Sorry to be so
blunt, but you promised me a collab.
Hope it's okay I'm bothering you
on your cell phone. I'll behave, I
promise. Especially if you let me
take you to dinner.

                                    XX
```

"She's already not behaving by using your personal number without permission," I grumble.

CJ chuckles. "Don't worry. I'll take care of it."

"I'm sure you will."

CJ folds his arms on his chest and leans back in the chair. "You sound judging. Or jealous." The devilish grin returns to his lips. "Let's go with jealous."

Jealous. Keep dreaming, CJ.

"Just make sure however you plan to *collaborate* with Aiya doesn't distract you from Project Viper." I head to the bunks.

Crap! My sketchbook. I turn on my heel, return to the nook, and grab my bag.

"Don't smile like that." I point at CJ's smug face and swipe all the almonds into my palm.

CJ rises from his seat and bars my way. "You're definitely jealous."

"Dial down that ego and go to bed already."

He chuckles. "You didn't answer my question." He uncurls my hand and takes two almonds.

I stuff the whole handful into his mouth. "What was it?"

CJ has to chew through the almonds before he can talk again. While he's at it, I savor his mock-indignant glare. "What kind of secrets would you be willing to keep for me?"

"Nothing criminal or scandalous, but you can trust me." Even if I don't fully trust him myself.

For the first time ever, I witness him wavering. CJ keeps eye contact, but there are shadows in his gaze and lines between his eyebrows. It's enough to cool down my agitation over the fact that there's barely any space between us.

"Don't tell the others, okay?" he says eventually. "That I'm in the dumps right now. Would you keep this one secret for me? It's not even a secret. I'm not hiding it from everybody that I'm not exactly…okay. I told you." He exhales hard at the end of it.

I wanted to know why he couldn't sleep, so I guess it's fair I pay for his secret with something more than a few chocolate-covered almonds. "On one condition."

"Which is?"

"You will not dwell on it, and you will do your best to kick the creative slump to the curb if it bothers you so much. And will you tell me how it's going?" No, no, no. What am I thinking? This will be way too much CJ exposure therapy.

"That's a lot of conditions, but I accept."

Oh. Okay.

I shift my bag on my shoulder. "Who won then?"

"I think you did. I should've known. Give me a week or so to get your prize. And if you reconsider about that kiss, just let me know."

I glare at him, but CJ only laughs. He admitted defeat, but I think he won this time. He's not the one full of regrets. I am.

▶ Track 11
A Hopeless Snoozefest

I watch Fiona disappear behind the door to the bunks. Sometimes I can almost believe she cares for me outside of work.

Like tonight.

I drop onto the couch and settle under a fluffy throw. Sometimes I go too far flirting with our manager's assistant. Far enough to have to push down hope that Fiona will look at me with something more in her eyes than *Cut it out, you stupid player*. I'm not the kind of guy for her. She's careful with relationships and seeks commitment. I've only met one boyfriend over the time I've known her. He didn't last, and to me he seemed to be exactly the kind of guy Fiona would like—respectful, hardworking, and dressed in business casual even in his time off. Her bar is high.

Oh, well. So I'm not the one for Fiona. I don't lack attention. I don't fall in love, nor do I want to. My heart seems to have become numb to real feelings after all the heartbreak I've been through as a kid. A father I never knew, an indifferent mother, lack of interest from other family members, foster care, zero friends. Plus, there's all the nagging that comes with an established relationship. Do this, don't do that. Fiona's already telling me off any time she can. I do enjoy her pouting about Aiya though.

Speaking of which. I turn to my side, take out my phone, and reread Aiya's text. If there was ever a person to perfectly fit the description of a vixen, Aiya would be it. I will be careful with her. She may be fun, but I know the danger of getting myself in over my head when I see one. She'll get a song from me, and that's it. No flirting and definitely nothing else. Despite what some people may believe, I can control myself around the opposite sex.

Music though…

Are you going through a creative crisis?

I died a little on the inside when Fiona asked that. So caring and genuine, ready to jump in and put out the fire even though she has no clue what's causing it. Heck, I don't know what's burning on the inside.

Sofia, Bulgaria

I stand on the stage, feeling completely dead. I might as well be a stone statue or a robot. Music means nothing. It's all noise. The fans—faceless masses. What do they even want?

I take myself to Marshall's side, because doomsday or celebration fireworks, we've been through it all. He's been there for me and with me no matter what. Fully in the song, he grabs my shoulder and steps close, sings in my face, not knowing I'm desperate for his energy and voice to puncture through the numbness in my soul. I can hear him, loud and clear, but…

It doesn't work.

I stalk away. Marshall returns to dominating the stage and engaging the crowd and leaves me in a bubble of this frightening calm. Simple creative crisis can't account for this, can it?

Seven years.

Seven years I've lived and breathed this, every note, every string, every clap. The fingertips on my right hand prickle with pain, and I discover a massive load of tension in my shoulders. I pace to the left of the stage, whip around, go the other direction. There's nowhere I can turn to slap myself out of this nightmare. Audience ahead, Graham behind, the rest of the band and techs on the sides.

Approaching the bridge that's a little more subdued than the rest of the song, I sit on the edge of the stage, eyes closed, and focus on the guitar solo. The yearning screams buffet me, but it's me and my six-string girl, and nothing matters.

Someone sits with me and leans their back on my left side. I keep my eyes closed, but the tickle of hair brushing my strumming arm tells me it's Alexandra. A chill sweeps over me. She can never know how I feel. She already thinks I want to leave the band. I won't. I'll get through this. I promised Fiona I'll do something about this, and I will.

In the week that follows, I send Aiya her song, play a lot of guitar, listen to a lot of music, dig through my old recordings stored on the cloud to get some fresh ideas and inspiration for the new songs I'm supposed to be writing. I actually compose a few things, but at the end of the week, I can't bring myself to show the guys anything. I'm not only not proud of what's pouring out of my soul, I know it's all forced garbage. No hits will happen out of stuff like that.

Vienna, Austria

We go through a radio show appearance, but I peel out of the studio as soon as possible and all but run downstairs. The walls were threatening to crush me. My bandmates promised the audience that we're working on a magnificent new album. They heard me tinker with melodies all week, so they assumed that everything's on track. Yeah, well, life is always on track. It's just a matter of what kind. I don't know where mine is taking me, figuratively or literally.

Chris follows in my steps, polite and all, never asking where I'm going or if I'm feeling okay—no questions asked unless there's a visible injury. Throwing the hood over my head, I navigate the building's hallways until I find a side exit, then find myself in a narrow alley, in the late afternoon shade between two buildings. That's it. This is the end. I'm done as a musician. It's only a matter of days before someone realizes that, and what use will I be to the band when they do?

I draw a deep breath, forcing air into my lungs until no more can go in, then let it out loudly and swear. Chris lingers by the door and gives me a steady look. Thanks for that, my man. Somehow it helps that he doesn't comment.

My phone rings. Who needs me right this instant?

More like, who doesn't?

I can't hide here forever. I don't even know why I ran in the first place. What was I going to do? Hitchhike back to the United States across the Atlantic?

The phone keeps ringing, but it's none of my bandmates or Rick or Fiona.

"Hey, Aiya."

"And he picks up," she jokes with her syrupy voice. "I listened to that demo you sent me."

Just now? I sent her the link to the file almost a week ago. "What do you think?"

"I love your voice, you know that?"

Stop flirting, woman, and tell me what you thought about the song! I clear my throat and swallow the irritation before I go on. "Yeah?"

"Sure do, but anywho. That song of yours? Oooh-la-la."

A triumph-flavored rush spreads through my body. It's not as if this is the first time somebody said they like my song. I make a living by having millions of wonderful, generous, crazy people listening to my music. Still, as soon as I hear Aiya purr, the fog in my head seems to lift. The shadows between buildings change from menacing to promising. I haven't lost all of my touch with music yet.

"You want it, then?" I ask her, already knowing the answer.

"Of course I do. Can you imagine me and Marshall with those lines on the stage? It'll explode."

"About that." I'd better burst her bubble now since I seem to have forgotten to mention this song is not something the whole band will record with her. "If you want the song, it's just you. I wrote it. The guys…thought you'd love it. So it's yours, but no Project Viper in the title."

A second of silence, then Aiya drawls, "You will help me record it, won't you? I need your guitar. Your sound. I'd really appreciate it if you did that for me." Aiya manages to surprise me by losing the flirtiness from her voice. She's in business mode right now, and she gains a bit more respect from me for that.

I stare at the far end of the alley, where cars and pedestrians pass by now and then, unaware of the frail webs I spin. The door behind me opens once more. I face the newcomer—Fiona.

"Thanks, Chris," she says to my guard, who must've told her where I am.

"Still there?" Aiya asks.

"Yeah. Guitar only? We can figure something out. I'll talk to you later." I end the call under Fiona's watchful eyes. She's not frowning, not questioning me with a what-the-crap-are-you-up-to look, or exuding impatience at me talking while everyone else is raring to leave. She's just waiting, always ready to deal with the next storm without a complaint. We got lucky with her. Fiona's steadiness is a true gift for those of us who misplaced their anchors.

"Go join the others, okay?" Fiona says to Chris. "I'll bring him back in a minute."

He nods and returns inside.

Fiona steps toward me. "Are you okay?"

"I'm fine."

Aiya likes the song, and I'll get to goof off in a genre that's not typical to mine, and my whole body feels lighter at the prospect.

"Looks like it'll be a nice evening." I scan the darkening sky, clear with a sliver of the moon, and walk down the alley in the direction of the street.

"Where are you going?" Fiona follows me.

"We're staying overnight. Some exploring sounds fun, don't you think? I could use a walk that doesn't involve a treadmill."

Fiona crosses her arms on her chest and bars my way. "You need to go back and get as much rest as you can, not meander the streets of a city you don't know by yourself."

"Me being gone for a couple of hours won't derail our schedule. And if you don't want me to go alone"—I give Fiona my second-best smolder. A second-best smolder is imperative. A first-rate one might earn me a cold shoulder forever—"come with me."

Fiona takes a step back. "What?"

The second-rate might have been too much, but it's too late now. I have to go with it. "Live a little. Besides, you said you'd bring me back, so you have to come along." I hook my arm through hers and step out onto the street. "We're in Vienna. When else are you going to have a chance to visit this place and make yourself sick on marzipan? With me?" That last bit, the with me part, usually works like a charm. On any other girl. I'm not even sure where this burning desire to get Fiona to say yes comes from. It must be her uptight black tee and flattering but still boring gray slacks. I know she has a wild side to her. What will it take to coax it out?

"Are you saying, again, that I don't know how to have fun?" She hangs onto my arm and, squeezing hard, walks beside me. "You seem to think I'm this utter, hopeless snoozefest. That all I do is work—"

"Prove me wrong."

Turning to me, Fiona laughs. The arm I've been holding wraps around my torso while she claps my shoulder with her other hand. Warmth shoots all over me, and before I know it, I place my hands on her waist.

"I dare you," I say, forcing my eyes away from her heart-stopping smile but keeping her in our unforeseen embrace.

A lemon-yellow cab drives by while several people, mostly elderly, give me and Fiona kind smiles as they walk around us. Our surroundings don't matter. I got this one moment with her. I never knew I wanted something like this to happen between us, but now that we're here, I'll cherish it forever. Even if she'll haul me back to the band by the collar, it's worth it.

"Prove me wrong," I say again to Fiona, leaning closer to her face. Close enough to feel the heat radiating from her. I don't want this to end.

I expect her to scold me, but Fiona places both hands onto my upper arms and whispers back, her lips grazing my ear, "Be careful what you wish for."

Her devious comeback sends a wave of goosebumps over my arms, and I'm the one to pull away first, before I do something she'll definitely kick me for. Such as claim that kiss I chose to forfeit the other night.

Fiona laughs again and walks down the street.

I catch up and thread her arm through mine once more. She doesn't flinch. She never does. Fiona knows me and doesn't care for me. My earlier rash desires cool down. Since I have no chance with her, I'm safe.

Since we only have a few hours left of the day, we decide to hit some of the touristy spots and catch a cab. As soon as we settle in the back, Fiona's phone rings. She looks at me while she fishes it out of the front pocket of her messenger bag. "Make your bet. One of yours, Rick, or Kiera?"

"Neither." I prefer the options that aren't on the list.

"Neither. Sorry. I don't think I can decline this call, but I'll try to reschedule the conversation," Fiona says, her expression a dark cloud after she sees the caller ID. "Hi. I'm sorry, but it's not a good time to—"

Snippets of someone's energetic voice reach my ears. Fiona opens her mouth to insert her response but never seems to get a chance. As the one-sided conversation goes on, her eyes grow wide, and her mouth even wider.

"Really?" Fiona exclaims at last, turning away from me.

Her surprise causes unease to crawl under my skin. I predict trouble at home—it doesn't sound like anyone managing the tour calling for help with something spiraling out of control.

"Yes," Fiona adds. "I want to hear all the details later, but thank you so much for calling me. I kind of started fearing opening your emails. After so many that were bad news… I can't believe it."

I'm not so certain it's something terrible anymore. She sounds relieved.

"Yes. I'll talk to you later." Fiona hangs up, slumps onto the seat, throws her head back, and closes her eyes.

"Is everything okay?" I ask, dying out of curiosity.

She gives me a sideways look, eyes aglow with excitement. "I was offered a publishing deal."

"Publishing what?" That's the first time I've ever heard about Fiona trying to publish a story, a self-help guide, a children's book, or whatchamacallit.

"*Dimensions of Darkness*. My graphic novel. Oh. My. Gosh." She presses both hands to her mouth but almost immediately yells, at the top of her lungs, "I'm going to be a published artist!"

With a peeved grunt, the cab driver swerves toward the curb, and I'm just as shocked, but Fiona keeps laughing.

I laugh with her. There it is. The wild side.

Whoa.

All it took was a dream come true. I'll never be able to compete with that. If there was ever a point in trying to impress Fiona.

"Fiona Knight, a published artist. Mmmm. Published. Artist." Each time Fiona repeats the words, she savors them a little more. Then she buries her face in her hands and starts crying.

"That'd better be tears of relief or something." I pat her back.

"You have no idea." She sniffs. "Years of sketching. Years of querying. Years of doubting myself."

I can relate to trying hard and giving it your best effort only to be rejected over and over and over again. Project Viper did not succeed overnight.

"Well, congratulations!" I keep patting her back, unsure if she'd welcome anything more.

"Thanks." Fiona sits up, wipes under her eyes, and torments me with another smile that has me thinking one thing only.

Holy sustain. Is this girl beautiful or what?

Her short, straightened hair is slicked back, giving me a perfect view of her smooth forehead, sculpted cheekbones, upturned nose, shining hazel eyes, and full lips that— If I could fall in love, this would be the moment I'd lose my senses.

The cab hits a bump in the road, jostling the world around me. Me having an inkling of deeper feelings for someone so disinterested in me...?

"It's not fair," I mutter.

Fiona pulls a confused grimace. "What's not fair?"

Feigning calm and control, I try to rescue myself. "It's not fair that you got such awesome news in a taxi. We have to celebrate. My treat. Don't even try to argue." I stare her down.

"Fine. I'm gonna let you get me that treat." Fiona issues another sigh, dreamy and wistful. "Ice cream. I haven't had ice cream in almost a year. I promised myself it'd be my ultimate celebration reward for landing a publishing deal. All the ice cream. With all the chocolate. Chocolate-flavored custard, fudge, sprinkles, chunks, shavings, chips."

My soul groans. Marshall mocks me for my addiction to all things dairy and chocolate on a regular basis, but the combination is the stuff I use to patch my world when everything feels broken. For Fiona to say chocolate ice cream is a special treat she'd choose to celebrate a creative milestone is not fair. Like I said.

85 Euros for 3 Minutes with Your Guitar

Fiona

Callie's ID flashed on my phone screen, and I could swear she was calling to check on me. I haven't responded to her in a while after all. It was the best news ever instead. Maybe I'm dreaming.

Yes. That's more likely. After so many no's, finally a yes? While I'm abroad? That would be my luck.

I'm still not convinced I'm not dreaming. CJ standing next to me at the top of the Danube Tower is more proof I'm experiencing something unreal. His shoulder is pressing against mine, his leather jacket warmed by the contact. He doesn't say much, letting me sketch the intricate patterns and structures of the city below. While he seems pretty relaxed, the tension in my head, and my body, is unbearable.

I didn't ignore his reaction earlier, in the cab, when he was so timid in his attempts to help me calm down. I was a moment away from kissing him. I wish I did. I could've blamed it on being too high on good news. But I'm nothing special to him, never will be, and I bet I freaked him out with my emotional outbursts.

It's all right. I like him, but not so much that it'll hurt me to see him with someone else after we get back home. All the more reason to keep him at bay and correct my thoughts. Just friends is what we are.

Just friends is what we should be.

I realize I've been holding my pencil over a blank corner of paper for a long time. I step away from CJ and focus on outlining the bridge that crosses the glittering Danube River. Now is not a good time for a romance with anybody. I'm going to be even busier, preparing for publishing. CJ and I aren't a good match anyway. He's fleeting and thrill-seeking, and I like consistency and the comfort of someone steady by my side. That's why I've been reluctant to date.

Although my thoughts keep looping back to how CJ and I wouldn't work, I can't deny I wish we could work, somehow. Drawing in silence only fuels these thoughts, so I stuff the sketchbook into my bag and turn to him.

I wish I wasn't so hasty in putting the sketchbook away. The way the sunset hits CJ creates beautiful, soft shadows on his face.

"So, what do you want to do next?" I ask in an attempt to fill my headspace with something else.

"Forget me. It's all about you tonight. Ready to get that ice cream? What about dinner? I'm starving." CJ threads his arm through mine as we walk toward the elevator.

He's been doing this—linking our arms—the entire evening. I wonder if he's trying to get a reaction out of me, as if it's his new way to rile me up. If it is, I won't give him the pleasure of reacting. If he figures out how much his closeness affects me, who can tell what he'll do?

"Dinner? With you?" I equip my best doubtful look.

"Hey." CJ steps away and hugs himself with one arm, making a splendid show of portraying hurt feelings. "No one turns me down. Usually."

I laugh, and immediately his expression lights up.

Crap.

He's good. Getting me to lower my guard around him like this.

"Don't do that," he says with a victorious smile. "I already saw you crack, and you're having fun. Why do you always need to be so serious?"

I'm not. "I don't need to smile all the time either. You don't. Nobody does."

CJ nods. "True."

We get into the elevator, and I say, "About dinner. Let's not get it yet, if that's okay with you. I want to see more of Vienna before I have to go explain to Rick and our security chief why we bumbled around without any of your guards." I shot them a quick text of our plans for the evening, just in case something happens, but I'm certain I'll still get an earful for our escapades.

"I'll take care of it," CJ says.

"No."

This response earns me a confused stare, so I explain. "I solve your problems. It'll be strange if you cover for me."

My stomach flips as the elevator rushes down. Not because CJ leans close enough for there to be less than six inches of space between us.

"First of all," he starts, "us having a night out during the tour is not a problem. I've done this before. So did the other guys. We're not puppets that belong to some almighty master. And secondly, you told me to stay put, and I dragged you along with me. So if that's going to cause you any issues, I'll take care of it. Remember, Fiona, I may be your responsibility most of the time, but since you're kind of my employee, you're my responsibility too."

I turn away, at a complete loss as to what I could say. I have never thought about me and Project Viper this way. It's always been me in charge of their wellbeing, dealing with the madness, resolving schedules, and ensuring the guys have everything they need. I don't know yet how to handle the idea that I can rely on CJ in return.

Our prowl through Vienna continues. My emotions simmer down a bit as we exchange jokes and gab about where we go and what we see. The darkness attempts to claim the streets, but there's plenty of lights around the city's attractions. A wild, jittery feeling accompanies me everywhere, and after a while I recognize it as cautious excitement at being out and about late in the evening in the middle of the week instead of being stuck at home watching Nia.

I give that thought a correction.

I'm not stuck with Nia. I'm giving my niece love and safety and helping my brother.

It's still amazing to feel the evening air caress my face, to have no set hour I have to be home, and have no shadow of regret poking me as I hear my friends recap their fun. I can do whatever I want for once. Such as bother CJ by pausing here and there to sketch out a shape, a plant, a china figurine in the shop's window, or CJ's profile as he looks up at the sky.

"You know," CJ says during a drawing break, "taking a photo would be much faster."

"You know," I angle the paper away from him and resist the urge to erase and spend forever getting a perfect line, "taking a peek on Google Maps is also much faster than roaming the city."

"Touché." He offers me a bite of a sausage he's managed to hunt down while I sketched.

Grilled onions and sauces glisten on top, the savory smell makes my mouth water, but I push my hunger down. I don't want to take food away from CJ. He told me earlier he was hungry, and in my selfish desire to see everything, I turned down dinner.

"No, thanks."

"Come on, Fiona. Live—"

"A little." I don't even try to hide how much that phrase grates on my nerves at this point. "Fine!"

I exchange the sketchbook for the sausage and take a large bite. "Happy?" The dang thing is so delicious, I almost groan. The onions are sweet, the sauces are just the perfect kind of tart, and the sausage itself is plump and juicy. I laugh and say, "You are never getting this back."

"I already ate mine." CJ wipes a bit of sauce from the corner of my mouth with his thumb.

Something tells me he's lying and letting me have the whole thing because I like it so much, but the most important part about this is, "Use a napkin. Napkin." I whisper, unable to find my voice. Would he stop touching me left and right, any time he felt like it? "Boundaries. Please. Just because it flies with all the other girls doesn't mean you can do that with me."

CJ stares at me for a second, mouth slightly open, then steps away. "I'm sorry."

I reclaim my sketchbook and hurry down the street. Embarrassment rages through me. Even if a reminder to keep his hands in check was in order, I could've joked about it, not be a massive wreck instead.

The night cools down, same as our moods. CJ must be regretting his choice to bring me with him. In silence, we continue along Burgring and past a sprawling palace. Then we pass a park with a statue and a large treble clef laid out in a section of the lawn in front of it.

CJ declares, "I must check this out."

Naturally. That's how we find out that the statue depicts none other but Mozart himself.

"No pictures?" I tease him when unlike the other tourists he doesn't take his phone out.

He shrugs and continues on. "I almost never look again at the pictures I take, so no need to waste time on them."

That's one of the most negative things I've ever heard him say, and it enforces my belief that I ruined his fun.

We move on. CJ walks beside me, at a proper distance, and whistles a tune. He keeps repeating a section and trying different endings with it. It sounds cheerful but with a hint of warning here and there. I foresee sinister lyrics later.

As we round the corner of the plaza that houses Vienna's State Opera, I remember the only other time CJ and I went out. Same as back then, I let him get into my head too much. It must be the proximity the tour forced on us. I finish the sausage and toss the wrapper in a trash can, pretending I throw my feelings in there as well.

Once past the State Opera, we stroll down a tiled pedestrian street. A lot more people are out and about here. There's even a guitarist sitting nearby, barely audible over the laughter and loud conversations that pour from every corner.

"You play better," I tell CJ as we approach the musician, who's not that bad, but not fun either. I think it's his voice. Not strong or articulate enough. Also, I've always been terrible at apologizing. Especially when I feel guilty. The words will never come out even though I know I should tell CJ I'm sorry. Giving him an honest compliment is the best I can do. "You sing better too."

CJ scowls. "He's trying. You know how terrifying it can be to play for all to hear?"

I'm glad he reminded me to respect the effort. "You're still better. Would you play for me?"

"Right now?"

"Why not? You love an audience, and there was this one song you played at The Label once. You were waiting for some meeting to start, and there were a couple guitars someone else left in the meeting room. They probably didn't plan on you goofing around with them, but—" I'm rambling. "I heard that song on the radio later. I like yours, the acoustic, a lot more. Something about fog in the woods, foxes in the fog?"

"Foxes in the fog?" Recognition paints a faint smile on his face. "*Stranger Danger* by Gilly Hoak. But I have a full gig tomorrow. Two and a half hours."

"So?"

"Don't even think about it." CJ gets in my face, warning but not threatening, and close. Too close and yet, somehow, not close enough.

For that I won't let him off the hook. "Come on. Live a little."

I skip toward the performer who sits on one of the four benches that form a square around a tree. He's a dark-haired young man with an unfortunate, thin mustache, and his guitar is a scratched, old thing with a chip on the bottom. At least it sounds decent. "Excuse me. How much for five minutes with your guitar?"

The guy stops mid-chord and issues a dry chuckle. The kind that means, *Very funny. Keep walking.*

"She's joking." CJ tugs on my jacket sleeve.

"I dare you." He won't back down. Not after the same challenge he issued me earlier. I dig up most of my cash and offer it to the street performer. "How about sixty euros for a few minutes? Maybe five?"

"Three." CJ sighs, resigned.

The young man looks between us, wary and ready to run. Or call the police.

I dig in my bag again. "Okay. Eighty-five euros for three minutes with your guitar." I wave the cash in front of him.

He reaches for the money, but I pull my hand back. "After the guitar is in his hands." I nod at CJ.

The guy shakes his head and offers the poor instrument to CJ.

He drops on the bench and strums once, surly as it gets. "What were you doing with this? Chopping wood?" He twists the tuning pegs and nods at the space next to him. "Stranger danger indeed."

If he didn't regret my company before, I have no doubt he does now. I take a seat. "But I'm not a stranger. As for danger, I warned you to be careful."

A spark of something dark flickers in his eyes. I hold my breath and recognize I should've taken my own advice about being careful.

He whips out a quick, sharp riff, flamenco style, that turns many heads toward us. The guitar owner frowns even harder. I give him the promised money and an apologetic smile. We might have destroyed his chances for a good audience—after CJ, he'll have no luck whatsoever.

CJ's voice is low and husky, tamer than Marshall's, who renders heavens speechless with his vocals, but as soon as it reaches my ears, I get that feeling of my soul being filled. I didn't think much of this song or him playing it months ago, but it all came tumbling down memory shelves, and the only thing I can think of now is that I could listen to him forever.

CJ's fingers are confident and precise as he strikes out fluid, attention-grabbing arpeggios, and by the middle of the first chorus, there's quite the crowd around us. I allow them exactly two seconds to distract me before letting go of everything.

I got CJ to sing for me. On a dare, but still. Shut up my heart, and if you won't, the remaining minute is all the time you get to be in love with this guy. CJ's not one to settle. If he ever decided to surrender his heart, it wouldn't be to me.

Loud whispers and excited exchanges start circling around us. I blink, and we're surrounded by a thick crowd.

"That's Project Viper's CJ Sanchez."

"Are you kidding me? Why would he be here?"

"They're playing a show here tomorrow."

"It's just a guy who looks like him."

Still singing, CJ smiles and shoots me a lightning-fast but potent glare.

"It's totally him. CJ Sanchez."

He closes his eyes and slows down the song on the last chorus, as if wanting to prolong the moment. As soon as he hits the last note, though, it dawns on me he hasn't been trying to prolong anything. He's been delaying the inevitable. People around us explode with deafening applause. Everyone aims their phones at him and surges forward to ask for a picture or whatnot. I jump to my feet, ready to be his bodyguard, but CJ gets up too and raises one arm, calling for calm.

"Thank you, everyone, but one moment. Please." He returns the guitar to its owner, then pulls out his wallet, takes out whatever money he's got, mostly hundreds, then presses it into the guitarist's chest. "Buy yourself a good one, man. And good night, everybody. Come and see our show tomorrow," he shouts to the crowd before grabbing my hand and jumping on the bench behind him.

We run across the wooden planks to the other side of the tree and tumble through the thinner crowd. Squeals follow us, making me feel like a rabbit chased by hungry wolves. My heart races as we dodge the pedestrians and tear into the nearest building. CJ pushes me around the first corner of a brightly lit lobby and drops to the cream marble floor, pulling me down with him.

Crouching, he hovers over my semi-outstretched legs to peek around the corner and presses his shoulder against me in the process.

I squeeze my face to the wall and fail to ignore his scent that induces all kinds of beach dreams. Ocean breeze, palms, couple's hammocks—

CJ lets out a loud huff and eases back. Thank goodness.

"You owe me. Big time," he murmurs in my ear, doing what he knows will get me ticked off—pushing the limits. He's pretty much sitting in my lap.

I jerk back, but there's a wall behind me. I'm already pressed hard enough against it to not have any space to even clonk my head and knock me out of the wishful stupor that descends on me.

Anger stirs inside me. One song is all it took for me to lose my mind? I won't be under his spell.

"Move," I demand.

CJ arches a playful eyebrow. "Which way?"

"Are you flirting with me?" Actually flirting with me?

He grins.

"Don't you dare enjoy this." Useless flirt. "Move."

"Which way?"

I regain control over my arms and try to shove him away and realize he's been holding my hand this whole time. I curl and uncurl my fingers, my face on fire. My palm is sweaty. Fantastic.

A hot guy holds my hand, and I— Oh, whatever.

"Either get off me or kiss me," I snap at CJ. That's bound to shock him into coming to his senses.

"I would, but you told me to mind the boundaries." He moves to go.

My hands shoot to his upper arms, and I hold him in place. CJ stares at me as we become suspended in tension that's too thick for threats or jokes or anything at all. My heart climbs up my sternum, stunned and scared and excited and overdosed on CJ's warmth. His gaze dips to my lips.

He doesn't like me *this* way, right? Of course he doesn't. I wish he'd already say it and help me stop imagining that there's a shy something in his look. CJ Sanchez doesn't do shy.

"Do you…want to kiss me?" I say, having lost my mind.

"Can I?"

His eyes lift up to mine, and every atom in my body stops moving, afraid to wake up from this dream. Only in a dream could I still be holding his arms, and he'd be leaning a fraction closer, his hands tugging at the sides of my jacket.

This is what it is.

This whole day has been one huge dream. I must've taken something to help me sleep, and now my brain is conjuring up every wild notion I've ever entertained.

"Is there any reason why not?" I say.

CJ's hand slides over my arm and up to my neck, sending a hot, heady feeling down my spine. I close my eyes. There's probably a thousand reasons why we shouldn't kiss, but none of them matter. I'm not just a boring manager's assistant. I strike enough of a spark in CJ for him to want to touch me.

He never closes the distance between us.

His fingers tense on the back of my neck, then CJ lets go and slides away. "You almost tricked me again," he mutters. "But I'd rather have all of my fingers in working order tomorrow."

He rises to his feet and offers me a hand.

I stare up at him. He thinks I was messing with him just now? What?

"Excuse me." A woman in a strict, black suit approaches us. "Do you have a reservation?"

I grab CJ's hand and get up, taking a good look at the lavish, gilded decorations, fancy furniture, and dark wood panels on the walls. Where are we and what kind of trouble did we get ourselves into? At the same time, it's difficult to care when my pulse can't decide whether to burst my heart from the rate of acceleration or come to a full stop.

"Actually, they do," Zach says somewhere behind me.

Wait. Zach?

I glance over my shoulder. There he is, coming toward us with a small square box in his hands. He's wearing a loose white shirt, relaxed jeans, and fluffy slippers. Honestly, this is how I envision him right before bed or on a lazy Sunday afternoon.

"Ah, Mr. Tang." The woman smiles at him. "Do these young people belong to your party?"

"Yes. Have some Sacher-Torte." He shoves the box into CJ's hands and drapes his long arms over our shoulders. "Cristian Sanchez and Miss Fiona Knight are the names you should find on the paperwork. Might we get some room keys?"

Oooh, nice. I'm Miss Fiona Knight, while CJ is Cristian.

CJ's reaction is immediate. He drives an elbow into Zach's side. "Is this our hotel?"

"It is." The pianist rubs his side, but a satisfied smile tells me jabbing CJ was worth it to him. "Sacher Wien."

"Well, whaddaya know," CJ continues, calm and relaxed, unlike me. "What's the cake made of?"

That's what he cares about right now? Cake! And he accused me of messing around? If anyone here is guilty of that, it's not me.

"It's a Sacher-Torte, dude," Zach explains. "Only all the chocolate. Just how you like it."

CJ passes on the box to me. "In lieu of ice cream?"

Forget the cake. "We are very sorry if we caused any trouble," I say to the hotel employee who had to investigate our insane arrival, along with whatever that was that followed.

She gives me a courteous smile. "If you would please follow me for your keys."

We go after her in silence, although Zach's expression screams, *What the heck did you two do all evening together?* And probably, *Why didn't you take me with you?*

The thought makes me laugh, but I stifle it.

Later, when I'm showered, full of chocolate cake that must be laced with drugs it's so good, and in the softest, smoothest, cuddliest bed in the universe, I text CJ.

```
Thanks for the foxes in the woods.
        It was worth every euro.
```

Lying in darkness, I try not to think or feel foolish about the madness in the lobby, but my burning eyes and increasingly stuffy nose won't let me fall asleep. Great. A night out in a new place seems to have brought on an allergy attack. I crawl out of the cloud-like white comforter and dig in my bags for some antihistamines.

CJ wouldn't kiss me, and I'm happy he didn't. I lost it for a moment, down there in the lobby, and couldn't see that us kissing would be disastrous. Even worse than that.

The intensity of relief of having dodged that mistake hurts all over, and now I regret taking our games this far. That kiss would have ruined us. CJ must've realized that too. His player nature notwithstanding, he's got more common sense than I do.

I dig up the allergy meds and take one, then chant, until I drift away, "Published artist, Fiona Knight."

An Honest Scoundrel

Fiona is cruel. She friend-zoned me so hard, it doesn't faze her at all when I touch her. Unless I get in her face, then she threatens death. She said nothing, asked nothing, when I wouldn't kiss her. That dare to kiss her was another test for her. A battle of wills. Even if I kissed her, she wouldn't care. But I couldn't kiss her because, apparently, I do care. We work together, and I know her standards, and I couldn't play with her like that.

More than any of that, I realize with a ping of anxiety, I want her to care.

I'm stupid for worrying about Fiona when I have songs to write for our next album. That's where my heart should be—figuring out how to restore my balance with the band, not worrying about what to do about the one girl in the universe who gives zero bleeps about me.

While we're in Vienna, there's plenty to keep me busy and avoid thinking about Fiona, but as soon as we're back on the bus, I can't seem to take a breath without sensing her, seeing her, hearing her talk, knowing she's mere feet away from me. I must have too much free time on my hands, as weird as it may sound.

I'll double down on writing that new album of ours.

I scribble for a couple of days, play guitar, listen to music, survive another show, and come out with zero useful lines. Again. This lack of any kind of progress keeps me from sleeping. I will pass out eventually, around four in the morning, but my skin itches from restlessness induced by being stuck in the bus bunk. Fiona's prize arrived this morning. I could give it to her if she's up right now. I hop out of the bunk, tiptoe to the door that separates the lounge from the sleeping quarters, and slip out.

Fiona's at the breakfast nook, sketching. It's almost one in the morning, and even though the door slides closed behind me with a solid click, she doesn't turn toward me. I spy earbuds in her ears, and have a much easier time resisting the thoughts about how I'm little more than an annoyance to her. If that.

Twisting the square, cardboard envelope with her prize in my hands, I approach the nook. Fiona smiles but doesn't even glance at me. She's outlining some buildings she drew earlier in pencil. Her fingertips are marked with black ink from a super-thin pen she's using. I do my best to not jostle her or anything around her as I take the other chair at the nook. Her drawings are good. I've seen her do quick outlines and intricate renderings. Every time her pencil hits the paper, something new and beautiful comes out. I used to be able to do that.

My phone buzzes in my pocket. A text.

> Aiya: My recording label is in love with your song. Same as I. Can we record it before July? Pleasy, please, please?
>
> XX

I put my phone away. I'll have to talk to Rick or Fiona about the band's schedule first, which won't be tonight. I'm done working for the day.

The bus rolls along, fast and smooth. Its gentle, quiet rumbling put the rest of our team to sleep long ago. I don't mind being up anymore as my eyes take in the lines of Fiona's left hand leaving precise marks on paper.

To me, Fiona is the real work of art here, and I allow my eyes to freely admire the curves of her arm and shoulder peeking out of a wide-collared shirt. Her neck is slender and long.

I'm getting a little too sidetracked.

"I want to read your graphic novel," I say after pulling one of the earbuds out of her ear.

"You can't." She still doesn't look up from her task, not even to glare at me for disrupting her music.

"Why not? It's going to be published anyway. I'll just buy a copy and read it."

"Then buy a copy. I'll get some money for it. Why are you up again? Go back to bed."

"Nope." I set the envelope next to her sketchbook, move to the couch next to the nook, and take out my guitar case from underneath.

"Okay, let's talk then," Fiona says.

"About?"

"How's it going with your…challenge?"

"I'm working on it. I've been trying to compose."

"Yes, you have. How do you feel about the outcomes? Good? Bad?"

I trace the bridge of my guitar with my fingertips. I've had it for almost five years now. This isn't my only guitar, of course, but it's like an old friend or a comfort food. It's always good, always sounds right, always fun to play with. I strum a chord, then another. They both sound boring.

"You seem to be out of sorts the last couple of days. Normally, you put up a solid competition to Zach in terms of talking. Endlessly." She's clearly making fun of me, but her voice is gentle. "Is it because I wouldn't kiss you?"

Oh. Excellent move. I will repay in kind. "Excuse me. It was me who wouldn't kiss you."

Another small smile makes an appearance on Fiona's lips as she continues outlining, but she still won't grace me with a single glance. That moment in Sacher Wien really meant nothing to her.

I give myself a mental kick. I promised I'd stop worrying about it. And her. And us.

"I'm stuck," I say. "Usually, I can whip out a song faster than you can count to ten, and being on stage—" Too much information. She doesn't need to be burdened by every detail of my issues. Describing them in general terms will do.

"I've been there." Fiona swivels the chair to face me at last. "Artist block sucks. I know mine is probably not the same as yours, and I bet you have better strategies—"

"No." My voice comes out sounding a lot more annoyed than how I'm feeling.

She swivels back and returns to drawing. "If you're going to be grumpy while I'm trying to cheer you up, get out of here."

So fierce. I approve very much.

I return the guitar to its safe spot under the couch and sit with Fiona again. "I'm sorry. I meant to say you shouldn't assume your problems are somehow less than mine. Just because our challenges are different, doesn't mean yours are less than someone else's. But you're right. I've been in a mood all day, or two, or three, so it came out all dumb and wrong."

"Do you feel that maybe Alexandra has something to do with your artist block?"

"No."

My answer is too rushed. I know through Fiona's pressed lips and unconcealed worry in her eyes as she glances toward the bunk compartment with my sleeping bandmates.

"Because if you now feel that bringing her in might have been a mistake—"

"I don't feel that way. I'm happy she's here. Alexandra made my dream come true."

Fiona rests her upper body on her arm against the countertop. "She would be devastated, you know, if you ever started thinking she ruined everything."

I press a fingertip to one of Fiona's pencils and roll it around. "I would never think that." I don't think anything of the sort.

Then what is wrong with me?

"If that's the case, you need to do a better job acting like your life, as you put it, is a dream come true," Fiona says with utmost seriousness. "I don't recommend you lie, though."

I already know I should be careful about my attitude and Alexandra's perception of what's happening. "I'll figure it out."

"Are you going to bite my head off if I try to give you some suggestions, or do you want me to pat your head and say, 'Poor you. Tough luck, but you can do it'?"

"Can you pat my head *and* give me some suggestions?" I prop my elbow on the counter and whip out a dazzling smile. The one that makes all the other girls swoon. "I promise I won't bite."

"Are you flirting with me again?" Fiona asks through a yawn.

Ouch. "Maybe." Even though there is absolutely no point.

"Because…?"

"Because I love the way you snap at me whenever I do." Not because I want her to blush or giggle or flirt back with me. I can't even imagine her doing that. "I suppose it's a habit."

Fiona places a thin notebook from her shoulder bag and a mechanical pencil in front of me. "Make something terrible."

When I frown, puzzled with the abrupt change of topic, she adds, "Cheap paper, cheap pencil, no expectations other than that you'll make a mess. Throw it in the garbage later. No one will ever see this. If you want to, I won't look either. Just do whatever you want—doodles, lyrics, shopping lists."

I pick up the pencil. "Is this one of your artist block tricks?"

"Sometimes you just have to make something awful."

"I can do awful." Plenty of it.

Fiona picks up her pen. I flip open the notebook, divide the page into eight sections, and start scribbling random lines. This tactic landed us a couple of good tracks before. I'll write one line in each of the eight sections. Right now it doesn't matter how well they fit together. If the line is hot garbage, I'll rip the section out of the page and let the page underneath fill the gap. I like this for the chaos and savagery of it, for the tactile destruction of words. The sound of ripping paper is cathartic. Sitting beside Fiona without talking is useful too. Her indifference fuels the darkness brewing inside me.

I shred half the notebook before Fiona speaks again. "Why do you…? No. Never mind."

"Hmmm. Something you're afraid to ask me—"

"I'm not afraid of anything." Fiona stabs me with a glare.

"Well, that's a lie." I swivel toward her and rest my chin in my palm. "Everyone's afraid of something."

"I'm not afraid to ask you anything," she clarifies. "But some things may be none of my business."

How curious and intriguing. There are personal, uncomfortable things Fiona seems to want to know about me. "I forgive your rudeness beforehand. Go ahead. Ask."

She mirrors my pose. "Why do you do it? Date so many girls, settle with none?" Her voice is full of challenge, but her fingers clenching her knee betray her nervousness.

I'm an idiot to think there's a personal stake in her curiosity, but I can't help enjoying the idea that Fiona may be asking this in order to figure out a way to my heart. "Why should I? So I can have a girlfriend who'll nag me day and night? I already have enough people in my life who do that."

Fiona shakes her head, her earlier, subdued smile back. "That's not what girlfriends are for. Not the good ones, anyway."

I force my eyes to stay on the sketchbook next to her instead of her lips. "What are they for then?"

"Support, attachment, fun. You love fun. You always tell me to have some."

Hmmm. I would've considered this a general comment if it came from anyone else. Fiona's words, each and every single one of them, are intentional. Is she suggesting she'd be a good girlfriend— Yes, she would be. Just not with me.

"I have all the fun I want without a girlfriend. Any girl I want, any time."

She stares me down, with much disapproval. "You do realize what that sounds like?"

"Like I'm using them?"

"Yes."

"They know what they sign up for." I prop my sneaker on the footrest of Fiona's chair, right between her feet, realize it's the kind of behavior she scolded me for a few days ago, but before I remove my foot, Fiona plants her foot on my footrest. We're both wearing shorts, and the sides of our calves are touching. Her skin is warm and smooth. My breath is stuck in my throat, and when I look at her, Fiona's lips are pursed, one of her eyebrows challenging me. Again. She's determined to win every duel we ever have. Maybe I'll let her.

Maybe.

"I spell out my expectations and tell them what they can get in return," I say. "It's always, always up to them what happens afterward. I don't fall in love. Never have been able to. Getting their heads stuck in the clouds, breaking hearts, cutesy couple's rings, and googly eyes have always been for someone else. It's best if I don't let anyone believe they'll get anything long-term from me. Otherwise, I'd be lying."

"Oh, so you're an honest scoundrel."

Whoa. Easy now. "And you're a harsh judge." Now I know why I'll never have a chance with Fiona. She thinks I'm lower than dirt.

"I'm not judging you. I just don't understand you. Don't you want more?"

"More always comes with too high a price. Attachment isn't free. Especially when that girlfriend you recommend so much leaves for no other reason than she felt like it. Look at Graham. I don't want to become a wreck like him."

He fell madly in love, followed that model all over the globe, and she ditched him two weeks before the wedding. No thanks.

"That was a tragic instance, not a common occurrence." Fiona gazes out the window, a crease cutting her forehead. "It shouldn't be, at any rate."

I clasp my hands together to keep myself from reaching out and smoothing out her frown.

Fiona sighs and startles me by grabbing the page with the half-outlined picture out of her sketchbook and crumpling it into a ball.

"Why are you so angry all of a sudden?"

She laughs quietly and points to the page underneath my hand, where the pencil sketch still exists. I unfold the crumbled drawing and bring it under the lamp on the desk. Seeing the lamp base right through the lines, I understand why Fiona destroyed her efforts with such ease.

"Tracing paper. My heart almost stopped."

"You're so strange." She places a fresh sheet of tracing paper over her notebook. "And full of fear."

"Do you ever have anything nice to say about me? I'm a womanizer and a coward."

"You're very sweet with Alexandra. You're kind and generous with all the girls in your life, and all your friends. She needs it most, though, having no family of her own anymore. So thank you."

"Don't thank me. I'm not as nice to her as you think. I kissed her, too." I say that because…? Lack of sleep is to blame. Exhaustion is the only reason that can explain my unstable mind right now. Also, our legs are still touching.

Fiona's eyebrows climb up her forehead, then her gaze darkens with fury. She grabs the envelope with her prize and smacks me with it, hard, on the thigh. "How dare you touch her? Sweet, innocent Alexandra, and you—"

"I had a very good reason for it." I spin in the chair in an attempt to avoid her wrath. "Trust me. I wasn't doing it for fun."

Fiona hits me on the shoulder, but it only makes me laugh.

"Trust you? Uh-huh. Sure. You stay away from her. You hear me?"

"She's with Marshall now, but they wouldn't be together if I hadn't kissed her." I keep laughing. Fiona's sisterly anger is the best. It gives me another glimpse of her less restrained, wilder side. "And if I were you, I'd be careful with the envelope. There's something inside it I think you'll like."

Fiona checks both sides. White and carrying nothing more than the addresses, the envelope gives her no clues. "What is this?"

"Your prize for winning the secret-sharing game."

After one last glare, Fiona grabs the easy-open tab and rips the envelope open. Inside is a single sheet of paper, folded in four, wrinkled around the edges, and I seem to remember it had a tear on the bottom somewhere. Confusion settles over Fiona's features as she unfolds it. Then silence as she studies the weathered sketch of a long-haired character with a scar across her entire face.

I bounce my foot on the stool bar as I wait for her reaction.

Fiona sets the torn envelope aside and spreads the sketch under the light on the counter. "This looks like an early design of Elizabeth Richter, the banished vampire queen from Erik Cho's first comic series. And that looks like his signature." She taps the rugged Korean alphabet characters under the sketch.

"I didn't know the name of the character. I just thought you liked the artist—"

"How much did this cost you?" Fiona's eyes are wide with shock.

I chuckle. "Don't worry about it."

"Thank you."

She fingers the drawing so reverently it fills my chest with the warmth of success. I made the right choice when I decided to give her this gift. I knew she wouldn't care for jewelry or designer perfume. She's the same as Marshall. If you want to give them something meaningful, give them eye food and inspiration. Although, in case with Marshall, a twelve-pack of Diet Coke will work too.

Fiona's phone chimes. She swipes the screen to unlock it. "Kiera sent me an email marked as urgent."

Knowing Kiera, it's nothing urgent at all.

Fiona locks her phone. "Just a reminder about the Teen Faves Awards night in three weeks."

Nailed it. Not urgent. Nothing to be concerned about at all. What bothers me is how little I care about the awards ceremony. Most of the time, I love events like that. The afterparties are wild, and there's always an abundance of pretty girls. But just thinking of being in the crowd again makes me want to jump off the bus and run into the wilderness.

Crap.

"No more talking about me and why I'm such a loss to society, okay?" This whole artist block mess will go away if I stop feeding it, right? "How about some more creative block advice? I promise to not bite your face off, and you don't have to pat my head. You don't have to touch me at all."

"Try to do something new in your routine," Fiona says. "Listen to different music, watch a movie you've never seen before, try a new sport. Or do some of your favorite things. Dig up your guilty-pleasure vinyls. Hang out with some friends you haven't seen for a while. Shake up the rut, as much as possible given the tour restrictions. Feed your imagination. It's starving, so you're having trouble being creative. A car won't run on an empty tank."

I can't argue with any of that. "I'll give it a try." I thought I have been. Perhaps not in the way that works.

"Great." She yawns. "Now go to bed. Insufficient sleep inhibits your thinking ability and puts you in a bad mood. Been there, done that way too many times. Don't expect to compose masterpieces when your body wants a nap."

"I get the hint. I'm leaving." I get up.

"CJ," Fiona calls out when I reach the door to the bunks. "The thing about artist's block is that it's never permanent. You will be fine. I promise you."

Her kind voice and those simple words—*you will be fine*—knock off some of the weight that's been arresting my shoulders. I think I got the better prize tonight between the two of us, even though I haven't earned mine.

Barely Leveled Up

Fiona

Four days after I get the news from Callie, I finally get the chance to sit down and process what's happening to my artist career.

Rick took my favorite spot on the bus, so I've resorted to working at what we consider the dining area—a booth with a table and two benches next to the window. It's been a whirlwind of Project Viper activity. I haven't even told Xavier about the publishing deal yet because we haven't been able to align our schedules to talk. Still, Callie has forwarded me the contract. I've been reading it all morning, and even though I'm familiar with many legal terms because of work, I'm nervous about missing something. My whole life depends on me understanding what I'm signing up for. I don't want to accidentally give away the rights to my art for the next century.

"Hey, Zach," I call out to the Project Viper's pianist who's busy rolling up the universe into a ginormous ball of garbage in a video game. "Can you recommend a lawyer who won't cost an arm and a leg to help me decipher a contract?" He knows the best of the best. Being a millionaire and running his own companies since he turned thirteen helps.

"If it's something you don't mind sharing, email it to me, and I'll pass it on to our guy," Zach replies without ever taking his eyes off the TV.

"I don't want you to pay for—"

"He's on a retainer. Your little contract won't add to our expenses."

"Okay."

"What's the contract for?" Alexandra sits across from me.

I move my laptop to the side. "Well…" I haven't had the chance to share the good news with her either. With anybody but CJ.

"What's this? You look excited." Elise drops on the bench next to Alexandra, a bowl of something green with a brush in her hands. She wraps a wide hair tie around Alexandra's head and orders, "Chin up. Let's make sure all the makeup and sweating on stage doesn't ruin your skin."

Alexandra lets Elise paint her face with what's obviously a detox mask.

CJ slides on the bench next to me and says to Elise, "Me too."

"There might be enough," she replies in an even tone while Alexandra and I both stare at him.

He ignores us until the very end of Elise applying the mask, then laughs with Alexandra. I smile too. Alexandra's still getting used to living without privacy, and I believe he's masked up to help her feel less awkward. I love seeing him this down to earth and caring instead of purposefully charming.

"So what's going on?" Elise asks once more.

"She's got a publishing gig," CJ announces.

The girls gasp in delight, both of them aware, to a different degree, that I've been working toward this goal, and I love their reactions, but— "I wanted to be the one to tell them!"

Grinning, and it's the most absurd thing I've seen in the longest time because of the green paste on his face, CJ bumps my shoulder with his. "Would you, though? You had that look on your face, debating whether it's cool to tell everyone that you have a graphic novel."

"They know."

"Wait, what?" Zach tosses the controller aside and squishes Elise and Alexandra on the bench. "You make comics?"

Apparently, he doesn't know. I have no idea how. Zach's one of the nosiest people in existence.

For the next fifteen minutes, I fight off everyone's requests to show the story, explaining that by the time the publishing house editors are done with it, it'll be different anyway. But Zach. Oh, that Zach. He digs up my website and demands I make a graphic novel about Project Viper origins.

"Don't laugh," he exclaims when I dismiss his request. "It'll sell better than hot cakes."

"I don't know about that." Also, I'd better make sure he never sees my sketches of Project Viper. Ever. Otherwise I'll never hear the end of it.

"Tell her," Zach demands from CJ. "Nobody ever takes me seriously."

"I do," Elise pats his shoulder.

"Me too." Alexandra leans behind Elise—I don't know how she finds the space—and gives Zach a sweet hug.

"He's not asking you to do it for free, you know." CJ turns to me, the blue in his eyes vibrant and playful against the green mask, reminding me of the moment on the hotel floor when he almost kissed me.

I've done my best to not dwell on that mishap, and after our conversation last night I started feeling that we moved on, but anytime he gets close… My plan for this tour has been to get some mental rest and a break from the mundane, but now I worry I'll have to get therapy once I'm back home. He's tearing my mind apart.

"Go away. Both of you. I'm not doing it for any money in the world." Hiding my Project Viper sketches won't be enough. They must burn. If anybody ever sees them, I'll be forever labeled as the most desperate groupie. It's not my fault the guys provide me with abundant material to practice drawing sizzling-hot bodies and emotions.

At the same time, the notion of someone else working on the book, should that crazy idea ever come to fruition, bothers me. Really bothers me. I know these guys. I've witnessed their souls at both the brightest and dimmest. For someone else to come in and try to show the world what they're like would be an intrusion of the worst kind.

"She stabs me in the heart." Zach falls off the bench, with all possible drama, and crawls back to his spot on the couch.

"Not just you." CJ winks at me and wipes his face with the damp towel Elise has handed him.

What an ungrateful jerk. He unloads all of his insecurities on me, absolutely refuses to fall for me, then teases me?

"You have a heart?" I throw back at him.

Alexandra snickers from behind her towel.

"Not anymore. You've stabbed it right through just now, remember?" He presses a fist to the middle of his chest and throws his head back, feigning deep agony.

I love the acting, but I keep my tone cool as I say, "A plus for the drama. Now get going. I've got emails to write."

CJ leans forward. "Since you're already doing worky stuff, would you find me three good days to fly back to the States to record with Aiya? If I don't do it soon, she'll text me to death." His tone is one of deep endurance, but the smile in the corner of his lips negates the complaining attitude.

"You're excited about this project, aren't you?" Alexandra asks.

"I bet he is. I mean, Aiya." Elise bats her eyelashes.

"Yes, I am excited. A little." Wringing the towel in his hands, CJ steals a quick look at me, as if he's worried I'll lecture him again about his priorities.

The way I see it now, recording with Aiya is something new to do, and it may help him deal with his artist's block. He may have other plans as well when it comes to Aiya, but I forbid myself to think of him as my potential love interest. First and foremost, he's my responsibility. If recording with Aiya will help him feel better, I'll do my best to make it happen.

"Okay." I pull up the schedule app.

"You're the best." CJ thanks me with a playful wink.

"No, really. Go away already." I train my eyes on the laptop screen and wait with bated breath until he leaves. I don't care what he'll do with Aiya. I don't care, I don't care, I don't—

"Aiya's trouble," Alexandra mutters.

I don't disagree, but I don't want to talk about that pop star at all. "Don't worry about it."

"You want some breakfast?" Elise offers to us. "I haven't had any yet. I'm thinking yogurt bowls with fruit and granola."

"Sounds good," Alexandra and I say in unison.

Elise goes to put our food together, and I ask Alexandra, "How are you doing? It's been a few shows. Getting used to playing full stadiums with the guys?"

She cringes. "Every time I stand there, before that first song, I want to throw up. These girls that come to see them—"

"And the guys that come to see you." I've noticed a significant shift in the audience in terms of male to female ratio. The majority of concert goers used to be young women. Now there are more guys in the audience.

"That scares me too. When we meet the fans, I freeze. I can't entertain and bounce the jokes back like the guys do. I feel like such an impostor." She spreads out on the table.

"You're not an impostor," Zach says.

"And I told you before," CJ adds, "you're inexperienced and we're working on changing that."

"Oh my gosh!" Alexandra shoots upward and glares at them. "At least pretend that you can't hear us."

They chuckle and put on headphones. Zach continues with his game, and CJ pulls out his phone.

"They're right though," I say. "You are doing well. Relax. Have fun." I can't believe I'm using CJ's favorite lines on her. "If you make a mistake, it's okay."

Alexandra nods, but her eyebrows stay knitted together.

I try again. "It really is okay."

She sighs. "Oh, I know it's okay to make mistakes. I just…" She continues in a whisper, "Something's wrong with CJ."

"What do you mean?" I whisper back.

"Ever since that first festival we played with me in the band, he's been different. He acts happy, but… I just know something isn't right. I'm afraid he'll leave the band. I confronted him, and he told me he'd never do that, but Fiona, he's hiding something. He doesn't talk to me as much as he used to. He doesn't talk to Marshall either. To anybody."

He talked to me last night. He trusts *me* when he doesn't trust the others who have known him much longer than I have?

"Have you considered he's giving you some space? Marshall thought you two had feelings for each other. CJ may be trying to let the opposite solidify." I wish he hadn't asked me to keep his creative troubles a secret.

She frowns. "Could it really be that simple?"

"It may also be the tour blues. Go, go, go pace can be difficult. I'm sure you understand by now."

Alexandra nods. "I'll try to be less paranoid."

"And?"

She stares at me.

"You'll try to be more confident," I explain. "You earned your place on this bus, Alexandra. Enjoy it."

She smiles. "I'll do my best."

It makes me happy to see her worries go away, at least for now, and I hope with all my heart, CJ will find his inner balance soon as well. Project Viper is in a state of heightened emotions and going through growing pains. Same as me. We all get scared by success at times, it seems. But they're strong, and they're tighter than any family I know. They'll shine brighter than ever before. I'm sure of it.

My phone rings. I check the caller ID, and speaking of families, it's Xavier.

"My brother," I say to Alexandra, who nods and joins Zach and CJ on the couch. I tap the accept call icon. "Hey."

"FiFi!" Once again, Nia's the one greeting me. "Are you coming home tonight?" She sneezes, loudly, and even on the fuzzy video I can see the snot flying.

Xavier groans in the background and stuffs a tissue into her nose. She blows and laughs.

"Not yet, sweetie," I say when she's ready to listen again. "How are you?"

"I have sneezers. I love you!" At that, she jumps off my brother's knees and runs off.

"She's got a summer cold?" I ask him.

Xavier nods. "I took a couple days off and let Juliette have a break. I don't want her to catch it."

"What if you catch it?"

He shrugs. "So far so good. How's your vacation going?"

I wish I could punch him. If by vacation he means that I get exactly five and a half hours of sleep every night, then sure. "Great. Seeing lots. Doing even more."

"Don't forget to send us pictures."

He appears energetic and happy to see me, and tells me about their day-to-day shenanigans, admitting that taking a couple of days to be with Nia has been nice despite her mild cold. Our mom will be coming out for a week to visit too. He sounds like he's got it all figured out. By himself. As soon as I left, he started managing everything quite well. He had to throw a fit first, though.

Oh, yes. I need to tell Xavier about the publishing deal.

Something crashes in the background, followed by a quiet *uh-oh.* Xavier blurts out, "Love you. Talk to you later," and hangs up.

"Love you too," I mutter even though he won't hear me.

For some reason, I'm relieved that I couldn't share my good news. He would celebrate with me. Getting published has always been something we looked forward to together. Xavier always cheered me on when I slumped on the couch and watched TV for days, convinced I'd never make it. But just like there's an ocean between us, I feel like our emotions and our lives are half a world apart.

I wonder if that's how Alexandra feels about CJ. If he's only been nice to her in order to train her, I'll definitely kill him. I glance at him, still scrolling through his phone, letting Alexandra hug his arm while she's resting with her eyes closed. He must sense me watching him, because he looks up. I point at his arm. He looks down at Alexandra and smiles. All right. It doesn't seem at all like his affection for her is insincere.

I breathe out my worries and return to work. Alexandra may be overwhelmed from lack of experience, but I don't think she's got anything to worry about in terms of CJ. He coined Project Viper, and he's not going anywhere. Not when we all know they've barely leveled up.

I, on the other hand, am having my behind kicked by trying out this tour gig. Between relaying stuff from the United States to Rick and dealing with a fair share of his communications locally, I stay up late every night even when CJ doesn't want to talk. Then, of course, I want to draw, so cue the full-on night-owl-induced exhausted wreck. Tonight, it culminates in that weird state where my body demands pillows, but the moment I close my eyes, it resists sleep.

Sitting on the couch in the lounge area, way past midnight, I sketch Marshall from a photo I took at the last concert. He's unstoppable. What I love the most is the glow in his eyes when he's out there with a microphone in his hands.

A deep, consuming yawn almost pops my jaw. My eyelids droop. What I really want, I think, is my own bed. My room. No chance of anyone waking me up in the middle of the night for anything more serious than a cup of milk. I don't know how the band does this for months on end. Also, I have to admit I didn't think I'd miss being chained to Nia, but I do. The consistency was good.

So was the privacy.

But I wanted to fly free…

I can't pry my eyes open anymore. I should probably go to bed. Then I'll have to change, trying to be as quiet as possible, and climb into that tiny bunk, and… Nobody wants to wake up to me sleeping here, but at least the lounge is an open space in which I can throw my arms around, and…

I sag down. I'll set an alarm for four in the morning and move to the bunks then.

My head hits a squishy pillow instead of the couch's leather. Did we have cushions? It doesn't matter. I fight my pocket for my phone— can't forget to set that alarm.

A blanket falls on me. I force one eye open.

CJ sits on the floor, his back turned to me.

"I shouldn't sleep here," I say.

"Sleep where you can." He tips his head back to look at me, the top of it brushing against my thigh. His blue eyes are dark in the dim light and so warm.

"I'll wake you up when I go to bed." He strums the strings of his guitar.

The notes are light and soothing. I pull the blanket around my shoulders and under my chin. My body relaxes, but my mind struggles against the comfort. Dang the sleep debt. CJ's music might be to blame though. It's light but haunting. His voice is a notch above a whisper and all the more attention-grabbing. I fish out my phone and open a recording app. What he's singing, I haven't heard anywhere before. It may be someone else's song, like *Stranger Danger*, or it may be his own. I want to have a chance to listen to it later.

They say I have it all
Perhaps, I do, but there are days
I crash into the wall
They judge me when I bleed

I'm not supposed to show I'm hurt
And when I smile to make their hearts stop
Because that's what's expected
They label me a sinner, say I'm tainted

He switches to humming, even quieter than before. I tap the button to stop recording. My chest hurts with how hard my heart is beating, and my thoughts are in awe and shame. These words... Does he feel that way? That people judge him? That someone out there considers him ruined?

Tainted.

By fame?

By the way he handles relationships?

Even if he's not singing about himself, there's a bitter taste in my mouth. I've considered him a careless guy based on what I see from my hill even though he's not. CJ cares for his own. He guards Alexandra. He worries about my comfort, and he's quick to make amends.

If things were different, I'd jump off this couch and hold him tight like I do Nia when she cries, and tell him, somehow, everything that simmers in my soul.

I reach for his shoulder and stop a breath away.

Things aren't different. He's still a flirt. Or is he?

I told him he is full of fear.

So am I.

Not daring to breathe, I brush the outer side of my fingers against his cheek.

The music stops. My heart does too. I jerk my hand back.

CJ faces me, one eyebrow raised slightly, his expression smooth and calm.

"Good music," I say.

"I'm glad you like it."

Time crawls as CJ holds my gaze. I'm hanging by a thread, afraid that if I blink, I'll never be able to deal with my feelings again. I've been burying this attraction and fighting myself long enough. He doesn't have to like me, but I need to get this crush out of my system, and now is as good a time as ever.

"By the way," I say, desperate to dispel the tension that's about to shatter me. "I booked your flight to New York for tomorrow, four in the afternoon. Best I could do, and I hope you don't mind that you'll miss out on a radio show."

"Oh no. How should I live without appearing in public?"

His crooked grin and lighthearted tone set something within me to rights. "Have fun," I say. "Recharge."

"Thanks." CJ takes my hand and kisses it.

This gesture is not CJ's usual style. He winks and shoots smolders, but a tame, quiet, respectful show of gratitude like this? A brush of his lips between my knuckles that sets my skin on fire, pushes heat into my cheeks, and ignites my imagination?

He continues playing his guitar.

No, I don't mean anything special to him.

I tuck both my hands under the blanket, away from trouble and temptation. I should go to bed and never listen to his voice again, but I don't. I wish I was more reckless. That I'd throw this blanket aside and drop onto his lap and claim that kiss—

I'll drive myself insane. Maybe I should. That way, I'll be able to stop torturing myself with wishful thinking.

▶ Track 15
Empty Promises & We're Okay

I try to rekindle my affair with the strings until three in the morning. My fingertips throb by the time I decide to be done, and when I turn to wake Fiona up, as promised, I discover her hand an inch away from my shoulder.

What am I supposed to do with you, you impossible woman? Do you like me after all? Do you feel sorry for me? I didn't know what to make of that touch earlier, and I couldn't decide what her look meant. I did sense a bit of uncertainty, though.

That could've come from hearing me sing and assuming I'm spiraling into the depths of depression. I am a little. That's why she touched me too. A friend comforting a friend.

That cool shiver that whispered down my arms when her fingers brushed my face?

I tuck the memory away into my soul, into its attic, and forbid my hands to push the hair off her forehead.

"Fiona," I say, "time to go to bed."

She gives out a quiet groan that manages to pack a universal complaint. "Okay." But she doesn't even stir.

I return the guitar to its case under the couch. "Want me to carry you?"

She lifts one arm in a childish gesture of pick-me-up.

Fiona! You're wrecking me. I keep telling myself I'll ignore you, and you find a way, every single day, to sabotage my resolve.

Suit yourself. I will carry you, and you'll smack me so hard it'll leave a bruise, or you'll shriek so loud everyone will wake up regardless of the earplugs.

I chuckle imagining that.

"Let's go then." Sliding one arm under her back, the other under her knees, I brace myself.

Fiona's arms wrap around my neck. How tired is she? I do my best to not fixate on how warm she is or how well she fits into my arms as I stand up.

Fiona clings to me, her blanket pressed between us, and rests her head on my shoulder. "Just this once." She is awake enough to realize what's happening, at least.

I take her to the bunks. "Does it have to be once?"

"No. Wait. What?"

"Push the door button, will you?"

She reaches for the button and fumbles for a second before she finds it. I enter the bunk compartment and set Fiona onto her feet, but before I can step away, she grabs the hem of my shirt.

"You're not tainted," she says through a yawn.

Her verbal acknowledgment of hearing me sing those words sends a jolt of embarrassed prickles through my ribcage.

"I'm not?" I did not just ask *that*. What am I, a needy teen again? I don't need anyone's approval.

"You're not tainted." She drapes the blanket I brought her around my neck. "I know you're scared to death to let go of your bad boy shell, but there's a good guy inside you."

"You keep saying heartwarming things like that, and I might just kiss you." This will definitely earn me a smacking.

Fiona turns to her bed with an exhausted sigh. "All I ever get from you is empty promises."

My mouth drops. I reach for her arm, but she's already climbed onto her bunk, leaving me to stare at the black curtain that separates her from the rest of the bus.

Oh, Fiona. Stop making me smile like an idiot.

"When you come back, let's really dig into some stuff for our next album," Marshall says as he watches me pick a few things from my suitcases for my flight to New York.

"Yeah, sure." Where are my leather sneakers? If Shane's wearing them again—

"I've recorded a few ideas that I uploaded to our cloud. Have you listened yet?"

I got the notifications that new files have been added, but I haven't looked. I've been brushing off most notifications lately. "I will. On the plane. I didn't want anyone interrupting. You know how it is. The moment I'll start listening, someone will need something."

I freeze with a leather belt in my hands. I didn't lie to him, but I'm dishonest all the same. Not about his music. There's so much Marshall doesn't know. Weeks of my life, at this point, have been withheld from him.

From everyone but Fiona.

Something is seriously broken here.

Before, I wouldn't talk to anyone but Marshall about the kind of mess that's been brewing in my head. This time, I leave him out. I am afraid of what he'd say. I can't hurt Marshall's feelings, much, but I fear he'll feel betrayed by my struggle and uncertainty. I promised that bringing a new bassist would seal my stardom dreams. I begged for that change. I wanted Alexandra here. Everything has changed, for everyone, and I'm still not happy. Not happy, and it's getting harder and harder to breathe with each passing hour. Everyone wants new songs, but I'm dry and useless.

I stuff the belt into the duffel bag and zip it up.

Marshall may feel betrayed. I may be a traitor. Such scary thoughts.

"CJ." Marshall grabs my sleeve as I walk past him.

"Yeah?"

"You…" He looks away. "Alexandra and me. You really aren't in love with her? We're okay?"

I need to go, but I lean on the wall and look him straight in the eye. We had beefed out the supposed love triangle between me, Alexandra, and Marsh close to four months ago, but Marshall still doubts me. Or himself. I add this to the growing list of my failures.

"Yes. We're okay." I may be in need of alignment, but he and I are fine. "I'm sorry for giving you all this uncertainty. Don't think about me and her ever again."

He nods. "It just feels that you and I have drifted apart. Which is stupid, I know. We're fine." Marshall drops his hand onto my shoulder. "Right?"

Crud. Fiona was onto something with her whole pretend-that-I'm-okay-a-little-harder.

"Of course we are. Everything's great. See you soon. Hold down the fort in my absence and keep composing." Because I can't anymore.

I whip around in the middle of the bus. I should just tell him I can't write another song.

That would be honest.

That's what best friends do—have no fears or secrets between them. They shouldn't.

"Marsh."

He stops in front of the snack bar and picks up a pack of jerky. "Yeah?"

On the other hand, what if what I'm going through is completely normal and will go away in a couple of weeks or even after my trip to New York? But if I say something now, I'll open a can of worms that could never be closed again.

"Have fun. Don't get married without me."

The pack of jerky crinkles in protest when Marshall squeezes it in his fist. He glances at Alexandra, who, as luck would have it, ignores the rest of the world with the help of noise-cancelling headphones plugged into an amp that's channeling a signal from her bass.

I raise an eyebrow at Marshall's startled reaction. Wait. A. Second. "Don't tell me—"

"You'll be late for your flight." Scowling, Marshall rips the package open. He might do the same to me if I don't leave him be. Whatever plans he has, he's not ready to include me yet.

I feel a little better knowing there are things both of us don't want to share with each other.

The World's Next Most Dynamic Duo

CJ

New York, United States

"Hey there," Aiya greets me as I enter her house.

It's quite the welcome—arms around my neck, eyes caressing my face.

I peel her away from me. "I'm here to work."

"Of course," Aiya purrs. "And we will. But do we really need three days to record one tiny song?" She intertwines our arms and guides me deeper into her white house with furniture pieces based on the latest trends.

One tiny song? I should've listened to everyone who told me this would have a questionable outcome.

"Aiya." I stop and wait until she looks me in the eye. "I'm here to work. Only work."

"Cristian, I do appreciate your professionalism, but you don't need to pretend with me." Leaning against me, Aiya tries to cage me with her arms once more, but she's done the one thing I don't tolerate.

"It's CJ, not Cristian." I hate it when people call me Cristian, no matter who does it. Not even Mrs. Tang can, and she's the only woman I consider to be my mother. My biological mother called me Cristian. She preferred the bottle to her own son, and I don't need any reminders of those days.

Also, just because I'm someone who enjoys pretty girls doesn't mean I want every female hanging on me every second of my existence. "Because I respect you, I'll tell you how it is. I'm not in the mood to have a fling right now. If I gave you a different impression, please forgive me."

Aiya blinks, appearing deeply stunned. She hugs her middle, and a shade of pink manages to make an appearance on her cheeks. "Thanks for the honesty. I get it. You don't care to fool around. Are you at least hungry? I made some barbecue pulled pork lettuce wraps."

"You cook?" I didn't take Aiya for the cooking kind of girl. Or one who eats, for that matter. She's on the starved end of skinny.

"I'm not just a ditz who happens to have a bit of singing ability."

Aiya flashes me a confident smile that eases the awkwardness between us. I hate to make anyone feel embarrassed, and it's a relief she can recover quickly.

Aiya proceeds inside the house, hips swaying, heels clicking, shoulders outlined by the straps of her tank top, exuding allure. If I'm honest with myself, a few weeks ago, I would've given her what she wanted. She is stunning. She is also shallow. She'll chew me up and spit me out. It's the case of takes one to know one. I'm her.

Heck. Is that how Fiona sees me? Careless and heartless? I'm not. I care. Every girl I date, I treat with respect. I tell them outright what I want, and never push if anyone says no.

Does it make anything better?

It takes all of me to not turn around, hop onto the flight back, and tell Fiona I'm not all sweet talk and lust impersonated.

She already knows it.

She told me I'm not tainted.

The memory pulls my lips into a smile. No matter the ocean between us, Fiona cheers me up.

I won't prove her wrong.

"You coming?" Aiya reappears in the arch that connects her entryway with the main living area.

"Yeah. Food sounds good."

I follow her into a spacious kitchen with faux fur–lined barstools and dangling, single-bulb chandeliers. It smells of warm meat and sweet sauce. I approve. A setting for two—white napkins, bamboo placemats, square black plates, and wine glasses—waits at the table.

"No alcohol," I warn her.

Aiya fills the wine glasses with water and gives me a curious look. "It's true, then? You guys never drink?"

"Safety measure. Can I help with anything?"

Aiya nods at the sink. "Wash your hands and grab the lettuce. Safety measure from what? Doing something you'd regret later?"

"Yes." I soap up, rinse, and wipe, then grab a bowl of lettuce leaves sitting near the sink and bring it to the table. "Drinking has ruined too many bands. Too many people in general." Including my mother. "We choose to stay away from things that'll damage what we have." It took us too much to get where we are to throw it away.

"Smart." She places a platter of juicy meat between our plates. "Can you eat cheese? Or is dairy also off limits?"

"Dairy is fine." I narrow my eyes at her, making sure she knows I'm onto her. Every time the no-booze policy comes up, people mock us.

"Don't get touchy." She smiles. "Teasing you is all I have left since you told me nothing's gonna happen." Which doesn't stop her from walking to the fridge with utmost flair, shiny black hair swinging down her back.

After a quick dinner, Aiya shows me to the guest house. Like many well-earning musicians, she has a recording studio at her place. To save some commuting time, I decided I'd stay with her for the duration of us recording.

"Now, I need your phone," Aiya says.

"Don't even think about it." I don't know what she's planning, but she's not getting my phone.

She takes out hers, along with a self-sealing plastic bag. "We'll swap. Since you're so insistent on work, that's the only thing you'll do. No girlfriends, no social media, no distractions. We only have three days." Aiya turns off her phone, drops it in the bag, and seals it. "Hurry up, will you?"

"How will I set my alarm? What if something happens back in Europe?"

"They'll manage a couple of days without you. Your phone, please."

Whatever. It's only for three days. I power the phone down, seal it in the bag, and we trade.

"Great. Now get some sleep. We'll start at seven."

"I like the business you a lot more than the flirty you. It suits you."

"Pft." Aiya tucks a lock of hair behind her ear, a gesture so timid, it takes me aback.

For the next three days, I play guitar, we sing, we goof around with different effects and chords and everything we can think of. Aiya, it turns out, has many opinions and a good ear too. Together with a couple of recording techs from her label, we churn out a solid track.

Having this break from the tour is nice, building something new helps me feel alive again, and having Aiya watch me every second lifts my spirit. I know I'm a horrible guy for loving attention like that, but

I cleared up Aiya's expectations, and if she wants to waste her time on me, it's her problem.

Aiya sees me off with a disappointed pout. Three days of sultry glances, skimpy outfits, and romantic dinners got her nothing. It got me an almost finished song. It's in the hands of the sound engineers now. We'll perform it at the Teen Faves in Amsterdam in two weeks, and I can return to my band having satisfied a mental itch.

Walking through JFK on my way back to Europe, I turn on my phone and discover a media storm. I shouldn't have let Aiya cut me off from the world or followed her then-reasonable suggestion to fast from social media. Who knew that missing one radio show could be so precarious? Fan posts are full of speculations that not all is well within Project Viper, and tabloid sites' headlines are the stuff of my nightmares.

Is Project Viper's New Bassist Here To
Replace CJ Sanchez?

The Six Vipers To Become Five Again?

Sanchez Brings In A Replacement To Pursue
Solo Career

Project Viper Founder Moving On

Being tuned in wouldn't have helped. Once the rumor fire is stocked, no matter how insignificant the catalyst is, nothing helps. The only course of action is to wait it out. I can only imagine what has been going through Alexandra's head. I hope Marshall confiscated her phone too.

"Next time you're gone," Marshall says, "we'll tell them you're sick. Or in a coma. Or that werewolves ate you."

I take a huge bite of a chocolate ice cream bar. "I vote for the werewolves. It's the most exciting option."

We're milling outside a gas station late in the evening. Our bus driver is topping off for the rest of the night while we take an opportunity to stuff our faces with cheap European snacks. The flavor of my smooth chocolate ice cream mixes with the stuffy but cooling summer air, exhaust, and the sharp scent of gas. The only one not present is Graham. He chose to stay attached to the real paper book he found somewhere. The cover looked grim, shadows and possessed faces.

"All we did at that radio show you missed was to say you were away for a quick help on a collaboration. It's not like nobody else does that. In fact, everyone constantly works on new projects together. Yet you take one step to the left, and it's the end of the world as we know it," Shane comments. "This is the stupidest side of this business—having to deal with the rumors."

"Well, let them have their fun." I wink at Alexandra.

She gives me a weak smile. "Yup. Fun."

"Does anyone know what happened to Monopoly?" Zach starts his second bottle of some flowery soda. "I turned the bus inside out looking for it last night."

"He really did," Fiona says. "I cleaned up after him."

Zach pulls his head into his shoulders and offers her one of his candy bars. He cannot leave a gas station with just one item. He must have a bit of everything.

"You're welcome, everyone," Shane grumbles. "And if I see that stupid game ever again, I'm not responsible for what I'll do."

Perfect timing. This story should cheer our new bassist up.

"Why did you make me get rid of it? I want the full story," Fiona says as she unwraps Zach's peace offering.

"You helped him?" Zach presses a hand to his heart. "How could you?"

"Thank you very much, Fiona. I'm not playing Monopoly again. With any of you." Shane points at all of us in turns.

"Calm down." Elise pats his back.

"Will you tell me why already?" Alexandra groans.

Marshall huffs. "Last game happened on our last tour. It took hours and hours, split over three legs of the tour, and they had to bribe us to talk to each other again. We were playing for real money, and Zach, of course, hoarded Park Place, Boardwalk, and half the other monopolies."

"Oh yeah, I remember Kiera flying out for this," Fiona says. "It was the only time real mediation was required. Not girls." She shoots me a hinting look. "Not drugs or royalties. A game of Monopoly."

"What?" Alexandra turns to Marshall, a solid grimace of disbelief on her face.

"It's true," he says.

"It was the best game of Monopoly ever," Zach declares.

"Because if we stuck with the real cash, we'd owe you money for the rest of our lives," I add.

"Seriously?" Alexandra leans into Marshall as she laughs. She is so happy with him. With us. I would never ruin that. Stupid rumors. Stupid artist block of mine too. "You had a major band crisis because of a board game?"

I kick her foot. "Don't laugh. Being stuck together twenty-four seven for almost a year is a pain in the butt."

"Speak for yourself," Zach says.

He's the only person I know who's okay being surrounded by

people all day every day. Even extroverts get worn out before he does. He's a super-vert.

After this little blast from the past and once we're back on the road, Marshall corrals us to work on a song for a little bit. His lyrics suck, but I help him find better rhythm. We come up with a solid tune too, social media is forgotten, and everything feels normal again. Perhaps Fiona was right—I needed to recharge.

We hit Tallinn, Riga, and Helsinki. The shows there feel better than any of the previous ones this summer. We come up with two more new songs, and I start believing I'm cured. Fiona gives me encouraging smiles here and there. She must notice I feel better.

Until I don't.

Stockholm brings darkness all over again. I feel bored on the stage. *Bored.* That's even worse than the earlier numbness and the artist block combined. I can't bear to make eye contact with anyone in the band or the crew. The strangest, most stupefying feeling of not belonging follows me everywhere. Every time I smile, I feel like such a fake. I avoid Alexandra because I fear that the moment I talk to her—about anything—she'll figure out I'm falling to pieces and blame herself.

None of this is her fault.

Amsterdam, Netherlands

We play Warsaw, then finally drive to Amsterdam for the Teen Faves Awards.

"Ready to get together with Aiya again? I bet it's not just marketing sense that pushed her label to release your song so fast," Zach says while we unload from the bus and into the hotel since we'll be in Amsterdam for a couple of days.

Shane hoots. Elise rolls her eyes at him, but he only grins.

Marshall grunts as he hefts his bag. "You can do so much better than Aiya," he says to me.

Alexandra nods, then Marshall startles all of us by sneezing. He's got one of those sneezes that wakes the dead. Fiona offers him a tissue pack.

"Thanks. Allergies have been killing me." Marshall wipes his nose and goes on. "All I'm saying is that all Aiya's got is her looks and her voice."

"Says the guy with the looks and the voice," Graham mutters, opening the hotel door for us.

"He's right, you know?" I say to Marshall as we enter the hotel lobby. "She's still a person."

"Barely. And how would you know that anyway in just three days? I doubt she gave you a chance to talk." He raises his eyebrows, insinuating everything we haven't done.

"For your information, not that I owe you an explanation, we didn't do anything you think we did." I grin. "She called me Cristian."

"Well, that just won't do," Fiona says as we arrive at the reception desk.

While she retrieves our keys, Shane continues the onslaught.

"Are you scheming to be the world's next most dynamic duo with Aiya? Marshall and Alexandra stole all of your thunder, so you're out to overthrow them?"

"Funny." I turn away from him. "Fiona, can I have my key now?"

"Of course." She hands me one of the key cards. "Here you go, Cristian."

Everyone wants to mess with me right now.

"I will not take you to the awards afterparty with me," I say, pointing my key card at Fiona.

She shrugs. "Good. I have better things to do. Okay, guys. Let's go. Your beauty sleep awaits."

"You really wouldn't go to a party with me?" I ask Fiona once we get to our floor and the rest of our group has gone ahead.

"Especially with you." She slips behind her room door.

Before it closes, though, I catch her stealing a glance at me and the teasing smile on her lips. If I'm not mistaken, and I don't think I am, I've finally witnessed an instance of Fiona flirting. I'd give anything to test my theory tonight, but she closes the door, and I remember how exhausted she's been lately. So, okay. I'll let her rest and catch a few winks myself. I hope.

Tomorrow, though, all bets are off.

Fallen from Bass, Fallen from Grace

CJ

At breakfast, I discover that Fiona won't be accompanying us to the Teen Faves show. Three of the tech crew have caught a stomach bug, and she has gone to our venue for tomorrow's show to help set up.

"She doesn't know anything about equipment," I grumble to Rick. "Couldn't we have hired anyone local to fill in the gap in the staff? Is it really helpful to substitute three pros with one inexperienced person?"

"Don't worry." He gives me a reassuring smile. "Anyone can help carry equipment and tape off things. Besides, she's on tour with us to learn everything she can about how things operate. It'll be good for her. She needs to see what it's like outside the luxurious tour bus and your starry glamor."

That is so not what I meant. I wasn't trying to insult Fiona's capabilities. I just… I thought she'd be here for the big day and was all geared up to explore that new expression she gave me yesterday. Now she's gone.

I drink my protein shake and listen to my bandmates complain about beds that are too hard, and when are we going to do something fun together while we're in Europe?

"We haven't been able to go out and about as a gang yet." Zach frowns at Rick.

"Sorry," our tour manager says. "I'll figure something out. What are you thinking? Something wild or something to unwind?"

"Wild!" Shane exclaims. Elise supports him with enthusiastic nods.

Graham and Marshall mutter, "Unwind." Marshall uses nasal allergy spray and straps on a black face mask. I can see why he wouldn't want to go crazy.

Alexandra and Zach are of the opinion we need to do both. Everyone looks at me.

"Whatever." As long as Fiona's back with us.

That is new. Needing someone specific by my side like this.

Is this…?

Attachment?

Connection?

…

Love?

The next glug of the shake goes down like a boulder.

I don't know what I feel about Fiona, but I don't fall in love. It doesn't happen to me. I enjoy flirting and catching attention and, yes, the chase. The hunt for that admission that someone feels a spark for me. None of those conquests caused me to miss them or sent me climbing the walls after an argument. Every goodbye has been easy.

As for Fiona, we haven't gone far enough for goodbyes. I doubt we ever will.

"Oh, yes. There's a package for you from home." Rick places a chunky bubble mailer next to me before he leaves our suite.

The return address belongs to The Label. This may be something official or urgent. I rip it open.

Inside, is a small card and the softest, mustard-yellow sleeveless T-shirt. Nice. Or so I think until I see the front, where the bold, black letters state,

FALLEN FROM BASS
FALLEN FROM GRACE

What the…? I check the card.

```
Hey, deserter. How's the six-string life
treating you?

                        Kel, CC, and T
```

Kel is Kelmore Schutz, CC—Crystal Coleman, and I bet T stands for Tristan Bailey. Bassists of Sinners Anonymous, Watch It!, and Acid Churro Dreams respectively.

How nice. A friendly jab from fellow bass players.

I'm not a bassist anymore.

Leaving the breakfast table, I throw the shirt on my chair but pick it up again a second later. The three of them knew I'd never wear the thing. I will. I strip out of my plain blue long-sleeve tee right there and then, and pull the yellow on.

"What is this atrocity?" Elise exclaims through a bite of pan au chocolate.

"Some friends of mine thought it'd be funny to give me this." My million-dollar smile on, I turn and face the band.

Shane sputters whatever he's drinking and laughs, Zach pulls out his phone to take a picture, and Graham gives me a glance but otherwise ignores me. Typical. Marshall frowns. I'm surprised he doesn't laugh. I thought he'd jump on this opportunity to mock me along with the people who sent me the shirt.

When he glances at Alexandra, I know why he's not joining in. Her lips are pursed tight, hands fisted next to her plate.

"It's just a dumb joke." I crouch in front of her and, smiling, take her hands. "A really stupid joke. They don't mean it, but I'll wear it anyway because I don't want them to win, no matter how childish it is. Also, this way, I take the blame, right? I'm the one who decided to change everything."

It's true. I am the one who wanted to shift the dynamic in the band and fix what wasn't broken.

"It is childish. Take it off. Nobody wins if you wear this." She rises from her chair and walks out of the suite.

"Alexandra," Marshall and I call after her together.

She pauses in the doorway. "I'm going to get a massage in the spa downstairs. We have a couple of hours before we're needed anywhere, correct?" The door closes behind her.

Marshall turns to me. "I don't know how to stop her from reading all the negative stuff people say about her online. All the comments have made her touchy."

"I'm sorry." My apology is for Alexandra feeling upset, of course, but my whole body vibrates from everything I'm hiding from him. What if I never get over this creative crisis? How will we go on? Anyone can play guitar. Shane could be the lead again. They wouldn't need me at all.

Did I make a mistake after all? Not in wanting a new bassist, no, but in thinking it'd fill whatever void I thought there was?

Marshall gives me a long, steady, and very much questioning look.

I smile. I have to. "Well, we might be finally getting ourselves a Teen Faves Award. What category though? Rock or Boy Band?"

"There's no such category as Boy Band." Marshall chuckles, and the tension melts.

For now.

We agreed to show up at the awards ceremony in full tuxedos. Everyone gets fresh haircuts, chins get shaven, nails are buffed. Everything. We're only playing three songs—I'm doing four, counting the one with Aiya—so we'll have no excuse to look like trash as we often do, sweaty and crumpled after a two-and-a-half-hour gig. I turn into a mark on our otherwise spiffy appearance by wearing that stupid yellow tee instead of a black button-up and a tie.

"This statement of yours makes my eyes hurt," Elise complains, running a lint roller over my tuxedo sleeves in our hotel suite.

"Then don't look," I say and close my eyes.

The lint roller stalls an inch above my right elbow. Quietly, Elise asks, "You okay?"

I wish Fiona were here.

I wish Marshall didn't worry about Alexandra.

I wish Alexandra didn't worry about me or her perceived damage to the band.

"Yeah. Thanks." I give Elise's hand a quick squeeze before approaching Alexandra. I can't fix my darkening mood, but I can do something for my bass successor. "We need to take a picture. Right now."

Her eyes, loaded with glittery green makeup, widen in surprise. "Why?"

"Just you and me." I throw my phone to Marshall and scoop his girlfriend into a one-arm hug. "Because you need more pictures to remember how you started. Because tonight we're probably getting an award, and"—I whisper the next part in her ear—"because Marsh is already turning red with jealousy."

Alexandra laughs. I turn to Marshall to wave for him to take the picture, but he's already on it. When he lowers my phone, I brace myself for a glare over the mask he's still wearing. Instead, I get a grateful nod before Marshall's eyes return to Alexandra. I made her laugh, and he'll forgive me for getting cozy with her. One last time.

"Me too!" Marshall jumps in, pulls off his mask, and aims my phone for a blurry, laughter-filled selfie.

"One more try," Alexandra requests. "I want a crisp one."

So we squish together and embed this moment into our souls forever. At least I do. Faces touching, Marshall's mug half-hidden by his unruly hair, but the brilliant grin is there. I throw in my signature wink. Standing between us, Alexandra has her hands on our shoulders, and her face is shining with delight. It's perfect.

I post the picture to Insta. No matter what anyone says, this is how we are. Happy together. These two are my heart and soul. So is Shane, Zach, and Graham.

And, not to leave anyone out, I add to my comment.

```
Thanks for the dopest rags! > @ccbassey,
    @kellmore_schutzzz,& @tb_is_free
```

It's this feeling of happiness and being part of a family I cling to later when we arrive at the venue, pose for the photographers on the red carpet, and shake hands with the fans lining the entrance. It's loud, and the excitement levels are dialed to eleven. Just how I love it.

Usually.

Shane's got Elise with him, both of them shining and posing for photos with abandon. Marshall stays next to Alexandra, but since they haven't announced their relationship to anyone, they keep physical contact to a minimum. Marshall doesn't want people thinking the only reason Alexandra's in the band is because she's the frontman's girlfriend. I wish Fiona was with me.

With *us*.

Smiling, I grab the next notebook offered for an autograph and leave a swooping signature. "So nice to meet you," I say to the teenage girl who presses her fists under her chin, barely containing herself. "Thank you so much for coming and waiting. We owe it all to loyal fans like you."

"Please, a photo?" she asks.

"Of course." What's a photo compared to the millions of dollars I have in my bank accounts thanks to girls like her?

More autographs. More photos. I push my mind to not dwell on Fiona. To not wonder if she'd wear something dressy for the occasion or stay in business attire. To not imagine her sharing jokes with some easygoing roadie while they all eat dinner together. Somebody take me away from here and make me do something that involves more mental effort than what's required for brandishing a marker.

I wave away the next photo print being shoved into my hand. "I'm sorry, but I should go now." I blow them all kisses and walk away.

The happiness I've shared with Marshall and Alexandra starts to fade. Dang it! I am so tired of hitting highs only to crash with a bang moments later.

"Long time no see." Lex Romero claps my shoulder as we enter the venue. He writes music for video games and does a lot of chart-topping EDM.

"Hi. What are you working on these days?" I ask.

"I'm tied in with Galvanized Games and *Access Denied III* that comes out in November. It's almost done. Just laying on finishing touches to the theme track. I've been struggling with the bass line for it, though. I think I need it to be the real deal, not synth. Speaking of which." He stops in front of me. "Want to help me out? Galvanized Games will pay for your services, of course. One track. Two at most. I already have it all written. Just play it for me, man. You're good stuff."

I chuckle. "Thanks, and tempting." Dipping toes in video game music does sound fun, even if I'm needed solely as a performer.

Lex shrugs. "Message me on Club if you decide you want to do it. I'm giving you a week to make up your mind—I'm on a deadline. If you don't want to do it, I'll find someone else. You know how it is."

I nod. "I do know."

Rick appears out of thin air and motions for us to join him on the side of the crowded entryway. The grim frown on his face warns that something has happened.

"See you later, man." I part ways with Lex and hurry over to Rick and my team.

"Change of plans. Rachel LeClaire, the opening act, is… indisposed, apparently," Rick says. "You've been volunteered to fill in for her. A little more warning would've been nice, of course, but— Get backstage right now."

"They're plucking us from the middle?" Graham squeezes his drumsticks in his hands. This development gives him a lot less time to achieve zen required to perform, so this is not good news for him.

I throw my hand back, signaling for him to settle down. "Why can't Aiya open? She's second on the schedule."

Rick subdues an enduring sigh. "They want someone with more bang. Rachel has been on top of all pop charts most of the year, that's why she's the opener—"

"The point here is Rachel *has been*." Aiya appears from behind me and stops between us and our tour manager. "I can do the opening." Chin raised high, arms crossed on her chest, what she's really saying is, *I will do the opening. Rachel's not here. Too bad, but it's my turn.*

Which I couldn't have agreed with more. Setting the mood for a show like this? It's big. We've done it before. And while Aiya is quite popular, she's still on the rise. She needs this opportunity more than we do.

"Let her do it," I say to Rick.

He checks with the rest of the band.

"No offense, Aiya," Marshall says, "but the opening is ours."

Now he wants to be stubborn? Then again, he always does.

"This is still good for us," I say to everyone. "If Aiya goes first, she and I still have a song together. Everyone's been speculating we're losing our touch, but this will show them we're simply experimenting."

Graham shrugs. "Experimenting isn't always a good thing."

I shoot him a glare. Would he keep his brutal honesty to himself for once?

"Come on, boys." Aiya grabs Marshall's arm and resorts to pure, old-fashioned, big-eyes, pouty-lips pretty please. "Give me a chance. You wouldn't do a full-on collab with me, so can I please have this?"

I pull Aiya to my side before Alexandra incinerates her with her glare for touching Marshall. "It'll be good," I promise.

Straightening out his tux sleeve, Marshall looks at me, at Aiya, at me again. It's hard to catch his full expression because of that mask he's been sporting since morning, but there's some wariness in his posture. "Okay. Go for it. You know what you're doing," he says to me.

Aiya jumps and hugs me. "Thank you."

"Yes, yes. Very cute that you figured it out between yourselves. Let me see if the organizers are okay with that. As if I'm in charge of anything here." Rick jogs off.

Aiya grabs my hand and tugs me to follow him. "Come on. You heard the man. Less than twenty minutes until the show."

"See you in a bit," I say to the band before Aiya drags me away.

Backstage, they outfit me with an in-ear monitor and other fun stuff, then Aiya shoves a pair of black jeans into my hands. "You're too dressy for my act."

She's wearing tiny shorts, again, a white halter, a gauzy black scarf, and several pendants of randomness, like a Fanta bottle cap and what looks like an edible red lollipop. There's no time for me to argue, so I go to swap the trousers for the jeans. Super-frayed jeans. I hate that kind. They bite into the skin in all the odd ways and places. Oh well. Things refuse to go according to the plan today, and it's only for one song.

When I come back to Aiya, five minutes before the opening time, she's a ball of energy, rolling her microphone between her palms.

"It's gonna explode!" She smacks her lips, exhales loudly, and throws her arms up for a couple of stretches. "I have to give you a heads up about something. No biggie. You'll handle it just fine. You composed all the parts, after all, sans the drums, and you're so good on guitars, it shouldn't be a problem at all."

"O-kay…"

A tech hands me a guitar. I fling the strap over my shoulder. Whoa, it's heavy, and the strings are thick under my fingers. I do a double take, count the number of strings in case I'm seeing things somehow. Four. E, A, D, G. It's a bass, all right.

Sharp dread stabs me in the gut. "What's this?" I demand.

"Don't frown so hard, handsome." Aiya walks her fingers up my chest, flirty-flirty.

I grab her hand. "Explain right now."

Aiya wiggles away. "We switched a couple of things in the song. That guitar solo you did apparently sounds way better on bass. It's got the oomph and a sexy kind of—"

"I can't do bass!" The strap of my former weapon of choice digs into my neck, a dead weight dragging me to the bottom of a quicksand pit.

"You have to. It's been re-recorded and will be published right after I perform. Your name's still on the title. Don't put up such a fuss." She tosses her shiny hair behind her shoulder, plants her hands on her hips, and glares to the side.

What is wrong with this girl? Never mind that she changed my song behind my back. Doesn't she understand what me playing bass after I stepped down as Project Viper's bassist will look like?

What it may do to Alexandra? How it'll fuel the rumors of me leaving even more?

"I won't *fuss*." I adjust my earpiece. "But this is the last time you and I perform together. Everyone told me this was a bad idea, but I advocated for you. Why did you have to go and stab me in the back?"

Aiya's defiant expression drops. She reaches for my arms—to comfort or to plead with me. Not caring either way, I raise my hand and step back. Her possibly hurt feelings are the least of my concern. Out there in the audience is the girl who will be panicking a lot more than I am right now once I set foot on stage with this bass.

The drumline punches the air, and I jump.

Aiya squares her shoulders. "We're still doing this?"

I wish I could walk away. I should walk away, but the organizers already had a musician bail on them at the last moment.

"As we practiced," I say. "Soulful agony with a hint of desire." I don't know how I'm going to pull off the desire. There's plenty of agony, though.

Aiya exhales. "Thanks."

I don't respond. We have no more time left for chit-chat, and I don't care to talk to her ever again. But I will accept all responsibility for what happens next, no matter what it is.

The crowd chants and claps and demands entertainment. I pull out my phone.

Aiya throws her hands up, the gesture asking, *What are you doing?*

"Messaging my band."

> I'm sorry about this. I'll explain when I'm back.

I slide the phone back into my pocket, ruffle my hair into an angry mess, then storm onto the dark stage. The lights won't turn on until we're in our proper positions, but when they do and blind me for a few seconds, I feel like I'll never emerge from the darkness, no matter how hard I try. I only make everything worse whenever I try to fix my artist block, my dream, my band.

Somehow, I keep a smile on my face. Somehow, I deliver a buttery, smooth bass solo. My hands shake the whole time, and I can't get off the stage fast enough. So fast that I forget to change back into my fancy trousers, which I don't notice until I drop into a seat next to Zach. Eff the pants.

"Alexandra." I reach across Zach for her hand.

She takes it. "That was amazing!"

Even though her calm smile takes the edge off my nerves, I still type them a long text. Several times I stumble over the wording and fight with the autocorrect, but never get to send the message.

First, we get summoned to receive our award for Best Pop Rock Artist, where we shuffle awkwardly for who gets to deliver the acceptance words. None of us have practiced a speech. We never do. It's either me or Marshall going for a couple of jokes and lots of thank-yous, but he points to his mask and shakes his head, and I'm holding Alexandra's hand, refusing to budge one inch away from her. In the end, Zach grabs the trophy and charms the audience with his cute salute of gratitude in Korean, promises them even more fun music, then points for us all to get off the stage.

Marshall squeezes my shoulder hard as we go down the steps. I face him.

"Another one to dust on the shelves," he says, fiddling with the straps of his mask.

I chuckle in response, but something about him doesn't sit right with me. He's not his usual confident, energy-exuding self. He doesn't shake hands or high five everyone he passes. When it's our turn to perform, Marshall is stiff and rarely interacts with me, keeping his attention on the fans in the pit in front of the stage. He must be ticked off at me for my bass fiasco with Aiya after all.

I run to catch up with him after our segment. As soon as we're out of the view of guests and cameras, Marshall drops to his knees and presses his forehead to the floor.

"Marshall!" Alexandra rushes to him along with me, along with everybody else.

We manage to convince him to lift his head. His face is paler than pale. His forehead is on fire.

"It's not just allergies," I berate him. "You're sick."

Graham and I support his arms and help him up.

Wincing, Marshall rises to his feet. "I hoped it wasn't anything serious."

Rick clears the way for us to one of the green rooms and demands for the first person with the venue staff lanyard to get the first aid administrator. Everyone and their dog walker hover nearby, barely giving Alexandra enough space to help Marshall drink some water.

Now I know why he wanted to go first, and if I managed to talk myself out of feeling like a complete traitor before, there's no longer a way out of that now. I chose someone else's success over my best friend. I didn't even see him hanging by a thread.

Let This Day End

Fiona

It's been quite the experience to switch my assistant hat to a roadie one. I've still run around all day, making sure everyone got fed and whatnot, but I also lugged cables, learned how the crew tests equipment, and watched Jedd stomp on all pedals and play all guitars, imagining the Vipers screaming in terror. They wouldn't scream. Jedd's paid to make sure their equipment works. He even subbed for Shane for a couple of shows when Shane got sick on the previous tour. But thinking of either Shane or CJ fainting is still a good laugh.

Late in the evening, we take five minutes for some snacks and a restroom break. We're not quite done yet, but everyone's starting to run out of steam a little. I sit on the edge of the stage and pull out my phone to scroll through Insta. There are a lot of fun posts. People must be having a good week. Dangling my feet with abandon, I tap hearts and comment on my fellow artists' adventures, even post a bunch of collages of Warsaw architecture and my sketches of it.

A new post pops on top of my feed. Yes! It's from Erik Cho.

Just as quickly as my enthusiasm flared, my mood plummets. He posted an announcement that his imprint, Speech Bubble Publishing, is open for submissions. Callie already pitched my project to them. They passed.

It's okay. Someone else decided to give me a chance.

I set my phone on the stage floor beside me and unwrap a protein bar from my hoodie pocket. A lot of lights are on, highlighting rows and rows of seats that will be filled with cheering fans tomorrow, but right now, the silence owns the arena. It's eerie and humbling. I'm a part of something big, complicated, but inspiring. I do a lot for Project Viper, but this opportunity to participate in setting up their sound and visual effects seems to add more weight to my contribution to their success.

My phone rings for the first time all day. The cascading chimes of my ringtone sound downright violent in this peace. When I see the caller ID—Kiera Denver—I can't help frowning. We exchange emails almost daily, but she hasn't called me since the beginning of the tour. Something must've happened.

"Hello?"

"What's going on?" Kiera's tone is harsh and impatient.

Adrenaline spiking, I abandon the arena in favor of the side hallway to be able to speak in private. I put her on speaker and check everything. No new text messages. "It's all under control." Whatever it is. I'm not sure yet what she's upset about. Better check social media.

Holy!

CJ played bass at Teen Faves, Marshall passed out after their segment of the show, and there's a million comments all saying the same thing—the band's breaking up.

"It's overblown." I close all social media apps. "Everything's good. A little drama for a bit of attention."

Kiera remains silent for the longest ten seconds in history. "Only a little drama?"

A bit of doubt creeps in even though there hasn't been anything problematic on this tour until now. I guess there's CJ. He's been having some roadblocks, but they have nothing to do with what happened at the awards event. I don't think. "The guys are fine. A little tired, but—"

"A little?" Kiera's tone becomes unforgiving. "Marshall fainted."

I don't know what to say about that, other than, "He's been fighting allergies all week."

"Allergies." Kiera sighs.

"Kiera, we got this." I head back to the arena. I feel bad for abandoning the crew, but I need to get back to my guys. "I promise you, everything's fine. Did you get to talk to Rick yet?"

"He won't pick up. That's why I called you. But since you say everything's okay, I'm going to trust you. Keep me posted."

I'd better be right. I never lie to Kiera. I love the band, but they're not paying my paychecks. In return for my honesty, Kiera stays out of the way as long as she knows what's happening and I'm handling things. I'll handle this curve ball as well.

I catch a cab to the hospital Marshall's been admitted to. The speed-limit-friendly ride gives me plenty of time to investigate videos and posts about what happened at Teen Faves. Kiera's freaked out, but I can see Charlie, our social media coordinator, jumping all over this and spinning it to the band's advantage. It's not her job to mitigate every instance of spooked public attention, but she'll love this mess. To her, the more drama the better. To me, I hope Marshall is okay. And Alexandra. CJ too. I hope they're all okay.

Rick meets me in the hospital lobby and takes me upstairs.

"I'm so happy you're back," he says as we ride the elevator. "Maybe you'll talk some sense into CJ."

That doesn't sound good. "What's up with him?"

Rick frowns. "You'll see."

That does not sound good at all. If I were prone to biting nails, I'd start doing so now.

Somewhere upstairs, down a long, quiet, dark corridor, we pass Chris on a chair at the door and turn into a large room. There's a bed and all the usual medical equipment, a rather comfortable-looking sofa, some leafy plants in white pots, a couple armchairs, and a coffee table. Alexandra's curled up on the sofa under a peach-colored blanket, eyes closed. Asleep, I hope. Her face is lined with shadows that have nothing to do with the dimmed lights. Marshall occupies the medical bed and is the proud owner of an oxygen mask. He's also asleep.

Next to him, resting his forehead on his folded arms is CJ.

Rick waves at him. "He won't leave," he whispers. "Make him come with me. The rest of the band is at the hotel, resting and chugging NyQuil and vitamins for a bedtime snack in case they've picked up what Marshall has."

We all have been on the same bus with him. Maybe I need to take something before bed as well. It doesn't matter right now, though.

"Can you get her to come with me too?" He points at Alexandra.

I shake my head. "Nobody will pry Alexandra away from Marshall unless brute force is involved."

Rick sighs. "Fine, but see if you can talk CJ into leaving. He doesn't need to be here."

Smiling, as if I totally got this, I tilt my head at the door. "Give me half an hour?"

He nods and leaves. I don't think I'll be able to bring either CJ or Alexandra with me. I just wanted to get Rick out of their hair. He doesn't seem to understand the dynamic here at all.

CJ looks up the moment the tour manager is gone. There's a permanent kind of frown between his eyebrows, and his jaw is clenched—he's ready to fight me. I leave him be, for now, and approach Alexandra.

"You're right," she says, eyes still closed, when I sit on the floor next to her. "I won't go."

"You don't have to." I take her hand, and Alexandra opens her eyes. "Marshall will be okay. What does he have anyway?"

"A sinus infection with a moderate case of bronchitis," she explains. "They're giving him antibiotics and a bunch of other stuff. I can't believe he was able to sing being this sick."

"That's Marshall for you."

I get the distinct feeling of someone watching me. I turn around, and sure enough, CJ is peeking over his folded arms. I wave for him to join us. He shakes his head.

"Get over here," Alexandra says to him.

He moves away from Marshall's bedside, to walk out of the room altogether.

"What happened?" I ask Alexandra. "I know the gist of it, but I don't quite understand the undercurrents yet."

She pulls the blanket under her chin and takes a couple minutes to relay the details. "Aiya screwed CJ over. She changed the song and put him on the bass, and CJ's been feeling…guilty, I guess. About me. I told him on the way here that me joining the band doesn't mean he can't ever play bass again. Many people see him as a bassist first. He won't listen to me, of course." She tips her head back and groans quietly. "These guys! What is it with them and never listening to anyone? They get something in their heads and— You know?"

"I know." I tuck the blanket around her. "Are you really okay, though?"

"No fear." She musters a grin. "Remember? You told me that before I met the guys. I won't be afraid now. What will be will be." Her smile snuffs out, hands bunching up the blanket. "What if I should've never joined them? What if we all took this too lightly? Have you seen the streaming reports? The sales haven't been good. The fans aren't super happy—"

"You're still thinking of last month's numbers." Relocating to the edge of the sofa, I pull her into a hug. "You shouldn't be thinking about them at all right now. Rest. When I'm tired, everything seems so much worse than it is, especially since the guy you love has pushed himself past all reasonable limits."

"For Project Viper." She brings her knees to her chest and hides her face in them.

"Look at me." I have to use my stern voice. "Repeat after me. Everything will be okay."

"Everything will be okay."

"Do you believe me?"

Alexandra draws a shaky breath. "Yes." She doesn't, but that's understandable.

"It'll be fine. Rest. Can I get you anything?"

"No. Thank you."

"Should I stay for the night with you?" I rise to my feet. "I'll be happy to."

Her eyes dart to the door. "Make CJ get some rest. Rick's right. There's no point in us all dropping sick, from infections or fatigue."

Something cool in her tone prompts me to ask, "Are you upset with CJ?"

"Yes. Why is he so dang set on thinking everything is his fault?" Her tone rises in volume. "We all knew Aiya was trouble—"

"Shhh." I don't want her getting wound up all over again. "Don't worry about it. I'll take care of him."

I exit the room, slowing down my steps to mouth to sleeping Marshall, "You get better soon."

The hallway is empty, with the exception of Chris. Where did CJ evaporate to? When Chris sees me frowning, he nods to the right.

I pass a few rooms and come into what looks like a waiting lobby with more of the same armchairs that I saw in Marshall's room. CJ's perched on the wide windowsill, hand resting on a bent knee, staring out the window. His pose is begging for a sketch. I allow myself three seconds to embed the image into my head—it would be massively inappropriate to take a picture—before I approach him.

"You seem to have had a day." I'm going to take this slow.

CJ doesn't respond. That's not good. Out of all the people I know, he's the least prone to shutting down.

"Come on. Let's go to the hotel. I'll let you keep me up while you explain to me in detail what happened." I tug on his arm.

CJ starts losing balance, as I knew he would, and has no choice but to scramble to his feet and stand up. "Hey!" He jerks his arm away and stuffs both hands in his jeans pockets. He's taller than me, and in this sour mood, has no qualms about towering over me.

I know he's not mad at me and don't take his attitude personally. "Would you like a hug?"

He reels away, glaring, as if I've offered him… I can't even pick a comparison.

Even slower then. "What's with the shirt?"

Fallen from bass, fallen from grace.

CJ tugs at the low collar, still saying nothing. His shoulders are tense, jaw tight with anger. Or frustration. Or both.

Rick was right. It won't be easy to take CJ away from here no matter how clear it is that he needs to leave. He needs to let go of what happened instead of being by himself and fueling his dark emotions further.

Still, I don't know how to approach him. On any other day, he'd spark to life if I touched him. He'd give me *that* look and launch into something playful.

Because this is the worst time ever to do so, my mind latches onto that notion. CJ might have been enjoying our banter and *me*?

No, no, no. This is really not the time to investigate this. I box my speculations for later and smooth out CJ's disheveled hair. Fiona the manager's assistant is here to save the day. "CJ, let's leave. You don't have to talk to anyone, not even me. You don't have to do anything." I want to hug him, too, like I hugged Alexandra, but I don't know if he'd appreciate it. My confidence deflates. He refused to listen to Alexandra. Why would he listen to me? "Would you please come with me?"

CJ's eyes narrow for a moment, then he exhales hard. I brace myself for an outburst, an order to get out of his face, or similar, but he wraps his arms around me.

I hold him as tight as I can. Forget the job. I can't stand seeing him like this, void of all the joyful energy that accompanies him everywhere.

We stand in the empty, quiet lobby for what feels like a long time. A couple of hospital staff pass by, but we don't move. A dark, desperate attitude wafts off CJ as he clings to me, his every muscle tense.

"I've ruined everything, haven't I?" His voice is quiet but full of suppressed emotion.

"That's impossible. No one can ruin *everything*."

"There's a mountain of gossip about how Project Viper is breaking up. Alexandra says it isn't a big deal, but I see her anxiety. I know she's terrified she's the reason for the gossip. Marshall's sick, and I didn't even realize he was going down. I'm his best friend, Fiona."

"Nobody's blaming you for anything."

"Yes, they do. It's all my fault. All of it." His fears are so raw, tugging on my every heartstring.

"I'm sorry—"

CJ scoffs. "It's definitely not your fault."

"I meant I'm sorry you feel this way, but I understand. I think. You must be so overwhelmed."

CJ pushes away and startles me by issuing a string of potent swear words.

I never took him for a cusser. He must be wound up past his limit.

"Fiona, I don't need you to pity me."

He's definitely in that mindset that escalates everything out of proportions. Time for tough love.

"What do you need then? You want me to say you're a screwup? Is that what you need? Do you want me to say it's all your fault? That you're a careless jerk? That you deserve to feel bad?"

CJ stares at me.

Heat creeps up my cheeks. That might've been overboard.

He laughs. "You're Kiera's assistant for good a reason."

My *comforting* tactic worked?

I curl my fingers around my shoulder bag strap for support. "Ready to go?"

"Okay."

"Good boy." I turn toward the elevators.

"Yeah. Not even close." The shadows sneak back into his voice.

"Stop it. Let this day end. Let it all end. Don't hold onto the negative."

"Fine."

He gives me the obligatory agreement, but I know, of course, he's doing it only to pacify me. That's fine. I'll take it. Little victories.

CJ takes my hand. My mouth goes dry as soon as he intertwines our fingers. So warm. A little rough from all that guitar playing, but there's no hesitation. His grip is gentle but strong, and... Not five minutes ago we were all wrapped around each other, and what unravels me is a little hand holding? What's wrong with my brain?

This is so different, though. CJ needed someone to help him settle down. Now some of his flirty confidence is back. And no. I haven't just had a naughty speculation rush through my mind about his hand sliding up to my shoulder. Maybe caressing my neck—

Enough! I won't fantasize about him. Not here, not now, not ever.

CJ doesn't let go of my hand, though. Not while we ride the elevator, not during our ride to the hotel. Not once.

My palm begins to sweat. I try to work it free, but he refuses to let me, and I swear, I *swear*, my favorite grin, the one that combines mischief and confidence, makes a quick appearance in the corners of his mouth.

Fragile

CJ

Lismore, Ireland

You don't have to do anything.
Nobody's blaming you.
Don't dwell on the negative.
Let it all end.

I don't know how she did it, how she always does it, but Fiona yanked me out of spiraling into darkness again. Her presence and her knowing, no, understanding glances keep me together as we go through rescheduling the next two weeks of our tour.

We relocate to Lismore, Ireland, where Marshall's been given two weeks to recover his voice that all but disappeared after he pushed himself in Amsterdam. He needs this break even if it costs The Label astronomical amounts of money, which it will—we're renting a castle.

"How's this for something fun to do in Europe?" Rick asks as we assemble in the square courtyard of the royal fortress.

Shane rubs the back of his neck. "Just how much are we paying for this?"

I'm curious, too. We're not struggling for cash, but still. A castle for a two-week vacation? Especially the one like Lismore Castle. It may be ancient, but it's in immaculate condition—shiny windows, not a pebble out of place on the driveway, trimmed bushes, and a small staff in black-and-white uniforms waiting for us at the entrance.

"Nada!" Zach announces. "Well, almost nada. A friend of a friend of a friend— Anyway, it's ours for two weeks. The only but is—"

"Out with it," Graham snarls at him.

I'm siding with the guy who wields the sticks. Zach has many friends with deep pockets and nice connections, but a free castle for two weeks is too good to be true.

Hands in his pockets, Zach takes a few steps away from us. "It's the twenty-first birthday of his Whatever Royal Highness Cousin What's-His-Name, who's fifty-seventh or something in line for the throne of England. Here. Tonight. Our presence at the Royal Birthday Bash is the only payment that has been requested. It's cool, right?" He takes another few steps away. "It's just a party."

"How many times did we tell you to not make decisions without consulting the rest of us?" Graham pulls drumsticks out of his side pocket—he often carries a pair with him like a comfort blanket—and chases after Zach. Those sticks are going to connect hard either with Zach's forehead or his thigh. It'll burn for hours no matter where the strike lands.

Alexandra laughs beside me, for the first time since we've left Amsterdam. My heart sinks again. Fiona told me to let it go, but I haven't been able to. I wish I could. I see no way out of what I've done. I apologized a thousand times, but it doesn't feel like enough. The comments online haven't stopped. Marshall attempted to curb the gossip about me leaving and the band breaking up by milking his hospital stay for all it's worth. Plenty of photos of him suffering in the hospital bed and being paraded around in a wheelchair even though he can walk just fine, but the dumpster fire I sparked to life keeps burning bright. I suggested I post something too. Kiera forbade me to do anything on that front. I'm not supposed to acknowledge to the public that anything went wrong, with Aiya or otherwise. The legal team will take care of her creative freedom and hopefully teach her once and for all to be considerate of her actions.

I need to learn some of that too. Fiona's been right.

Boundaries, please.

Trust you? Uh-huh. Sure.

All I ever get from you is empty promises.

I've been a careless jerk, and it doesn't matter that I didn't want any of it to turn out this way. Now my life has entered a dark tunnel with no light at the end. Who am I kidding? Entered? I've been in the tunnel all along.

The rest of the band heads inside.

"You coming?" Marshall rasps over his shoulder when I hesitate to join them.

A single thought dances on the edge of my clouded mental state. Maybe I shouldn't. I can't leave and abandon the tour, but I can't bring myself to be with the band either. Everything is so fragile. I used to be able to lift mountains for Project Viper. I'm afraid that the next thing I do or say will break us.

Get Over Him

Fiona

Once everyone settles in, Alexandra, Elise, and I huddle down on my bed. We have four hours until the guests start arriving. My legs are pretzeled so I can lean forward to type on my laptop. Project Viper's lawyer reviewed my publishing contract and gave me a green light a week ago, but I haven't had the time to sign it yet in light of everything that transpired.

"Do it already." Elise elbows me in the side. "The contract is good. Sign it and send it. It's your dream."

"Do it, do it, do it," Alexandra chants on my other side.

I exhale and use my fingertip on the mouse pad to sign the last remaining files. Last step—click submit.

"No fear?" Alexandra raises a mocking eyebrow at me.

I stare her down. "How dare you use my own words against me?"

She shrugs. "Easy."

"Come on!" Elise groans. "Do you want to publish your story or not?"

I do.

So very very, very much.

Thinking of this new reality is kind of paralyzing, though. My dream is going to become real. There will be even more work toward it than before—

I click submit.

"Yay!" Elise cheers.

Alexandra claps.

Everything from relief to wanting to jump off the bed and run around this stupidly lavish castle screaming in joy floods me from my toes to the ends of my hair. I fall backward onto the plush duvet. The girls do the same.

"You deserve this," Elise says. "You really do. You've worked so hard."

"I did."

Breathing, the mundane, second-to-second task most bodies do on autopilot, feels different somehow. Easier? Lighter. There's a lightness in my body I don't think I've ever felt before. I close my eyes and imagine thumbing through a printed copy of *Dimensions of Darkness*, its colorful cover, the smell of ink. Designing bookmarks, ordering merch with my characters, going to conventions.

Now that I've signed and sent the contract, I'll tell Xavier. That odd hesitation to share the news with him is gone. Probably because the whole thing feels real now.

"What do we do now?" Alexandra asks.

"Party prep." Excited flames come to life in Elise's eyes. "Let the guys call it the Royal Birthday Bash—"

"We'll call it Fiona's Victory Party!" Alexandra catches up.

"Exactly," Elise replies. "Let's go all out, so that everyone's heads turn. You're always so conservative." She pokes my shoulder with her long, black-polished nail.

I frown at her. "I'm not conservative. I dress appropriately for my job. If I don't wear business attire, people don't take me seriously because I'm so young." Twenty-two is much too young for most people when it comes to someone bossing them around.

"Fine, fine. What do you have then for special occasions?" Elise gets off the bed and upends my entire suitcase on top of it. "Did you even bring any red carpet attire?"

"Are you mad?" I protest.

"Look." Alexandra's hand dives into the midst of my clothes and fishes out a black garment bag folded in half.

Oh no. Not *that.*

Elise must read the look on my face, because she snatches the bag away from Alexandra and shakes out the cocktail dress before I can even think the word *stop.*

"Fi-o-na," she sings. "This is a far cry from business attire. What have you been saving this for?"

I swallow at the sight of the cherry-red sheath dress with a wide strap over one shoulder. "I bought it last year, hoped to wear it to The Label's Christmas party, but ended up not being able to go because both Xavier and Nia had the flu. The tags are still attached."

"Oh, that's right." Compassion softens Elise's voice. "I remember you not being able to come."

"There was a Christmas party for everyone at The Label?" Alexandra pushes her lower lip out in a perfect baby pout.

"You don't get to complain. You went to Zach's house and got spoiled by Mama Tang," I say. "Nothing beats being spoiled by the Tangs."

"True." Alexandra tugs the dress out of Elise's hands then rips the tags off.

Both Elise and I gasp at her barbarics, but she laughs. "There. You have no choice but to wear it."

I never planned to accompany the band anywhere fancy, at least not this-kind-of-dress fancy. I always thought I'd be in the shadows, not on the red carpet. The only reason the dress went into the suitcase at the last moment is that I got fed up with three hundred of my hard-earned dollars collecting dust in my closet. I was determined to take the dress out of the country at the very least.

Elise's eyes narrow. "You're not concocting an excuse to ditch the party, are you?"

"No." The girls are right. I should celebrate. I earned some fun for all the sleepless nights and pen calluses I developed.

I hold out my hand, and Alexandra deposits the dress into it. I will wear it. It's bright, red, and bold, and CJ won't be able to say anymore that I'm boring.

I'm not wearing it for him. I don't care what he'll think. I don't. I *won't*. He won't even notice me with all the other girls in the room.

My hand prickles at the memory of his hand around mine. He wouldn't let go.

Sheesh. What is wrong with me? He was upset and needed support. Nothing else.

Elise waves a hand in front of my face. "I don't know who you're thinking of, but I never thought I'd live to see you blush."

"I'm not." I press both hands to my *burning* face. Unbelievable.

"I know who she's thinking about," Alexandra declares with a huge smile on her face.

"You don't." She can't know anything.

"CJ," the two of them say nonchalantly, leaving me frozen on the spot.

"Did you seriously think no one would notice the little glances you two have been exchanging? Or that he'll sit with you anytime he can? Or that he sang you to sleep—"

"How do you know about that?" No one was there but us.

Elise smirks. "The bus lounge isn't what I'd consider private. I needed a drink that night and—"

"I didn't hear you."

"You were ninety percent gone."

"Whatever." Alexandra grabs our arms to get us to shut up. "You two are perfect for each other. No need to hide anything."

"You're wrong. We will never be together." When they both face me with confusion in their eyes, I add, "You know what CJ's like. I don't want to get invested in him."

Elise sits on the edge of my bed. "Forgive me for being blunt, but I think you judge him a bit too harshly. He's different with people he cares about."

I smooth out the dress. "I know that." He frets over his bandmates, he protects Alexandra, he even cares about the feelings of the girls he dates, kind of.

"You've gone out with him before," Alexandra joins in.

"If you mean that opera outing in February, that wasn't a date."

"No fear," Alexandra says once again.

"I'm not scared." A little.

"It'll be fine." Elise pats my hand and starts collecting my belongings back into the suitcase, folding each piece as best as she can. "Just go for it. One party, Fiona. It's not as if you wearing a red dress equals a love confession or a need for something permanent. Flirt a little, play a little. You're way too uptight."

"That's my choice," I remind her. How I behave around guys and what my expectations are in a relationship is no one's business but mine.

Elise raises her hands in surrender. "True. But at least tonight allow yourself some fun?"

I run a finger along the delicate red fabric. The truth is, I am terrified, absolutely chilled to the bone with fear of opening up to CJ, showing him I'm interested in him, allowing him to flirt all my common sense away. He won't care. He may have sung to me the other day, but I don't know if it was for me or because he was stuck with me in the same room kind of deal. To him, even if I let him closer, I'll eventually become one of many. He'll move on without a second thought. That's what he does. I'll be heartbroken.

Crap.

Crap, crap, crap.

I already let him get inside my head, inside my heart, too much.

But I won. I jumped through a million hoops and earned a publishing contract. What harm is there in relaxing a little? What's one evening with a guitar-playing tempter compared to that?

I need to stop pining for CJ.

Since I'm awesome and finally a winner, I might as well be brave and brazen enough tonight to claim that kiss that never happened. One kiss is all I'm expecting from him. No relationship, no promises, no commitments, but it will help me get over him.

Not Seltzer Water

Fiona

The castle throbs with lights and sound. I feel like a celebrity, decked out in my former Christmas gown, knee-high black boots, and a lightweight, cropped leather jacket that Elise loaned me against the cool summer evening. This heady feeling fills me with a buzz that tempts me to pretend for the night that I'm one of the rich and famous.

Almost. I don't know what it is—maybe I'm afraid of CJ seeing me like this, or worse, not noticing me at all. Or maybe it's the growing worry that I'll feel like an outsider. Whatever it is, I step away from Elise and head for the front doors as soon as we come downstairs. "I need to make a phone call." I'll check how Xander's doing. We haven't talked for a few days.

Elise follows me and grabs my upper arm. "Don't slip into the shadows. We're not working. Go party. And don't make CJ wait too long."

"He's not waiting." I regret revealing to her and Alexandra I'm interested in him.

Elise shoots me an argumentative look but doesn't say anything and keeps dragging me along.

"Okay, okay!" I free my arm. "I can walk on my own."

She smiles and adjusts the collar of my jacket. "That's better."

We enter what was described to us pagan Americans, in a language we'd understand, as the reception hall. Music flows around and carries me away. I love loud parties and having no obligations, if only for one night. I spot the Vipers in various corners. All but Marshall, who's still confined to bed, and happy about it too. Those present, however, seem to enjoy themselves. Even Alexandra looks like she's having fun, laughing with a microphone in her hands. I guess Zach roped her into singing karaoke with him, much to the delight of those gathered around them.

"Someone's too distracted to notice," Elise murmurs in my ear before dragging me toward a group of young women and—I brace myself—CJ.

He looks… I remind myself to breathe. Skinny black pants, a gray long-sleeve shirt, sleeves rolled up, of course, and a black vest. A black tie is still hanging around his neck, but it's loosened in a major way, and his recently bleached hair glows in the party lights. The girls in his circle crowd him and hang on to his every word, fully under his spell.

So am I. A little. Unlike them, I've had a couple years to develop some immunity against those blue eyes. Or so I like to believe.

One of the girls laughs and plants a smooch on CJ's cheek. He shakes his head, as if disapproving.

As if.

He loves the attention. Every little bit of it. I'm dressed in the same fashion as these young women who flirt with him, and who'll never-ever get to be with him, breaking their hearts for five minutes of his smile. That's what I decided would be enough for me.

Suddenly, the red dress is too short, the boots are too high, and the jacket is downright ridiculous. I scan the space for an escape route—

Oh, my gosh. No way.

I refuse to quake in fear or embarrassment or anything else. I pull my arm from Elise's grip once more. "I told you. I can walk on my own."

"Sorry. I'm just so excited."

She's excited? What am I feeling, then? "I love you, but go be excited somewhere else."

Elise chortles and sails off to Shane.

Okay. No more stalling. I relax my shoulders and walk toward the chatty ladies and the apple of their eyes.

What will CJ do when he sees me? What will *I* do? I desperately wish I had a purse or my phone, something at all to occupy my hands currently attacking the zipper slider. The plan was to dazzle CJ, for whatever insane reason, but past that?

"And that's when—" CJ stops talking abruptly. "Fiona."

Mouth half-gaping, he fixes his tie in one quick motion. Then our eyes meet and... CJ raises an eyebrow, an appreciative smile appearing on his lips.

My physical reaction is automatic. I roll my eyes. Inside, though, I don't know where to run. Into his arms? Out of the castle? Back to the United States altogether to pretend we've never met?

The young women turn to me, cold eyes assessing what level of threat I represent. This is the first time I've been under such a catty examination. Usually, girls dismiss me after a second's glance. CJ's reaction makes their scrutiny worth it. Whether it's the dress or something else, he's noticed me, Fiona the girl, not his manager's assistant.

"Are you all having fun?" I ask the girls, smiling and knowing full well I'm teasing the hyenas, but I'm in the mood to take risks tonight.

"Who's this, CJ?" asks a tall, curvy blonde.

"It's just..." He clears his throat into his fist. "This is our manager's assistant, Fiona Knight."

"That's your assistant?" says another girl, also white-haired and curvy. "No wonder you don't have a girlfriend. Is having an assistant like her one of the perks of recording with your label?"

Seriously?

The group laughs. CJ doesn't. He doesn't acknowledge the speaker at all, his whole attention still on me.

"Now, don't make him blush too hard." I can't resist offering CJ a teasing smile before detaching from the group. I'm not here for them.

Will he follow me?

"Excuse me, ladies," CJ says to the girls, who groan with disappointment as he ducks through the opening I left in the group.

He *does* follow me. I can't decide whether what I feel is relief or more anxiety over what will happen next. Good question. Where will we go from here?

"You're going to bait them, then leave me to be eaten alive?" CJ catches up with me. "Are you at all in the mood to dance?"

I thought he'd never ask. "Maybe a little."

CJ takes my hand and wraps his other arm, firmly, around my back as we approach the dance floor. "Thanks," he says in my ear, his hot breath tickling my skin. "I thought I'd never be able to escape them."

"You? Escape?" With me.

Who replaced my heart with a hunk of molten lava?

He purses his mouth to the side and looks up. I'm hopelessly in love with the enduring, half an eye-roll he often does with me. I also love the speed with which his gaze returns to me.

"Someone mentioned dancing," I say.

CJ grins and guides me deeper into the mass of dancing bodies. We're swallowed by the revelers and generic pop beats, but the music isn't important. CJ rests his hands on my waist and steps close, then closer, until there's no space between us. I place my hands on his shoulders, feeling awkward, nervous, and hesitant. He guides me in slow, circular motions that better fit a ballad than a dance floor bounce. I soak in every second, every brush of his skin against mine, every time our glances collide in the shimmering lights of the party.

"So." I have to get even closer to CJ for him to be able to hear me speak. "You would dance with me?"

"I would do anything with you."

Is it the blood rushing in my ears or is he being awfully quiet? "Anything?"

His fingers press firmer against my back, for the briefest moment, before his hold on me returns to careful gentleness. "Everything."

I pull away a little to be able to look him in the eye. My heart throws itself against the wall at the sight of the open, sultry blue hints in his gaze. Does he…? What are we…?

What was it that Elise had said earlier? *Flirt a little, play a little?* Easy to do when I have a willing participant in that plan.

CJ gives me a knowing look, as though he can read my thoughts, and chuckles. I laugh along, and we dance more. Unrestrained moves all over the place, touching each other as if we've done this a hundred times before. Get over him. Who was I kidding? CJ steals my heart for good with his real, eye-crinkling smiles. I can't believe I can make him let down his guard enough to be carefree and relaxed like that.

"Is it hot in here or what?" I say when the DJ dials the music down to some light tune.

"Should we find some fresh air?" CJ holds my hand and leads me through the castle. "Want to see the view from the top? Zach said it's great."

"We can't leave. People want to see you."

"They've seen me. Alexandra, Shane, Graham, and Zach can take care of the rest. Come on."

We run through the hallways. I manage to snatch a drink from the tray of a member of the castle staff as he rushes past. A short cup of what appears to be seltzer water and citrus slices in a clear plastic tumbler with a straw. White and black glitter shifts between the tumbler's double walls as we hurry up the stairs. I haven't felt this reckless and eager for trouble since high school. It's amazing to let go of everything.

We emerge at the top of one of the castle towers.

"Zach was right." CJ places both hands on the moss-covered blocks of stone and leans far out.

"Careful." I grab the back of his vest and rein him in a bit. "How am I going to explain it if you fall from here?"

"Tell them I hit on you and you slapped me."

I laugh. "That'd be quite the slap." Remembering the drink I snatched earlier, I take a sip from the tumbler. Citrusy, piney fire races down my throat along with sharp, highly carbonated bubbles. "This"—I cough a couple of times—"is not seltzer water."

CJ takes the open sides of my jacket, pulls me closer to him, and leans over to catch the straw with his mouth for a long sip. "Definitely not seltzer. Well, not only. Gin."

"I don't need any more help to misbehave." I tuck the drink behind one of the square teeth of the tower.

He leans his back against the rocks and folds his arms. "Do you ever misbehave?" His tone, smooth like first-rate chocolate, lures me closer.

"Want to find out?" I don't even try to contain my playful smile, but at the same time, I can't face him. The lush, green view of the Lismore Gardens and its clever geometric layout of shrubs and other plants really is breathtaking, and a perfect excuse to keep from ogling CJ.

"You look very beautiful tonight."

His tone shifts to an intimate murmur. That's what I wanted to hear at the beginning of this evening. Or so I thought. When he's like that, and no one else is around, and he takes my hand, tentatively, asking permission… I can hear him smiling. I can see it in my head, his honey grin that makes hearts flip.

I have to clear my throat before I can speak again. "Sure."

"You do look beautiful. Always."

I shake my head. "Stop it."

"Nope. Can't you take a compliment?" He stands behind me and rests his hands on the edge of the tower in front of me.

My knees buckle. Good thing there are tons of rocks to support me. "I can."

"But you won't?"

"I'm just your manager's assistant."

He actually did me a favor by introducing me as such earlier. The comments weren't good as is, and I can only imagine what those people would say had CJ introduced me as anything else.

Still, I can't help enjoying toying with him. He messes around with me anytime he can. "Just the assistant. The person who'd stay up late in case you can't sleep again, wear these stupid clothes to a party for you—"

This is not a little bit of toying. This is me offering every little bit of my soul. That one sip of diluted gin must've done me in. I don't see why else I would've told him any of this.

CJ moves to my side, and his fingers arrive at the base of my chin. "You dressed up for me?"

I battle the urge to throw myself even more at him. "No."

He laughs. Loudly, head thrown back. "Oh, for crying out loud, Fiona! Enough of the back and forth."

"Don't you love it? I do. Every single bit of it. I love that you'll hold me like this, but won't actually kiss me or—"

"If you wanted a kiss so much…" CJ's hands cup my face, barely touching, then slide, still featherlight, to cradle the back of my head. "You could've gone for it a long time ago. I gave you plenty of opportunities."

"So it's my fault now?" I joke, taking handfuls of the sides of his vest. I have no idea how I still have it in me to banter. That's not what I want, but I will carry on with this useless argument for all eternity if it means he'll keep looking at me like there's nothing and no one in the whole wide world but me.

"It can't be all my fault all the time. In this case, you have to share the blame." CJ presses a light kiss against my lips.

Smoke & Gunpowder

I will be sorry. So eternally sorry. I resolved to not mess around with Fiona, but I have no defenses against her anymore. The moment I saw her, I knew she was up to something. Nobody wears a red dress and approaches you with a chin held high if they don't have a plan. I wouldn't let myself start hoping she'd cracked for me at last, but she's in my arms.

Man, I'm ready and willing to be sorry. I've been waiting for this moment for a long time.

"You call that a kiss?" Fiona murmurs, sending my heart into the stratosphere.

"You disagree?" A telling whistle cuts through the air. I hold her tighter. "It's going to get loud."

High above us, a boom explodes in a puff of white sparks.

Fiona jumps, then squeezes her eyes shut and laughs. "Fireworks."

Huge orbs of colorful light keep shooting up. Sparks blossom in my soul, not just in the sky. Fiona's hands warm my sides. I love that she doesn't move one inch away from me during all of this. The shine of the fireworks reflects in her gold-lined eyes.

Smoke and the smell of gunpowder slither by, igniting my longing for her, but I'll take my time. It took me a long time to get here, to be with her like this. I won't rush, but I can't stop myself from teasing her upper lip with another whisper of a kiss.

Fiona's lips move to the corner of my mouth. Hot, soft, excruciating. I take that back. I had no clue what excruciating was until her mouth seared a slow, deliberate path, a burn on my sanity, across my cheek and to my ear. If she's going to test me like this, no more teasing. No more playing.

I crush her against me and connect our mouths in a deep kiss. Fiona's fingers weave into my hair. I expect her to tug or grab or be otherwise demanding, she's more than welcome to, but she's soft. Not afraid to explore. Not at all. My hair, my shoulders, my lips. She breaks the kiss off multiple times, but always comes back for more. Her hands flit over my face, caressing my jaw and cheekbones, her thumb brushing over my earrings. Everything she does with me in this centuries-old tower is confident but gentle. So gentle, I start wondering if that's what it feels like to be kissed by someone who loves you.

The idea sends a shot of dizziness through me.

"Wait." I untangle myself from her, careful to not appear spooked. "You…" Too much oxygen after a restricted air flow due to the most amazing moment earlier hits me hard. My head starts spinning harder. I take a good, deep breath. "Why didn't we do this sooner?"

Fiona smiles and touches her lower lip. "We could've."

I take two steps away to give me enough space to raise Fiona's arm and guide her into a twirl to the music still streaming from below. The fireworks show launches into the grand finale, but it's nothing compared to the wonder in front of me. "We could've? Are you talking about Vienna?"

"Yes." Fiona finishes the twirl and leans into me once more. "Did you really think I'd be mad at you if you kissed me then?"

"I wasn't sure whether you were goading me. I wouldn't put it past you to lure me into a trap."

Fiona steals what's left of my supposedly still beating heart with her easy smile. "Yeah. I wouldn't put it past me either. No traps tonight though. I know your terms."

"Terms?" I kiss her temple.

We sway slowly, barely. I strain my every sense to catch Fiona's heartbeat.

She rests her head on my shoulder. "You always tell the girls what they can expect. I figured the same applies to me."

Oh.

Hmmm.

Normally, I'd just ask what my new date wants. Sometimes, I'd negotiate. The girl would get a night or a few out in town, no expenses spared. In exchange, she couldn't nag or tell me what to do or who to be. It's never too hard to convince them. They always want the same thing—someone handsome and popular to be their shiny accessory, even if only for a few hours. I have the hardest time believing that Fiona would want the same thing.

"I know you don't date," Fiona continues.

I stop moving. "Right." Suddenly, my stance on relationships feels less of a shield and more of an excuse.

Fiona smooths out my shirt collar. "At midnight my carriage will turn back into a pumpkin, but fear not. You don't have to be my prince. And seriously, I promise to not throw any shoes around so that you wouldn't have to feel obligated to return lost property to me. Let's have our fun and forget about it tomorrow."

She's giving me a good out. No expectations. Oddly, the relief that comes with her words feels too close to a nasty fever. Harsh, heavy, gutting. Forget about it tomorrow?

"Okay," I say.

She's right. It's best if we stick to what we were a couple of hours ago. Friends, colleagues, and maybe, someday, even strangers.

"Fun I will give you. I am good at fun," I promise, twirling her again then reeling her in for another tease of a kiss.

She laughs, and it's so easy to smile in return, but the whole evening—dancing with her, feeling the warmth of her hands and the willing softness of her lips—has intoxicated me past any reasonable point. I don't fall in love, so that's not why I'm so full of sharp unease. I haven't asked her out, she hasn't turned me down, there's no reason for me to feel rejected. I haven't done anything wrong. We haven't fought. She hasn't made me mad. I haven't made her cry. Feeling unhinged is out of place.

"Let's get something to eat." I've been depressed and not hungry all day, and the low blood sugar is probably to blame for the weird emotions circling inside me. "A proper food raid is in order, and we have to eat our spoils somewhere we're absolutely not supposed to."

"Yes! I'm starving."

Fiona takes my hand and leads me to the stairwell. She looks at me with a huge smile that makes her eyes shine even brighter and rips what's left of my bleeding heart into tiny, tiny pieces because now I know what everyone I ever dated felt like.

Fun with no expectations sucks.

They're Fries, Not Chips, Dang It!

Fiona

A quiet knock sounds at my bedroom door around two in the morning, after the party starts to wind down.

Sitting on my bed, I shove my sketchbooks and pencils into my bag. I had to put down a few of tonight's moments onto the paper. I had to. It's not often that I draw myself because nothing that amazing happens to me usually, but tonight—tonight has been incredible. The whole day has been fantastic. I signed the contract that'll bring me to artist stardom, and I kissed a rock star. *I kissed CJ.* On top of the castle tower. I would've gone on a thousand tours for that moment.

"Come in," I call out once sketches of me, fireworks, and CJ are out of sight.

Alexandra slides into the room and drops on the bed next to me. "Oh, oh, oh. Look at you. The smile. I take it tonight was good?"

"Yes. It's been great." Perfect. Everything's so perfect. I finally know what it's like to feel on top of the world.

I grab a pillow to hug.

Alexandra scoots closer and grabs herself a pillow as well. "You seem happy."

"I am. I never thought I'd get to this point. I know I should've been my own number one champion, but—"

"I know exactly how it is." Alexandra smiles. "What about CJ?"

"We had ourselves a…cozy evening."

After the tower, we devoured a mountain of cookies and finger sandwiches on a velvet couch in the library. More kissing. All the kissing. CJ is an expert at more than just playing guitar. No surprises there, but I bury half of my face in the pillow I'm hugging to conceal the blush scorching my cheeks all the same.

"How cozy?" Alexandra asks.

I bump her with my elbow. "Do I come and demand you tell me every dirty little detail of what you do with Marshall?"

"Sorry. It's just that… You're happy, and I saw CJ earlier. He seemed happy too. Are you a couple now?"

"He doesn't do relationships. You know that." I surprise myself with how indifferent I sound. I'm proud of myself for not clinging. It'll be easier to carry on tomorrow morning.

Her eyebrows come together. "So he says."

"No, Alexandra. You can't force anyone into something so personal and serious." Regardless of how much we all wish we could.

"I know that, but—"

"It's okay. I knew what I'd be getting. One evening."

"Don't you want more?"

Her words bring me back to my conversation with CJ on the bus a few weeks ago. "It doesn't matter what I want. He doesn't need anyone permanently."

She scoffs. "The ones who say such things the loudest are the ones who need someone by their side the most. Why would the Vipers be so tight otherwise?"

"A brotherhood is not the same as a romantic relationship."

Alexandra had to come and try to push me off my comfortable spot of where I am with CJ.

"It's fine," I say. Of course I want more, but I knew what would happen when I decided to pursue CJ tonight. Now it's time to talk about something else. I will not pine after CJ. Not anymore. "Why aren't you in bed yet?"

"I needed to find out how things went." Alexandra yawns. "But you're a meanie who won't tell me anything."

I laugh a little. "You're worse than Charlie." Our social media coordinator is the biggest gossip lover ever. It's hard to judge her, though. Charlie's funny and reliable, and being the nosy one is her job after all. "Let's do something fun tomorrow, okay? We'll grab Elise and go to town or something. Girls only. The guys can keep Marshall company. What do you say?"

"Okay…" Alexandra's voice drifts away. She's a second away from being asleep.

Don't stress out the talent.

I won't make her go back to her own bed. There's also something to be said about a friend feeling comfortable enough to fall asleep with you around. I smile and grab us a couple of blankets from the bench at the foot of the bed.

The next morning, we leave the castle grounds and drive an hour down to Waterford, a beautiful city on the River Suir. It drizzles the whole time we're here, but we've enjoyed our shopping spree and sightseeing all the same. Still, with the weather the way it is, I wish I could pull around me the warmth of the restaurant we chose for our late lunch.

The dark brown wood of the furniture and the wine racks on the far wall set a cozy mood, while the promising portions on the plates of other customers spur me to settle for the local staple. Fish and chips.

My choice proves true, but as soon as I have one bite of each, the crispiest chips and a divinely juicy fried filet of cod, my phone rings. I frown at it, wishing for it to combust because I'm ravenous and hope it's not some management emergency, but it's my agent. Oooh. She must have something important to discuss with me.

"I'll be right back," I say to Elise and Alexandra as I leave the table and step out of the restaurant with my umbrella in tow—there are too many people to be able to talk in peace and it's still drizzling.

Outside, I pop the umbrella open and take a few steps away from the entrance. "Hi, Callie."

"Oh, Fiona. I'm glad the call didn't go to voicemail. I have some news for you." Her voice is staticky and quiet even after I crank the call volume all the way up. I can't figure out her tone. Is it good or bad news?

"Okay. What is it?" Probably nothing bad. I just barely sent off the paperwork, and Callie can be chatty at times. That being said, I appreciate her desire to communicate. She's never left me wondering if she's actually trying to help me.

"The publishing deal for *Dimensions of Darkness* has been rescinded. They said they could only take so many projects this quarter, and yours competed with another story in the genre by Kat Runn…"

The rest of her words meld together into meaningless hum. Kat Runn. A comic book team of Katelyn Smithson, the artist, and her writer boyfriend Ed Runn. Beautiful art, solid plots, breath-catching twists. Half a million followers. Sold out pre-orders.

"I understand," I mutter eventually.

Of course my story would have been pushed aside for Kat Runn.

They are guaranteed to recover every penny spent on them and fill the publishing house's bank accounts.

I take a few steps down the street, mostly to remove myself from the restaurant windows, awkwardly dodging other pedestrians I have to share the sidewalk with. The umbrella keeps me dry from the light rain, but it's not enough to hide me from the rest of the world.

"Fiona!" Callie exclaims after a few minutes of me not responding or even catching what she's saying.

I draw a deep breath of humid air, which feels too heavy and too sticky and fills me with lead. "My project competed with Katelyn and Ed's. That means we submitted similar stories. Did they submit before or after?" I ask but realize I don't want to know. It doesn't matter because it won't change anything. The publisher hasn't paid me anything yet, so they can ditch the contract whenever they feel like it.

"Fiona, I'm so very, very sorry. I can't even imagine how disappointed you must feel. I wish I could be there with you and give you a hug, but please don't despair. We still made it past the barricade, right? Got our foot in the door. We did it once, and we'll do it again. I promise you."

Her encouraging attitude twists me harder than the reason for her call. "No."

"What? I'm sorry. The connection isn't the best."

I fold the umbrella and, oddly enough, stop feeling like I'm suffocating. A cool breeze whispers over my face. I blink, and a hot drop of liquid rolls out of the corner of my eye and down my cheek. "Can I call you back?" My voice trembles. I can't control it no matter how hard I try. "I need to process."

"Of course, but I want to hear from you in two days, okay? Don't disappear or take this as failure."

"Okay." I hang up and shuffle back to the restaurant.

Alexandra and Elise are huddling over one of their phones.

"Look at those hearts," Elise exclaims. "People are starting to love you."

"No. Those are for Marshall," Alexandra replies.

"Half of his skinny butt is all that's in the picture—"

"But everybody loves his skinny butt—"

"No, everybody loves your curvy one."

They laugh. Somewhere in the back of my mind a light bulb lights for Alexandra's improving ratings with the fans, but the rest of me is darkness. I pick up the fish filet with my fingers and take a large bite, then eat the rest without pausing to savor. The food doesn't bring me any comfort. It's a temporary distraction at best.

"Are you okay?" Elise asks, and I realize that they're both watching me.

I nod, not daring to speak, knowing that if I so much as open my mouth, I'll dissolve into sobbing. I should've gone straight back to the castle.

It's just a contract. Callie's right. We'll try again.

"I don't want to try again," I say.

The girls exchange a frown.

"How many times am I going to have to climb to the top to be pushed back down again?"

"Fiona, you're not making any sense," Elise says gently. "Did something happen?"

I start stuffing the potatoes into my mouth. "They're fries, not chips, dang it! Chips are the crunchy stuff you buy in bags from supermarkets and gas stations. And why is there no dipping sauce? Twenty-four euros a plate and no dipping sauce. Who does this?"

Quickly, as if I'll bite if she doesn't hurry, Alexandra pinches my plate with two fingers and pulls it away from me. "What happened?"

The ridiculous amount of potato I managed to half-chew through gets lodged in my throat. I grab my glass of water and take a few painful sips to help it down, then clunk the glass on the table and bury my face in my hands. I haven't fallen apart like this in…ever.

"They took back the publishing offer. They…took it…back. And my agent… She's just…" I can't breathe. I grab the water again and drink the rest of the glass. "She says to carry on. Forget it. I'm not doing this again. Putting myself out there, like a beggar, pleasy-please, for years. No more!"

I pick up my bag, swipe another handful of potato pieces from the plate Alexandra confiscated from me, and march out of the restaurant. A few members of the staff and pretty much every other customer throw bewildered glances in my direction. I'm happy to be the basket case of the day. What do they know about what I've gone through to come undone like this?

Alexandra and Elise take me back to the castle. I leak tears the whole time and refuse to talk. Although, it's hard to call it a refusal when the girls don't try to engage me. Mentally frail and uprooted, I can't decide whether it's because they understand that nothing they can say would comfort me or because they think I've ruined their day.

When we return to Lismore Castle, I say, "Please don't tell the others. I wouldn't have told you either if you weren't around. It takes me a while to sort through things."

Alexandra says, "Of course," and Elise nods.

We go inside.

"Want some herbal tea?" Elise offers.

"Sure."

She goes to the kitchen.

I think of going upstairs to my room to take a bath or at least hide under the blankets for half an hour before I face everyone, but CJ runs down the stairs toward me.

"How was the—" He stops a step away from me and cradles my face in his hands. "Why the puffy eyes?"

I asked the girls to keep my end of the world from everyone, but there's no way I can brush off my swollen face.

"They wouldn't give her any dipping sauce with her fries. I mean chips." Alexandra flashes me a sympathetic smile.

"What?" CJ throws her a doubtful look.

"No, seriously. Fiona threw a fit at the restaurant." Her tone grows lighter and lighter. "She wailed like a toddler at the table."

Her attempt at helping is absurd, but not entirely unuseful. It gets me to chuckle even though my sinuses are still groaning from the tear overload.

Alexandra passes us and goes up the stairs.

"She's right," I say to CJ. "I did cry."

"Are you okay?"

No, and I want to tell him why, but I can't. I don't want to give the tears another chance to rage.

"Fiona?" CJ tries again.

"I'm fine. What did you do all day?"

He takes another moment to study me, then wraps an arm around me and leads me deeper inside. "Nothing. Can you believe it?"

Him touching me and worrying about me puts the war inside me on pause for one second. He doesn't do relationships. I didn't expect him to change for me, but our one fun evening is long over, and he's still here.

▶ Track 24
Just Wanted to Borrow a Bass

Fiona draws. When she's not shooting emails or helping Rick fix sudden kinks in our adjusted schedule, she fills her sketchbook. In the hallways, in the gardens, everywhere.

"I'm pretty sure you captured every stone in this place," I tease her the evening after the fireworks when I catch her standing in the middle of the entryway, sketching a chandelier.

"Not yet." She smiles.

My heart melts around the edges at the sight of that subdued smile, like butter in the sun. It's been a rough day for her, yet she smiles.

"Not yet?" I approach her from behind and draw her into my arms. "Does it mean you're determined to spend all of your time with your pencils in your hands instead of me?"

Fiona stiffens and presses her sketchbook to her chest. "What are you complaining about? You don't fall in love. You don't want a girlfriend. We settled on what you usually go for. No expectations and one evening of...of..."

I'm tracing her shoulder with my fingers. Is that the reason why she can't finish that sentence? I hope so. "Did it have to be?"

"Did it have to be what?" Fiona tilts her head back and closes her eyes.

"Did it have to be…"

I can't say it even though it's so simple.

Did it have to be one evening?

Could we not go on with the magic between us a little longer?

Could she, maybe, see more in me than a player?

I bury my face in the rounded corner between Fiona's shoulder and her neck and inhale the scent of her skin. What a huge mistake. I can't let go, chained by the subtle mint and berries lingering on her skin. To Fiona.

I don't fall in love.

What I feel for Fiona isn't love.Love isn't just wanting to touch her, hold her, have her lower all defenses against me, is it? Or wanting to know the real reason why she cried earlier today. The girls joked it off, and I didn't want to press the matter, but I know it must've been something big for Fiona to let anyone see her in such a dire state. I want to fix whatever happened or at least get her ice cream for moral support if she doesn't need me to save the day. Next time I'm sick or sad or angry, I want her to be the one to tell me everything will be okay. Last time she did, it held me together better than super glue.

All these little things have nothing to do with love.

I don't think they do.

"Someone's going to come in here and see us like this," she mutters.

"So?"

So? I've lost my mind. If anyone sees us together, they'll think all kinds of garbage. That I can't control myself around pretty girls, which admittedly has some truth to it. That's not even the worst thing. Depending on who comes across us, they might think unsavory things about Fiona. Things that would be in line with the comments at the party when Fiona dared to disturb the circle of glittering hopefuls to snag me for the night. She doesn't deserve to deal with that kind of gossip.

Bile rises in my throat as I reflect on my actions that earned me my reputation. It was fun, and I didn't want to commit to anything or be responsible for anything. I am a player. Untrustworthy.

I step away from her. "You know what? You're right. I'm being unfair. This is a rare opportunity for you to study cool elements and… What? Textures? Colors? I don't know what you practice. I shouldn't distract you. We won't stay here forever."

Fiona picks at the corner of her sketchbook. "True. I should draw as much as I can while I'm here." She looks at me.

Something invisible but tangible stretches between us, and I almost believe she'll ask me to stay and do something with her instead.

Her phone rings. Sighing, Fiona pulls it out of her back pocket. "Good evening. Fiona Knight speaking."

Somewhere inside the castle, Zach is playing piano. Insane Russian composer style—thundering, rolling scales and chords that are bound to make the keys quake in fear of falling out. He's a good guy. Lightheaded as no one would believe and a little crazy, but if any of us were in trouble, he'd bleed until the last drop to help us. That's the kind of person Zach Tang is.

What kind of a person am I? I don't do anything good. All I want is to play around.

I wave goodbye as I walk away, leaving Fiona to talk in private. I could help out Lex Romero. There's still time to let him know I'd record the bass line for his video game theme. It's anything but busy here right now. I shoot Lex a message on Club to let him know I'm in.

Half an hour later, Lex sends me sheet music and a few files with what he's done so far. Everything sounds great, and the mysterious vibes of the theme get me pumped to play for him. I set up in a room with as many carpets and as little wood paneling as I can find. The laptop and the software are good to go, the audio interface is hooked up, and all I need now is a bass.

Standing in the middle of the room, hands on my hips, I ponder my dilemma. The only person with basses around here is Alexandra. After Amsterdam, me asking her for one may come across as confirmation of my disloyalty to the band.

No. It won't. I explained what happened in Amsterdam. Aiya used me.

I go upstairs to find Alexandra, and the whole time I cling to the thought that I'm not doing anything wrong. What's so wrong about recording a bass line?

I knock on Marshall's bedroom door—that's where Alexandra's been spending the majority of her time, hanging out with my antibiotic-popping best friend.

"Come in," Marshall invites in a raspy voice.

"You still sound like a nightmare," I tell him when I come inside.

He gives me a thanks-a-bunch kind of grimace and mutes the TV. "What's up?"

I scan the room for Alexandra. She's not here. "Where's our *Matryoshka*?"

"Our?" Marshall heaves himself out of the bed and comes to stand in front of me.

"Will you relax? I didn't say *my*, did I?" I used to. Just to bug him. I knew from early days of Alexandra with us that he'd fallen for her, but he was a stubborn idiot and would not acknowledge his feelings. Plus, he thought she was in love with me. People come up with all kinds of delusions to avoid scary emotions. Either way, saying that we've had some tension over Alexandra would be putting sprinkles on a dumpster fire.

Marshall runs his fingers through his tousled black hair. "She's getting a snack." His doubtful green eyes are still gauging me. "Why?"

"I need to borrow a bass."

"You didn't bring any of yours?"

"Why would I?"

We engage in another round of staring.

"I suppose there's no point anymore." Marshall goes back to bed, where he smooths out the covers and drops on the edge with one foot curled under him. He coughs, deeply, before continuing, "Why do you need a bass anyway?"

"I don't need to report to you about everything I do." I bite the side of my cheek. Where did the defensiveness come from?

Marshall's eyes narrow. "What are you up to?"

"Recording a short bass line for a video game theme for Lex Romero. Remember him—"

"Yes, I do remember him. Fun guy. What I wanted to know when I asked what you were up to is what's happening with you and Project Viper?"

Stuffing my hands into my jeans pockets, I focus on not letting my breathing accelerate. "Nothing." He'll call my bluff. He knows me. He knows the way I talk and the way I dodge questions. He can probably already see it all over my face—my every fear about my role in the band. That nothing has felt right for weeks now.

"Nothing?" Marshall's eyebrows rise in sarcasm. "You could put it that way. You work on songs for everybody else but us."

"Two side projects don't make it *everybody else*," I snap.

"It's two for now." Marshall clears his throat with another cough. "When are you going to write songs for us? We still owe one more album to The Label."

"You can write songs too. Even Graham can push out a verse or two when he wants to."

"You're the one who writes the majority of our lyrics and music. Or who fixes what we come up with—"

"But that doesn't mean you shouldn't or can't do anything without me." I stalk deeper into his bedroom and stare out the window at the blur of green and brown outside. "I'm not our creative director."

"You kind of are."

I can feel his glare on my back. My blood's hot and pulsing in my veins. I'm too overwhelmed. There's too much pressure. "Do you even know what it's like to be that only person who constantly keeps everything together? Who's constantly responsible for everything the band does? What about you?" I whip around. "What about the rest of us? Why do I have to take care of everything?"

Marshall scoffs. "So you'll take care of nothing anymore? You'll just be a pretty face and chill with the girls while the rest of us work?"

"Why can't I? You have been!" I can't do this anymore. Carry everyone's burdens or think of everyone else before myself, worry about what they'll all think of me.

"Write the songs and do the work," I go on. "Don't wait for me. You don't ever have to wait for me."

"What are you going to do, then?" Marshall exclaims, and I freeze on my spot, certain that his question is global. As in, what am I planning to do with Project Viper long term? "You know what being in this band cost me?"

"Nothing!" He's going to play victim? Over my dead body. "It cost you exactly nothing. Since day one I've done all the work and what we have, it's all thanks to me, you ungrateful b—"

The door opens. Alexandra appears in the doorway. "You guys are kinda loud. I could hear you down the hall."

"Good," I say.

Alexandra blinks. "Sorry. I'll go—"

"No. Stay. He'll tell you everything later anyway. Might as well get the front-row seat. You haven't really seen us fight before, have you? I bet you believed we don't. Oh, but we do." I glare at Marshall.

He glares back. "Stop."

Alexandra comes toward me and reaches for me, but I sidestep her. "What are you doing? You wanted Marshall, so go and side with him."

My angry response cranks up the tension three hundred percent as I realize what my words could mean. That, in the end, I have feelings for her.

Alexandra's voice is small as she starts, "CJ—"

"That's not what I meant." I rub my face. I can't say a single thing right.

"Will you just stop?" Marshall rises from the bed and stands with us.

"Stop what?" I ask.

"Acting like a lunatic and say what you actually mean?" he spits out.

"Oh, nice. You want to hear that I haven't been able to write a line of lyrics? Or how I've been wading through doubt and fear and worry that I've ruined everything? Or that I haven't been sleeping because I don't feel like I belong with the band anymore?" I've been hiding what I've been feeling like these past weeks, but now I'm ticked off that he hasn't noticed. I know it's idiotic. I am, after all, the one who didn't want any of this to be seen, but he's my best friend. He should've noticed. "Which of these things did you want to hear?"

Arms crossed on his chest, Marshall remains silent, dark green eyes betraying nothing.

"Why do you think you don't belong with the band?" Alexandra whispers.

I swallow hard. I don't know where the feeling comes from, other than it's been rotting me. All these shows that have been nothing but drudgery. The worst part is that I know Alexandra will blame herself, and I don't care.

"Is that why this whole we-need-a-new-bassist thing started?" Marshall asks. "You were, in fact, looking for a replacement?"

Alexandra pales and glances between us, over and over again.

"And if I did?" I didn't. Back then, I truly wanted to be a permanent couple with my six-string on stage, but what's with the overly accusatory tone? As though me wanting to find an appropriate substitute *if* I did want to leave would be a bad thing somehow. "What then?"

"Please don't say that." Alexandra's face turns whiter, somehow.

"Why are you so worried about it all of a sudden?" I move away from them both to the far side of the room. Not far enough. "When you first arrived, you didn't care. You never once asked me if I was planning to leave. You grabbed your chance. Why are you so afraid of me leaving now? Even if I do, you'll be fine. You have what you want. You have more than you could've ever imagined." I wave at Marshall.

"Get out of here," he snarls, the ill gravel in his voice making him sound even more ominous than he would've otherwise.

"No!" Alexandra grabs his arm, but her eyes are pleading with me. "Please, don't leave."

"All I wanted was to borrow a bass!" I storm out of the room.

I have to go back.

I won't.

Why isn't anybody listening? Marshall outright ignored me when I admitted how impossible things have been for me. Some friend he is. Never mind my crisis. I've hurt his girl's feelings.

I halt in the middle of the stairwell.

It's not some random girl I lashed out at.

It's our *Matryoshka*. It's my kind, little sister, bass princess Alexandra. Who was actually worried about me.

Who asked me to stay.

I whip around and run back upstairs. Just as I approach Marshall's room once more, the door flies open.

"How is it not my fault?" Alexandra shouts at Marshall before noticing me.

My heart cracks at the sight of her tear-streaked face.

"You can have the bass back," she declares and pushes past me.

I follow her along the lush red carpet with golden flowers. "Alexandra, I'm sorry. I didn't mean—"

She disappears in the next room—her bedroom, nearly smashing my fingers off with the door in the process.

"Alexandra, please come out." I knock on the door. "I am really sorry I said all those things to you. I was a mean jerk."

Leaning on the doorjamb, I knock a few more times, even try the handle, but it's locked. "Alexandra?"

The door opens just enough for a guitar case to be pushed out, then slams shut again.

"Alexandra." My skin prickles, and I look up from the dark brown polished wood of the door.

Marshall stands in the middle of the hallway, hands on his waist—one of his usual challenging poses.

I draw a slow breath through my nose and force myself to approach him. "I…" I've been feeling like crap and like I've been toeing the edge of the abyss for weeks, but that in no way excuses my earlier outburst.

"Well?" Marshall asks, his whole pose indicating that he's ready to hear my explanation.

My mouth won't produce another word. The damage is done. Also, I wonder if there's anything I can say to make him or Alexandra believe that I haven't been scheming to leave the band despite all my fear that I might have to.

Marshall shakes his head and returns to his room, leaving me to stand alone in an empty hallway. Lonelier than ever before because before, whenever I messed up, I had him on my side.

With nothing else left to do, I pick up the bass Alexandra shoved at me and go downstairs to fulfill my commitment to Lex. There will be at least one person I won't upset today.

◐ **Track 25**

Not You Too

"You missed dinner," Fiona says when I come to grab a bite from the dining room a while after the others eat. The castle staff always keeps food out late for us in case someone's hunger flares.

"I'm pretty sure I did everyone a favor." I'd be danged if I sat at the table with them while both Marshall and Alexandra are shutting me out. "I'm being childish and defensive, I know. I should've joined them and tried to apologize again." I physically couldn't, terrified of having to explain myself to the rest of the guys, especially with some of the crew present.

"Alexandra won't come out of her room," Fiona says quietly as she makes a plate of steak and roast vegetables for me.

"Thanks. You really didn't have to." I take the plate, but my appetite is gone.

Fiona motions for me to sit at the long dining table. I put the plate down but don't pull out a chair. She stands next to me. I wish she would pat my shoulder or hug me or anything at all, but all she does is ask, "What happened?"

"Alexandra didn't tell you?"

Fiona shakes her head, and I'm grateful. Even when she's mad at me, Alexandra's got my back, giving me an opportunity to explain myself on my terms.

"I got in a fight with Marshall, and Alexandra had the bad luck of joining it."

"Ah. That explains Marshall's scowl during dinner. Do you mind if I ask what the fight was about?"

"I told him." I grab a piece of roasted carrot and pop it into my mouth. "That I've been off hinges. That I don't know how I fit with the band anymore. That I don't even know what's happening anymore, and—"

"You didn't tell me any of that." *Now* she takes my hand, concern or disappointment or something in her gaze.

I don't need it.

"Not you too." I free my hand.

"Not me too what?" She tries to take my hand again.

I avoid her touch by stepping away. "Don't accuse me of anything. I haven't done anything wrong other than yelled at someone who didn't deserve it."

"You told me you were struggling with artist block. Not knowing if you fit with the band anymore is not just a case of artist block, CJ. It's a big problem—"

"Don't I know it?" I hiss. "Don't lecture me. You're not the one—"

"Please don't get defensive with me." Her expression becomes calm once more. "I want to help."

"How can you help?" I come back to her and place my hands on her shoulders. "This is not something I myself understand. What are you going to do about it?"

"Don't wind up." She hugs me. "I'm not attacking you, remember?"

The coil of lingering feelings of failure won't let me relax. I push away. "I didn't lie about the artist block. I really can't write a line—"

"What about that notebook I gave you? There were some lines in there—"

"All garbage. Ramblings. Nothing useful." I pick at the veggies some more and chew through a forkful of broccoli. All I taste is salt.

Fiona goes to pour a glass of water. "Maybe you could—"

"I don't want solutions, Fiona. I know it's your job to fix everything, but I don't want you to, okay? Not this time."

"What do you want then?" Her voice is tinted with a bit of metal.

"I want you to not treat me like a kid." I want her to listen and understand. "And I want you to stop treating me as if I haven't done anything to fix this—"

"Have you?" Her beautiful eyes are so very much unforgiving right now. "Have you done anything to fix your mental state other than make your friend mad at you and make Alexandra cry?"

She saw me try, over and over again.

"Is this what you call not attacking?"

"You wanted me to stop treating you like a child." Fiona takes a long sip from her glass.

Nothing is ever easy with Fiona. I always knew that, but why can't we, for once, share a wavelength?

"All things considered, after this little tour ends, I think it'd be best if I stepped away for a while. To let everyone's emotions settle. Especially mine." I stuff another piece of carrot into my mouth. "I need a break from this gig."

"Ungrateful idiot," Fiona mutters.

I choke on the carrot. "What?"

"You're an ungrateful idiot." Fiona takes another glass, pours more water, and stuffs the glass into my hand. "You have everything you've ever wanted. Millions out there wish they were in your place— noticed, recognized, and sharing their art with the world. Yet being recognized as the cream of the crop is not good enough for you.

Earning millions on your music has become what? Boring?" Her eyes blaze with anger, and she bites her lower lip, restraining herself, maybe. How kind of her.

It hurt a lot when Marshall got mad at me. I still feel pretty wretched about upsetting Alexandra, but having Fiona bury me cuts deeper than anything. Out of all the things she told me—that I'm not tainted, that she doesn't judge me for my relationship habits, that she wants to help, I should've only ever believed one thing. Fiona doesn't understand me. She's not even trying to right now. Despite everything that happened between us, she has no mercy for me. Nobody does. It's possible I don't deserve any, but I sure as heck don't need one more person to make me miserable right now.

"You're fired," I say and force the images of fireworks and us kissing out of my head. In love with *her*? She says she's there for me then skins me. I don't think so.

Fiona frowns. "Fired?"

"Yes, fired. Pack your things and go back to the States right now." I let that sink in for a second before stalking out of the dining room.

"CJ!" Fiona trails me.

"There was never any real reason for you to come to Europe with us." My voice, loud and clipping, echoes down the wood-paneled corridor.

Elise peeks out of the side room. "Are you two okay?"

I groan, ready to rip my hair out. Can there never be an argument without others butting in? "You leave me alone," I tell Elise, my earlier plan of not upsetting everyone failing with a bang. "And you're fired," I say to Fiona again.

"What?" Elise squeaks, at which point Shane and Zach join her. That's just perfect.

"He's overreacting," Fiona explains, although her confident posture is offset by a slight tremor in her voice.

"I am not." I wish I could just disappear. Explode, evaporate, have aliens with flesh-annihilating lasers shoot one at me. I also can't stop. I either continue raging or collapse and weep. Rage is stronger. "Either you leave or I will."

"CJ, what the crap?" Shane demands.

Fiona throws her hand out to silence him. "It's fine. I'll go."

She walks away, leaving us all in stunned silence.

I almost run after her, but her unfair chastisements still echo in my ears, and my lungs are tight and heavy from her calling me an ungrateful idiot after I shared my pain with her.

I let her leave.

Dust Will Settle

Fiona

Something bites into my palm. I uncurl my clenched fingers and would've frowned, only my eyebrows can't be any closer together. My boarding pass is a crumpled mess in my hand, and I can already see the look the gate agent will give me.

A mental vacation, a chance to see the world, new skills, and an enhanced resume. Going on tour with Project Viper was supposed to give me all that. I'm incapable, however, of deciding what I got in the end. If I got anything at all.

Of course I'm being dramatic. I saw so many beautiful places in Europe and got a chance to do a few things I never would've been able to do otherwise.

I'm just not sure the price was worth it. If my shaking hands, the boulder in my chest, and the burning tightness in my throat that I haven't been able to chase away with any amount of water or Diet Coke are a fair payment.

The loud announcements remind me that I'm in the middle of a busy airport, for one second, before I plunge back into what passes for my thoughts. I don't know what I feel. I…

I don't want to feel anything. Whatever it is, I don't want it to take hold of me. CJ— I don't want to think his name. Not even that much. Not in the way my brain has an inclination to. I promised myself I wouldn't want anything from him, so I won't. Our…argument is between an employer and an employee, not lovers. Not even friends. Friends don't throw each other away to the other side of the world because of a disagreement.

The boarding pass receives another round of rough treatment at my hand. Rick got me a first-class ticket for my flight home. I'm sure he felt bad for me and tried to spare me the over-crowded economy cabin, but the luxury feels like an insult all the same. I know who's really paying for it, where the money comes from, whose face and music made the dollars.

"We invite all passengers with first-class tickets to board now," says a pleasant female voice.

A few other passengers grab their laptop bags and expensive leather Coach duffels and proceed to the gate. I stay in my seat and study the nothingness of the shiny, beige floor under my feet.

As soon as I'm on that plane, I'll be on the way home and away from trouble.

I hate to leave like this. It feels like I failed and like I'm giving up without a fight.

I chose to go because I could tell things wouldn't end well had I tried to stay. I also don't think I'd reach CJ.

The truth of it is, I don't want to. I don't think he wants to be reached. Not by me, at any rate.

The burning in my throat migrates to my eyes. I take the last swig of flat Diet Coke from my bottle and march toward the gate.

I'm going home.

At least there people don't toss me out of their lives as soon as I say something uncomfortable.

Home is where I should've stayed in the first place.

With Nia and Xavier, who need me.

Portland, Oregon, United States

Kiera picks me up from Portland International Airport. I don't know what Rick told her about my return, and not knowing all the variables of any given situation is the manager's worst nightmare.

"Wow." Kiera flashes me an oddly proud smile. "You're as tough as you always are. I expected eyes red from tears, angry glares, and you immediately complaining to me about them heartless Vipers."

"As if."

Kiera smiles wider as we walk to the baggage claim area. "That's my Fiona. Never surrendering to her emotions. I've loved that about you since day one."

Little does she know. I surrendered plenty. The reason why I'm not all angry and complaining is because I don't have any energy any longer. First class or not, I couldn't sleep, worrying about what I'm going to tell Xavier about my early return. Whatever I say, though, I know he'll huff about how it was a waste of time after all.

It wasn't. Not all of it. The pictures I took, the sketches I made. Although, I didn't bring them all back. I left whatever notes and drawings I had about Project Viper with Alexandra. The whole mess of it, dozens and dozens of pages. Other than the ones of me and CJ together. I didn't want the memories anymore, but I couldn't bring myself to throw them out either. So I gave them to her. They'll be a good reminder, hopefully, of all the precious moments she's had with the guys so far. She should have them. She's staying with them, not me.

"Do tell me what happened, though," Kiera goes on. "Rick said you and CJ had a disagreement and it was best to give you both some space. To me, that's a diplomatic version of you almost killed each other. What did CJ do?"

"He fired me."

Kiera's eyes widen in surprise or disbelief. She leans out of the way of a burly guy squeezing closer to the conveyor belt and grabs the edge of my jacket sleeve to pull me aside. "Fired you?"

I take a deep breath. Pressed to explain the situation, I suddenly don't know where to start. The best I can do is, "I told him he was an idiot."

Kiera parks her hands on her waist and looks to the side. "Well, that's hardly a reason to fire you. I've told him to stop being an idiot many times, and I'm still around as their manager."

"I don't know what to say." I turn back to the baggage claim that has finally started spinning, wanting to jump onto it and be taken away from the questions.

"Did it become personal?" Kiera's voice is quiet but firm.

"Personal how?" I know, I know what she means.

"See, you dodging the question is how you tell me that you and CJ got involved with each other. Oh, Fiona. It didn't even cross my mind you'd get in trouble like that with any of the guys. Two years and not a glimmer in your eye." Kiera sighs. "It's none of my business, of course, whether you make yourself available like that, as long as the work is still done and things are good—"

"Am I really in trouble, then?" I spot my suitcases—two thanks to all the souvenirs and cool things I got for Nia, Xavier, and a few friends—and remember how I teased CJ on the day of our departure from the United States about his heavy packing.

Kiera helps me grab the suitcases. Once we emerge from the crowd, she leans in front of me to make sure I'd look her in the eye.

"Yes. I think you know you're in trouble already. Right here." She points at my heart. "But you're not fired. Your contract is with The

Label, not with the band, and the only thing that can happen, if CJ is truly serious about you being off the team, is that we'd have to become creative with how you could stay out of the band's hair."

Guilt floods me. I wanted to have a summer adventure, and I made my manager's life difficult as a result. Everyone's trying to accommodate me, acting like CJ's throwing a tantrum, but I should've stuck with my resolution to not succumb to CJ's spell, and everything would've stayed perfect.

"I'm sorry." The tears launch a serious attempt to overcome me, but I had my fill of sniffling after my publishing contract was revoked.

Kiera takes one of the suitcases away from me and starts walking again. "Don't apologize. Conflicts happen. Dust will settle. Do bring me a latte tomorrow morning. I missed those. I've been getting my own this whole time."

I can't help smiling. "I'm sorry for your suffering. I'll make sure to grab a cranberry orange muffin too. My treat."

Kiera laughs. I'm grateful she's trying to help me feel better, but I know it's not over yet. I've been longing to go home, but that's where my brother is. My eager supporter and my harshest judge. And I don't know which he'll choose to be.

Punished. Banished. Rejected.

Fiona

I hold my breath the whole time I climb the metal stairs to our second-floor condo. When I point the key at the lock, my hand shakes.

Oh, for crying out loud. I stick the key in and turn the lock.

A dark entryway and silence greet me. I haul in the suitcases and switch the light on, then blink at the light green runner rug I bought on clearance last year. It's a good rug. Soft and washes well. I have to clean it a lot, same as other areas in our house. A toddler lives here. I expect the sound of running feet, but all I get is more silence.

"Xavier?" I call out. It's seven in the evening. My brother should be finishing eating dinner and getting ready for his shift.

No one answers.

Exhaling, I close the door. I've been granted a few more minutes to figure out how I'm going to explain why I'm home.

After I roll the suitcases to my room, I take a quick shower to get rid of the airport grime. The familiar simplicity of home—the silver shower curtain, the soft but worn slippers, cheap towels that do their job—is in stark contrast with the luxury that surrounded me while traveling with Project Viper. Even on the road, they always had top notch everything. I'm not complaining about what I have. My living situation is comfortable in every way. I just wasn't prepared to face it once more yet. The magic of Europe still tingles in my body, its remnants making me feel like I've been punished. Banished.

Rejected.

I comb my pixie haircut and refuse to succumb to that feeling. I wasn't rejected by CJ. I was turned down by a publishing company, but not by the blazing guitarist. He couldn't reject me because I never asked him for anything. I never offered to be anything to him. There was no point. He doesn't need anybody. He definitely doesn't need me.

I leave the bathroom and occupy my mind by curling under a blanket and thinking, thinking, thinking of what I'll tell Xavier.

Only he doesn't ask. When he and Nia return home, there's a lot of squealing and laughing and hugging. Xavier asks about my flight and what I brought them while we're all gathered in the kitchen for Nia's bedtime snack of bread and milk. He looks steady and happy. Maybe he forgot I was supposed to return two weeks from now. That's rather unlikely, but still possible.

"How was Mom's visit?" I ask Xavier.

"Good. Juliette got a break, and Nia got spoiled by Grandma. Too spoiled." He shakes his head, looking down at Nia who's abandoned her food and is now jumping with her arms stretched upward to me.

I pick her up. "They say that's what grandmas are for."

"Yeah. And therapists are for parents who can't rein in their kids later." Xavier offers to take Nia.

She refuses to go with him, so I help her get ready for bed. When she gets kissed and hugged and kissed and hugged again, I leave her singing to herself, as she often does, and find Xavier in his room. He's already putting his work sneakers on.

"See you later." He grabs his jacket and goes out the door.

I can't believe it. I'm off the hook. What in the universe has aligned to grant me this escape?

They Inspire Me

Fiona's not the only one to leave.

The day after our fight—or fights, I should say—Marshall and Alexandra pack a few bags and fly off to Hawaii. From the second-floor window over the castle entrance, I watch them load into a car that'll take them to the airport. I hate the dull ache that worms into my chest when Alexandra looks up and our eyes meet. The wind plays with her long, black hair and pushes it into her face, but it doesn't hide the betrayal, so clear and cutting.

I was afraid she'd feel that way. That's why I never mentioned anything in the first place. Until yesterday. Yesterday was a nightmare. I can't believe all the things I said, but at the same time, I don't regret them either. It's easier to come out and tell them I'm broken.

Easier, but not in any way better.

Marshall comes out of the castle with his laptop bag and climbs into the car.

Alexandra maintains eye contact with me. She takes a breath deep enough for me to see her shoulders rise and fall. Is she waiting for me to come down and apologize?

My every muscle protests the idea. There's nothing I could say to make any of this better.

When she glances at the car—Marshall probably asked her to get in, I push away from the window and run down the stairs. Emptiness rattles inside me. I don't know what I'm going to say, but I can't let them leave like this.

Tumbling through the heavy castle doors, I arrive just in time to see the back of the car disappearing behind the ancient wall. I flew over those stairs two at a time and the courtyard isn't that big, but my opportunity's gone all the same.

I jerk my phone out of my back pocket and squeeze it in my hands. What on earth am I going to say? I'm sorry? Am I? I am. For what? For flipping out? Yes. Of course, I am. Those two are my world.

For feeling what I've been feeling for months? For losing my way despite my best effort? I'm not sorry about that. I didn't choose to suffer insomnia and guilt.

I stuff the phone back into the pocket and storm down the path to the gardens, needing air and space to… I don't know what I want to do. I'm mad at myself. And sad. And lonely. That last feeling is the worst.

Graham catches up with me before I take two dozen steps. "Come on, man. Come back inside."

He grabs my upper arm, his grip strong and bearing no argument. I don't usually doubt Graham's loyalty or friendship, but he's not very talkative and doesn't engage himself in anyone's business unless something is terribly, terribly wrong. I didn't think anyone would be on my side after my performance yesterday.

"Don't feed the misery. Don't think the thoughts that'll rip you piece by piece." Graham tugs me back into the castle. "Eat dinner with us. Marsh and Alexandra will be back. Don't worry. We all had a bad day yesterday, but there's no need to let it escalate out of control. Let it go."

I nod. "Okay."

Only last week, Fiona told me the same thing.

Let it go.

I let her go.

It's for the best. She'd never love me even if I *ever* loved her. If I did love her, I'd never have let her go, would I?

Graham doesn't drag me along anymore, but he doesn't move again until I start walking. We end up in a room with a beige couch and a bunch of armchairs of different colors that still complement the red rug on the floor and colorful tapestries on the walls. Elise, Shane, and Zach are already there. I pause in the doorway, but Graham pushes me in the back.

"I'm going," I mutter under my breath.

Elise points at a light blue armchair next to the window. I obey and sit. She hands me a plate of what looks like a fancy version of chicken and rice. I take it. It's only the band and Elise. No crew, no Rick, no outsiders. I'm safe from the world. If only I could be safe from myself.

"You've never snapped at me before," Elise says. Her voice doesn't sound accusing, but I feel like a piece of crap all the same.

"I'm sorry." This one's probably easiest of all—to apologize to her. It was only a surface fight, her getting into the crossfire of my anger.

Shane clears his throat as he glares at me from an armchair opposite mine.

"I really am sorry," I say with a bit more conviction.

"Apology accepted," Elise says with a pacifying look for Shane. "But CJ, what happened?"

I stuff a forkful of rice into my mouth. Delicious and oh so helpful in buying me valuable time. Still, everyone watches me eat.

What *do* I say?

Everything. Marshall knows anyway. There's no point in hiding anything. I tell them everything.

After I explain my mental state, I realize, there never has been a need to hide anything. They're my family. I should've relied on them instead of making things complicated. If I can't ask them for help, then who? I've gone through enough crap in my life to never want to suffer alone again.

Yet I chose loneliness anyway.

"Okay," Zach says in the end. "So you're having a major case of burnout accompanied by a minor mental breakdown."

I squeeze myself into the armchair. Is that what it is? I've lost it? Something along the way overwhelmed me so much I couldn't take life anymore? "It's not a breakdown—"

"Yes, it is," Graham chimes in. "Don't even try to deny it."

"There's nothing to be ashamed of," Elise adds.

"I'm not ashamed." I might be. Mental health is no joke, and I always considered myself to be the one to be able to handle anything, yet here I am.

"Take the insanity plea," Shane says with a smirk. "Maybe Marshall will forgive you for causing Alexandra to fight with him because of you."

Elise throws a strawberry at him, and I scowl at him, but Shane's not too far off the mark. I have no idea what I'm going to do to fix my friendship with Marshall. Or Alexandra. Or…

I eat more chicken. I want to fix things, but at the same time, I'm afraid of doing even more damage.

"And what about Fiona?" Elise asks quietly.

"What about her?" Despite me knowing I'm in the wrong all around, the defensiveness flies like an arrow from a bow. "Kiera will find herself another assistant manager. It shouldn't be too hard. It's not as if we're so difficult to work with—"

"You're mad at her," Zach declares, eyebrows raised high in surprise.

I dial my flaring anger down. I'm trying to put out the fires, not make more.

"You're actually mad at a girl?" the obliging pianist continues. "You're never mad at any girl. Ever."

"Not true. I was mad at Aiya. I still am."

Hmmm. I take another bite of food. I haven't actually thought of Aiya at all since we left Amsterdam. I don't let people who are set on ruining my life linger in my thoughts.

"Okay, that's true." Shane jumps into the conversation again. "You didn't tell her to leave you alone, though, did you? You left first. But you sent Fiona home."

Graham shoots me a curious look, along with Elise and Zach. I throw my legs over the side of the armchair, which turns out to be less comfortable than I expected and pretty dang awkward, and focus on my food.

"What did she lecture me for? I have so much, but I don't want it? I would've understood her preaching had she been one of the musicians in our genre. What did I do to *her*? She's got her publishing deal. She's successful too." That's only the tip of the iceberg. I feel absolutely wrung out by Fiona turning against me yesterday. Twisted, hollow, and, well, sad.

"CJ." Elise laces every letter of my name with as much disappointment as possible. "You... I understand you've been having a rough time, but you—"

"I messed up everything with Fiona too. I know, I know." More rice goes into my mouth. Focusing on the dinner helps me avoid thinking of what I've lost.

Correction. What I've tossed away.

"Fiona doesn't have a publishing deal anymore," Elise says.

"What?" Zach thuds his plate on the small table in the middle of the room, shocked, maybe even as shocked as I am.

Elise picks up a roll and rips it in half before smearing butter all over. "She asked me and Alexandra to not tell you guys, but we were with her when she got the call. I've never seen her that gutted before."

My food becomes a rock in my stomach. The puffy eyes. The joke about crying. I knew even then something big happened, but this is much more heartbreaking than I thought. Her dream came true then came crashing down.

Something occurs to me. Fiona didn't want me to know. Is it better that it wasn't just me but everyone she wanted to keep in the dark? Who cares? I should've convinced her to tell me. I was there. We were good. I knew she was upset, so I should've done something right away.

"Well, that's lame," Shane grumbles.

Elise sighs. "Yeah."

For a while, we eat in silence. Everyone else eats, that is. I sit with my plate in my hands and study the rice grains. Fiona's indignation makes all the sense in the world now. It wasn't even anger but disappointment, and grief, and that despair of watching everyone else around you succeed while you skin your hands and knees to blood climbing to the top.

I'm no good at all.

"Speaking of Fiona," Zach says and waits to continue until I look at him. "She left something for you."

"She did?" I can't imagine what it could be.

Zach gets up. "Kind of. She left it to Alexandra, who said you should see it. Let me get it."

Alexandra wouldn't give it to me herself, though. She asked Zach to pass it on.

He takes only a couple of minutes to come back and bring a thick, black binder that can't even zip anymore from all the papers. A leather cord is wrapped around it to keep its contents from spilling.

"I don't know what it is." He hands me the bundle. "I didn't look."

I set my plate aside and untie the cord. The binder seems to breathe at ease as it's released, but a sharp fear grips my shoulders. I sense personal revelations and memories at my fingertips from the pile of papers bursting to come out.

Looking up at what's left of my crew, I find three pairs of eager eyes. I can just hear them all screaming in their heads, "Come on already!" I flip the front open. How bad can it be?

The majority of the papers are drawings.

Fiona's sketches of Project Viper.

The classic comics-style faces deliver perfect resemblance, and immediately I remember Zach begging Fiona on the bus to make a graphic novel about us. Now I know why her responses were so stiff—she had already started on something of the sort. It's not exactly a novel of any kind. Nor is it a story. The sketches depict real life events, but they're not in any particular order. All the same. They crush everything inside me. I don't even know why.

"That is insane," Zach breathes out. "And she refused to work on this for us? It's all but done!"

I squeeze the binder shut the best I can and rise from the armchair. "I'd like to look through these on my own."

Everyone nods.

In my room, I place the binder in the middle of the bed and let it fall open. Pages slide out. I've glimpsed the drawings, but there are also notes, on cheap lined paper, on cardstock, on sticky notes, and on napkins. I would've smiled at how terrible Fiona's handwriting is, she's an artist after all, if I wasn't terrified of reading what the notes say. Of the guilt they're sure to ignite.

Then again, the fire's already burning. I might as well let it consume all of me.

I sit with the sketches and read every snippet, examine every line. If I believe the notes, Fiona loves her job. She loves us.

They inspire me.

I love Graham's poise. He's got a classy scowl to accompany that.

As always, Marshall sets the crowd on fire. If he ever burns out, it'll be a real shame.

Zach's a total clown, but his kindness is the most amazing thing I've ever seen.

Alexandra's a true warrior, but I hope she won't always feel like she has to fight for her place.

Shane, stop bashing CJ with your guitar head.

That last one makes me chuckle. I try to find a description of me, but there aren't many notes about me at all. Why? Did I hurt her, somehow, a long time ago?

I honestly believed I couldn't feel any worse. Fiona proved me wrong even though she's not here.

She's not here. I want her to be. All I can do is continue with the drawings.

There are sketches of each of us with our instruments from concerts, and sketches of us as a group at our house back in Portland, and at interviews, and in pairs. There's even one that's dated a few days before we met Alexandra. The lines are rugged, penciled over several times, but the roughness somehow accentuates our individual characters. The six of us, Alexandra including, stand in a row as if posing for a photo. Zach and Shane are laughing at whatever Shane has on his phone screen. Graham is looking up, enduring Zach's and Shane's antics. Alexandra stands between me and Marshall. I have my arm around her shoulders while Marshall glares away. Alexandra holds her bass, head drawn into her shoulders, eyes huge with terror. Fiona's imagination painted the scene that would come to pass so realistically, it gives me goosebumps.

A lot of the notes are her impressions of moments she wanted to sketch later. There is a couple of drawings of me surrounded by excited girls. I stuff those to the bottom of the pile. I look too happy and fake. But there are more drawings of me. On stage, in the zone, with my guitar. Not all of them are comic book style. Some are realistic renderings—deep shadows and bright highlights. What strikes me the most is that I look alive on those, grasping every moment and breathing every note.

Fiona always knew what I was like, yet she drew me like that.

Closer to the end of the collection, I start recognizing recent events.

The charity show with its ridiculous games.

A bunch of rough sketches of us on the bus.

Me playing that borrowed guitar in Vienna.

The side of that page is covered in Fiona's chicken scratch, and I fight to decipher every word. She might've said something about me at last.

> I've heard CJ say that he'll never out-sing Marshall. He doesn't need to. His voice is powerful in its own way. His smile may be spellcasting, but to me, his voice is more dangerous. The way he plucks the strings is hypnotizing. I know exactly why so many girls fall in love with him. Project Viper would never be what they are without him.

Hands sweating, I put the drawing down. I understand why Alexandra wanted me to see this. These memories and warm feelings and Fiona's devotion. What I have is good. It's so much more than good, this family of mine. This dream of mine. I've been living it every day. No wonder Fiona had no mercy on me.

I reread that last note, eyes lingering on the part that says, I know exactly why so many girls fall in love with him.

Does it mean she could have had the same feelings for me? Our kiss under the fireworks pushes away all other thoughts. I remember Fiona's gentleness. She told me she never wanted anything more from me than that one evening. Could it be because she believed I wouldn't give her more?

Wondering, even for just one moment, about Fiona possibly being in love with me, having the same burning in her chest for me as I do for her, sends me curling up on my bed. If we switched sides and she was the one to banish me out of her life, I would've…died.

I pull out my phone again. I must talk to her. Fiona probably already knows, but I must tell her I've been wrong and scared of my feelings, both about the band and her, and I just couldn't cope anymore.

Even though I know I have to make that call, I toss the phone aside. I've ruined enough things already. Although I hate the distance, and I know I've hurt her, I'm too messed up. I'll slip into making it about me again, and it is about me, but I need to regain my footing. I don't want Fiona back so she can help me. I want to be the one helping.

I want to be the one to fix us.

At the very least, I want to do my part.

An idea pops into my head.

I sit up, arrange the drawings into a neat pile, and grab my phone again. I might've damaged whatever chances I had with Fiona, but I believe I can still do something about that busted publishing deal of hers.

A Nice Jerk

Fiona

Kiera gives me a week off to unwind. I start feeling lost and useless on the very first day of the break. It's odd to be doing nothing after weeks of keeping on my toes day and night. There is one thing I can do, though.

After lunch, I stick Nia into her bed for a nap and settle down at the coffee table in the living room to figure out an email to my agent. She asked me to call, but I can't handle even imagining hearing her cheerful voice. I'm spent on the publishing front. I either need to pause in my pursuit of public recognition or quit altogether. Another rejection will traumatize me for good.

"Can we talk?"

Xavier's voice startles me. I didn't hear him come into the living room even though he always makes the floor vibrate with his heavy steps.

"About?" I knew it. He remembers I wasn't supposed to come back yet.

"Well…" He scratches the back of his head and joins me on our floral couch. "When Mom was here, we talked about you."

"Okay." Maybe I didn't know what he wanted to say, but his somber tone doesn't inspire any confidence or relief. "What about me?"

"I'm going to take Nia to California. The tenants of Grammy's basement apartment are moving out in a month, and Mom said I should take the place. Mom and Grammy will help out with Nia—"

"I'm not good enough anymore?" I stare at the blank window of the email composer. Everyone's pushing me away. The publisher doesn't want me, CJ doesn't want me, and even my own brother doesn't need me anymore.

Xavier sighs. "That's not it at all. You're the best sister I could ever want, but Mom reminded me about something."

"What?"

"Fiona."

I close the laptop and face him.

"You're young. You need to be able to stay out late, meet people, fall in love, and make a family of your own, if you want to. Not take care of your older brother who had his chance to live a life, then made a ton of mistakes, and is now stealing your fun."

I can't argue with that, but I don't want to be all *Dang right you are* either.

Xavier goes on, "I am grateful for all that you've done for me and Nia, but it's time for me to grow up."

I can't help a smile. "Under Mom's wing?"

Chuckling, he leans back and rests his head on his hands. "Hey, baby steps. A lot will change for me, but I'll figure it out. I'm going to help remodel Grammy's house, and I'm going back to school for a business degree."

"Me too," I say, quietly, mourning and dying a little on the inside.

"No!"

Xavier's loud response startles me again. "Why? You've been telling me to do this all along. I'm ready."

"You're an amazing artist. Go to an art school. You already have an associate's in fine arts, so it won't take you as long to get your bachelor's degree. Or even a master's. I'll help you pay for it. I promise."

I shake my head. "You have a daughter to raise, and I need to get my head out of the clouds." In every sense possible. My art and my heart.

"Don't give up, Fiona." He scoots closer to take my hand. "You have an agent. Your publishing deal is coming."

I free my hand. "I had it."

Xavier frowns. "What?"

"While I was in Europe, Callie landed me a deal. It was solid. Until Kat Runn showed up on the horizon. Similar projects. Of course, they chose them." I take a deep breath and forbid my eyes to burn. "I can't do this anymore, Xavier—"

"But you've had so many rejections. What's another one—"

"You don't know what it's like!"

I jump to my feet and cross the room to stand in front of the balcony door, to stare at the building across the street, to register nothing. Why can't Xavier see what the publishing race has done to me?

"I'm exhausted to the bone with asking. Please, please, please. No, no, no. Always no. Only ever no. You have no idea what it feels like to always be rejected, compared, passed up."

My brother's strong, kind arms envelope me. "I'm sorry you feel this way. And I do know what you feel like."

Feeling sick to my stomach, I snuggle into his hug. "I'm sorry. I didn't mean to hurt you." Or remind him of the way his wife left, saying he'd always be a loser. "I'm just so frustrated. I don't want to fight anymore. I don't have to, do I?"

"Of course you don't have to." Xavier caresses my head. "I still believe you could do it, but you don't have to. You can take a break or you can quit. It's up to you. There's no wrong choice here. You don't need to hurt if that's what your art has become."

I breathe out in relief. "Thank you."

This decision would've felt like a surrender a few months ago. Right now, it's a healthy choice.

Gently, Xavier pulls away and holds me at an arm's length. "Is that why you came back? You got the publishing deal, then the bad news, and you needed to be home?"

Dang. Here it goes. "No." I suppress a groan.

"Did you get in trouble?"

"Kind of."

He gives me a skeptical look. "You never get in trouble."

"I do now."

We return to the couch.

"What kind of trouble?"

This is my brother. He understood when I said I'm quitting art. He might understand my fight with CJ too.

"One of the band members was being difficult. He's been going through what he called a creative crisis, but he lied. It was more than that. It was a lot more than that." I pull my feet up onto the couch and hug my knees. "I tried convincing him that what he has is so good, but…" Something rings wrong about my explanation. I pick at a hangnail and try to figure out what it is.

Xavier leans back, arms behind his head again, relaxed and taking my story in stride. "He didn't like what you had to say, did he?"

"No." The feeling of wrongness intensifies.

"Do you still have your job?" That's Xavier for you. He isn't digging deeper into the argument, but he is sticking with his pragmatism.

"Yes."

"Do you still want the job?"

"I do." Even if it means being around CJ again.

My response earns me a curious glance from Xavier. A few seconds of tense silence, then he asks, "What did you tell him? You said you tried to convince him. You don't get in trouble, but you don't—"

"Are you taking his side?" Unbelievable.

"Maybe a little bit, okay? Don't be mad at me. Hear me out, Fiona. You have a very set definition of what's right, what's wrong, black and white, light and dark. I think it's great—"

"But?"

"You can be hard on others who don't have the same understanding of the world. To you everything is clear, so sometimes you don't have the patience with those who struggle."

I push myself as deep into the corner of the couch as I can. "So what, then? I'm the one in the wrong?" Theoretically, it's possible.

Xavier shakes his head. "I believe you did what you thought was best."

"Just not what's right."

"Fiona, please. I'm trying to make a very convoluted point here. Let me get some drinks." He goes to the kitchen and brings two orange juice boxes. "A little something to dispel the gloom."

I pop the straw into the foil. "So what is your convoluted point?" What could have I done better?

"Is it possible you were too quick to judge? You put his situation into your perspective…" Xavier keeps talking, but it's not his words that I hear.

You're either judging me or you're jealous.

And you're a harsh judge.

Not you too.

I sip the juice to get some sweetness into my suddenly bitter mouth, but it doesn't help. I had half a reason to flip out at CJ—he didn't tell me the whole truth—before he cast me out (*that* still hurts), but I might've fueled his already raging pain. He wanted someone to be on his side, same as I when I started telling Xavier about the argument, but I joined the forces that were against him. Instead of supporting CJ and helping him get to a better place, I called him an idiot.

I called him a scoundrel.

I mocked him for his honesty and for his intentions about Aiya, which was completely none of my business. Neither was it my business to tell him what to do or how to feel.

"But we've become better friends." I look at Xavier for help to decode the conflicting ideas. "Don't friends tell each other when they're wrong? Or let each other try again after they mess up?"

"Oh, boy." Xavier rubs his face with his hand and leaves it there while he looks at me, at the very center of my soul. "Let me get more juice."

I grab his hand, forcing him to stay. "Why more juice?" That is the lamest explanation or response or whatever after that dreadful *oh boy.*

"This is not about his band issues at all. And if you insist on defining your relationship with that guy in such a kiddy way, we're going to start with kiddy solutions—snacks. More juice boxes in our case."

"Xavier!" He has lost his mind.

"Fiona. You're twenty-two, I'm thirty-one, we're all grown-ups here. Just call it what it is. You two bonded way past friends, or so you thought, and then that jerk threw you away after he got what he wanted. Had you started with that, I wouldn't have taken his side at all."

"He didn't get anything. He didn't even try." I keep eye contact with Xavier and get my vengeance by seeing him clench his jaw in embarrassment.

"Ah, so he's a decent jerk." He goes and brings more juice all the same. "Who still broke your heart."

I smile at how similar we are. I called CJ an honest scoundrel. Xavier called him a decent jerk. We're both right. We're both wrong.

Despite my earlier grumbling, I empty another box of juice in seconds. "He didn't break my heart. I knew I'd never get anywhere with him, so I refused to fall in love."

CJ absolutely and completely broke my heart. And I absolutely and completely fell in love with him. I can deny it all I like. Doesn't make it any less true. No matter how hard I tried to remember he's a player, I let him get under my skin and kiss me. I chose to taste that spark between us. The way he held me in that castle entryway, asking me if our time together had to end with one evening only—

"Oh."

No.

My thoughts race and trip over themselves.

"I see the light bulb turning on in the back of your mind," Xavier teases me.

"Oh, shut up."

He's right though. I don't know if I'm conjuring things up to put a Band-Aid on my wounds, but back there at the castle wasn't the first time CJ had asked me to do something with him again. On the bus when he carried me to bed (I still can't believe I let him do that), he did the same thing. He asked me why it had to be the only time he could do something with me.

I always thought he was flirting with me out of habit, but what if he meant it?

"No light bulbs." I slump against the back of the couch. "It doesn't matter. He doesn't fall in love. He told me so. Everybody knows it too."

Xavier laughs at the top of his lungs.

"Shush!" I hiss. "You'll wake Nia."

Shaking his head, he collects empty juice boxes and leaves the living room without another comment. How helpful.

Live a Lot

Fiona

The next morning I arrive at work.

Kiera gives me a disapproving look. "I gave you some days off."

I set her coffee and the promised muffin in front of her. "I can't be home. It's too easy to think there."

"I know what you're talking about." She takes a long sip of her coffee, then adds, "I won't complain that you're here. After lunch we have a legal meeting about Aiya's sting, so I'll take any reinforcements I can get."

I wish I had talked CJ out of doing that song with Aiya. It set everything on fire.

There's no way I have that kind of sway over him. Even if I did, I don't know if I should. I always tell my friends it's up to me whether I date or not, whether I do anything. CJ should have the same agency and the freedom to pay for his mistakes.

I sit at my desk and fire up my laptop. It's strange to be back. Comforting, familiar, but strange. Too quiet and too steady. Maybe this return to the routine is what I need. Answer easy emails that don't involve bookings, venue managers, merch emergencies, or refund issues. Compared to that, updating a press release feels like no work at all. Other than it's the one asking us to clarify CJ's status with the band.

The Label, of course, told me to say that everything is well and that should there be any changes in the band, the guys will be the ones to decide how or when to announce the news. My fingers pause on the keyboard. I don't think CJ is the kind of person to leave out of spite after what transpired, but he mentioned that it might be good for him to take a break from the band.

There have been too many times when bands took breaks to never reassemble.

I abandon the office for a trip to the bathroom. Cold water soothes my anxious thoughts, and I rinse my face despite my careful makeup. Knowing CJ could leave Project Viper plants a sharp worry in the center of my chest. If he does, I'm not sure how or if the band will go on.

If he does, I might never see him again.

And even though he lied to me, I'm afraid to lose him.

Cupping my hands, I throw more cold water on my face. CJ wouldn't leave. If he did, there's nothing I could do anyway. He doesn't listen to me. If he did before, he won't after me skinning him alive for feeling depressed, lost, confused—

I turn off the water and grab a wad of paper towels. They scratch at my eyes and skin, and the pain fuels my shame for how I acted. What if CJ is depressed, in a way where he needs professional help, not just a pep talk, and we all ganged up on him?

Whatever's happening to him, I want to say I'm sorry. It wasn't my place to tell him what he feels is wrong. Xavier gave me space to decide I didn't want to pursue my publishing career anymore with patience and understanding. Why couldn't I give CJ the same? I didn't have to dismiss his pain because mine felt so much greater.

Does he even need me to be that person who validates him?

I throw the lump of soggy paper towels into the trash bin and march out of the bathroom. I want to know. I want to hear him say, to my face, that he doesn't fall in love, not even with me. I'll be okay if he does.

If he does like me and we can pick up where we left off, I'd love to have more than one time when he sings me to sleep. I want to dance with him again and not because he needed to get away from the ravenous crowd. I want to enjoy his flirting and live a lot, not just a little like he always tells me to, and I want to see if we could do it together.

I push the door to our office with a bit too much force, causing the handle to slam hard against the rubber door stopper on the wall. Kiera jerks her head up from her computer.

"I know there's barely anything left of the Vipers' tour, but I want to go back to them," I say.

"Oh, good." My boss smiles and surprises me with how warm her expression is. "I booked you a ticket already. In time for their show in London."

"You booked me a flight?" I come to stand in front of her desk. "Why?"

"Can you survive until then? Hopefully Marshall and Alexandra will get back from Hawaii in time."

"They went to Hawaii?"

Kiera frowns and picks up her phone. "Don't even get me started. He's still on antibiotics, isn't he? Kids in love."

I hope that's all it is—a need to get away and spend some time without others constantly hovering, that the band isn't cracking.

"I knew you'd want to go back." Kiera hands me a printout of my flight to London. "You always fight to make things right."

"I don't know if I can make anything right, but I want to try. I'm sorry for going back and forth. Whatever the outcome is, I'll stick with it."

The fear of failure rakes my gut with its sharp claws, but I won't relent.

Do It

CJ

London, United Kingdom

Alexandra and Marshall don't come back until the day of our first rescheduled show. London. Royal Albert Hall. It can hold almost six thousand people, the gig is sold out, we're two hours away from the doors opening, and our sweet couple is still en route.

"They made the flight, it hasn't been delayed, they might get here a little later than preferable, but we're good to go," Rick says while we settle in the dressing room.

The red of the square leather couches ratchets up the tension already doing its number on me.

"I want to check out how our sound is shaping." Zach grabs a baseball cap and a can of diet ginger ale and heads out to the stage.

I go with him. Anywhere is better than in a room that's set to destroy my mood. As if it needs help. I haven't talked to Marshall and Alexandra for over a week. I didn't want to interrupt their time

217

together, but waiting and stewing in what I could say once they're back has been driving me insane. Fiona too. I won't present her with a pathetic, bumbling, uncertain version of me. *Matryoshka* and Marsh, though, will be back soon. I need to ground myself and come up with a plan.

Hours pass. The crowd starts filling the seats, and I still don't know what I'm going to do, if anything I'll say will be enough.

When Marshall and Alexandra don't make it to the venue when they said they would, I can't help wondering if I've gone too far. That I pushed those two away for good and broke the band despite my best efforts to keep it together.

Our fight couldn't have been *that* bad. Could it?

I pace the green room and destroy Elise's work by running my hands through my hair, over and over again. Our opening band is out there already. We're half an hour away from hitting the stage, and our lovers are still not here.

Rick throws the door to the dressing room open. "They're stuck in traffic. The roads from the airport are one accident after another. I checked the traffic on Google. There's a lot of red."

I breathe out in relief along with Shane, Zach, and Graham, but we still have a problem. There's no estimate of when the rest of our band will get here.

"Let's helicopter them," Zach suggests, tripping over a can of soda he placed on the floor earlier.

Elise jumps in with a towel to help him clean up the spill.

Rick shakes his head. "Where are you going to land a chopper? On a sidewalk or in a ditch? Sit tight and be ready for a double encore. And seriously guys, no more surprises on this tour. Only six more shows left. Let's breeze through them."

The door closes. I sit on the couch and close my eyes. Everything's okay. They're coming back.

Elise combs out my hair once more. "Are you ready?"

"Yes." I don't know what she means—too many interpretations, but I'm going to tackle it all tonight. All of it. If I fumble or say the wrong stuff, I won't get defensive but try again. No more hurting people around me.

Forty-six minutes after we should've started, Alexandra and Marshall run into the dressing room.

Struggling for breath from running, Alexandra says, "We're so sorry—"

"Later," Elise cuts her off. "Put these on."

Alexandra starts stripping with everyone in the room, forcing all nonessential helpers to leave while the rest of us face the wall.

"Did you have fun?" Zach asks, bouncing on his feet next to me.

"Sorry, we didn't miss you at all," Alexandra says with a smile in her voice. "It was—"

"I don't want to know," Graham grumbles, but when I glance at him, I see a devilish grin. "Let's just get out there before the crowd slays us."

"Yes," Shane adds.

Within five minutes, both Marshall and Alexandra change into leather and denim. Instead of her usual straightening treatment, Alexandra gets a few quick spritzes of what Elise named as beach curl spray, and off we go.

"One minute to do *the thing*," Zach pleads with Rick. "Just one minute."

Our tour manager pinches the bridge of his nose but nods an okay.

Once again only us in the room, we stand in a circle and name our strengths.

Marshall starts. "Fearlessness."

"Courage." Alexandra.

Then Zach. "Loyalty."

"Inner strength." Graham.

"Freedom." Shane.

It's my turn. "Inspiration. Let's make this show the best one yet." I sound pumped as much for their benefit as for mine, whether I feel inspired or not.

Shane, Graham, and Zach nod, Alexandra responds with a nervous smile, and Marshall responds with a deadpan stare.

Okay. He's still seething. I get it. So I smile at him. Bring it on. I'm ready to apologize.

Marshall smiles back. "The best one yet?" He arches a challenging eyebrow.

I see. He was making sure I understood I'm not forgiven yet, but not snubbed forever either.

"The best one yet." I clap his shoulder.

He responds in kind, and we start filing out of the dressing room.

As soon as we step out, Marshall stops.

I brace myself for him to blow a lid, at last, and lash out at me, but he steps aside and says to Chris, our chief of security waiting by the door, "Do it."

With all grave seriousness, Chris nods.

I hear Graham sighing behind me, "Oh, man."

"What's the matter?" I ask him.

Two pairs of hands like iron grip my arms.

"Don't make too much of a scene, okay?" Chris says when I try to rip my arms from his and another security guy's holds.

"What the— Marshall!" I yell at my best friend's back as I'm dragged in the opposite direction from the band, shoes slipping against the floor.

"Enjoy the show," he shouts without turning around, throwing a hand with a peace sign high over his head.

As I storm up the stairs to the top tier of Royal Albert Hall, two goons flanking me, all I can think of is that I want to make a scene. The biggest one ever. The one that the tabloids would chew on for months. I'm more than capable of it. I have been the driving force behind this band for years. What's one tantrum? Yet I oblige Chris and Amir—I remember the name of the second guy—and come along quietly.

They bring me to the gods' observation deck level, as high as it gets. There are a few people there, venue crew and some spectators, but I'm afforded a section partitioned off by black curtains.

"In you go." Chris motions for me to go inside the jail. "Don't try anything."

"You work for me too, you know?" I snap.

He shrugs. "Five against one."

I bat at the curtain and go in. A white armchair on crooked, wooden legs, a bucket of ice with a few water bottles, and a pair of noise-isolating headphones wait for me. How nice. I slide the headphones onto my ears—no need to hurt my eardrums in a fit of rage, grab a bottle of water, and throw myself at the banister to watch.

Everything is dark. The countdown timer has five seconds left.

Four.

Three.

Two.

One.

The air vibrates with the guitar intro of *Desire and Denial*. Standing on a foot-tall podium, Shane's illuminated with white light from behind in such a way that all you see is his silhouette. Marshall starts singing, but he remains dark. I could name this sequence if they woke me up in the middle of the night. Graham comes in, and he's silhouetted the same as Shane. Then Alexandra and Zach, two measures apart, and when the song swings into its full energy, Marshall becomes highlighted in red. The star of the show. Our resident divo.

My hands curl around the cool bottle. If only my aim was good enough and my arms were strong enough to fling this bottle straight at his forehead. How dare he box me?

I watch him sing our first hit, willing him to look up. He doesn't. He's too busy thrashing all over the place, as always, whipping his ridiculous hair, pulling his usual sexy—more like stupid—poses, and acting as if he's got the best voice in the world. I'll wipe that smugness off his face, preferably by dragging it across some asphalt.

The situation is worlds beyond idiotic, but I have to admit… watching my band from an audience's point of view is fascinating. I've seen the videos of our performances, but this is different. The air, the light show, the throbbing sound. Live music is a beast of its own, with breath, blood, flesh, and bones. Growling, snarling, howling, purring.

Out of my reach.

I'm back to wanting to punch Marshall.

Maybe the rest of the guys too for going along with him.

What am I now? An outcast? We promised to each other, ages ago, all of us, that no matter what happens, we stay true to each other. We stay honest and spell things out and deal with it in broad daylight. Our background, our shared misery of being in foster care, dealing with garbage families, and dwelling on the bottom layer of every totem pole of every school we've ever been to forbids what they're doing to me right now.

I glare at them all in turns. Even at Alexandra. She's the newest, and the only reason she's here is because I— Okay, fine. She's only following her lover's lead. And hiding behind a pair of wide shades. Feeling guilty, I bet.

I drink half the bottle of water and chuck it into the armchair.

Shane plays my solos, confident as ever on the stage. Strutting his stuff, caressing his guitar, and—

Wait, he's playing a black guitar.

All of his are green.

"Is that my Les Paul?" I shout, knowing perfectly well he won't hear me.

Shane riffs off crisp melodies and dances with my guitar girlfriend. He knew. Of course, he knew I'd recognize my baby. I will break his fingers. After I wipe the asphalt with Marshall's face. They're doing this on purpose. See how much you're missing?

The crowd sings along. Every single word.

For the first time ever, I don't see any faces up close. Only the tops of the heads, shoulders, and backs bouncing up and down, hands in the air, digging every last drop of the songs. Not missing me.

Why is it so hot up here? I can feel the breeze sliding over my face, doing nothing.

That's what I'm doing up here. Nothing. I should be out there.

Sweating, I drop my jacket to the floor and tug at my tee collar. It's low but somehow too tight. I can't seem to breathe right, not deep enough. I'm angry enough to attempt to fight my way out of here.

Chances are Chris would lay me out before I lay a finger on him.

Unwilling to entertain Marshall's scheme any longer, I drop to the floor and lean my back on the half wall that prevents anyone up here from plummeting to their certain deaths.

Traitors.

They threw me to the curb. Like they could ever do this without me. I kick the leg of the armchair, then one more time, then once again, as hard as I can, sending the heavy white monster a foot away from me. Violence for the sake of doing something is far from satisfying because the truth is, they can. They are rocking the show without me right now. Every position is accounted for. Nothing is lacking. That's how we used to be. Vocals, drums, bass, keyboard and effects, and one guitar. They're continuing with our old sound, which worked. There was nothing wrong with the band before. I just needed a change, wanted my dream to be complete.

I take out my phone since I didn't get a chance to give it to Rick for safekeeping right before the show and scroll through this summer's photos. Who knows what I'm hoping to find. A sign of some kind.

My eyes spot a thumbnail of me, Marshall, and Alexandra before that cursed show in Amsterdam. I tap it. The photo fills the phone screen as the sounds of my music, played without me, knock on my back. Teen Faves was a disaster, but this photo is proof of me trying, and succeeding, to do good. Proof of me having a family. Proof of some of my choices resulting in happy things. Marshall is happy with Alexandra. She has a new home and people to belong with. I got to do what I always wanted to do.

Until now.

Now I'm out.

Hard, bitter fear rakes through me. Them forcing me out of the show isn't a permanent banishment, is it?

I swallow hard and will my heart to stop accelerating. It won't. It can't. I've caused too many problems in the past year. I'm the only one who broke the promise to keep things honest and straight between us.

The music simmers down to a quiet drumroll. The crowd's cheers subside. I scramble to my feet to check what's happening.

"We are very sorry to put a damper on your evening." Standing in the middle of the stage, Marshall swipes his wild hair away from his face. "For starters, I want to apologize for being late. It is entirely my fault. I beg your forgiveness." He drops his arms to his sides and delivers a deep bow.

The audience eats up his gesture and showers him with a new round of applause and cheers.

"And secondly," he goes on, barely managing to speak over the cheering masses, "this next song—"

The front-row girls chant his name—Marshall! Marshall!—so he pauses and laughs and blows them a bunch of kisses. What a poser.

When Marshall can speak again, he says, "This next song, we can't perform it without CJ."

He looks up, straight at me. Our eyes lock across hundreds of feet and the crowd, and I want to shout, "Why the heck did you lock me up here, then?"

Someone bumps me in the shoulder. I swivel toward the person. It's Chris with a harness attached to a cable. Amir is also at the ready with an in-ear monitor.

I assess the equipment for a second. No way. Marshall has planned for this too. He's making a show out of our fight. Clever. I would do the same. I take off the headphones, lift my arms, and let Chris strap me in.

The Thunder in the Storm

They stick me in a harness, order me to stand on a platform that's twelve inches in diameter at best, and lower me to the stage. Graham keeps at it with the quiet drumroll, and the audience's heads snap up to watch me, thousands of hands reaching for me. I cling to the cable to the point of it biting into my skin. Lingering rage and adrenaline from being this high above the ground are a cranky combo. When I arrive at Marshall's side, I'm not sure what I want to do first—hug him because I made it in one piece or punch him.

Marshall high fives me. "Here's my best friend. Of course you all noticed CJ wasn't with us here for the first segment, but it's not because Project Viper is breaking up. CJ had a few things to take care of before he could join us, but now you're going to get the best show ever." He shoots me a wry grin.

Something to take care of? Why not? Let's call it that.

He turns to me and mouths, "Ready?"

Eyes locked with his, I nod. Am I ready? I was born for this.

Alexandra stands on my other side. She got rid of the sunglasses, and even in the uneven lighting I catch the red around her eyes. I reach for her face, to touch her cheek and say I'm sorry, but she offers me the bass.

Ah, right. *Devastation, Free of Charge* is next. They really can't play it without me. This is the one song where a six-member layout is a must. Marshall will play the guitar lead and be the backup singer for once, and Alexandra's the vocal anchor, the kind that doesn't allow distraction from anything else.

I take the bass and gasp from the zing that shoots through my arm. It could be a faulty cable, but the way my heart settles and burns with a different, powerful kind of fire makes me believe everything is going to be okay from now on. Or at least I will be okay no matter what happens.

I'm not banished.

As I fling the bass strap over my head and adjust it to my preferred length, Graham transforms the gentle drumroll into the *Devastation's* intro. We have no time to dawdle. All instruments go in right from the start, and the fat, rounded strings of a bass under my hands…

Lights hit my face, and I close my eyes. I'm the thunder in the storm once more.

Alexandra and Marshall command the crowd with their powerful voices, and I feel every note, soak in every drumbeat, bask in the colorful lighting. Every breath is easy. Every smile and desperately reaching hand is a gift. Sliding to my favorite spot at the edge of the stage, I revel in the weightlessness that fills my body. A determined kind of energy seems to power me through the stage's floor, up my feet and through my legs, into my heart. I belong here.

I sense Shane approaching me from behind. It's inexplicable. I don't have eyes on the back of my head, but I know he's there. When I swing around, our guitar necks clash together. My Les Paul! He dares to roughhouse with my baby and smirk about it? I drop the bass line for a few seconds to grab my cord and whip him on the thigh. Shane sidesteps to dodge it, but I deliver another whip, land it, then return to the bass line. Laughing, we smash our backs together and carry on, birds of a feather, two nutjobs in love with the strings.

Fiona was right. I've been an ungrateful idiot. Even on the bass guitar, I always did what I wanted to do—play music with my favorite people. The good old times aren't over. I hit a pothole, fell onto my face, and changed into someone new. Or something like that, I think. I'll need some help figuring out what happened. I do know one thing—I don't need any help knowing I'm sticking around no matter what. There's no other place I belong to more.

Fiona, on the other hand.

What do I do about her? Will she forgive me?

After *Devastation* ends, we execute another hostage exchange. I get my Les Paul back, Alexandra reunites with her Fender P Bass, and Shane receives his green PRS from one of the techs. We play the rest of the concert and give the crowd their double encore. I'm sweat-soaked and parched and aching everywhere, but Marshall was right. This is the best show yet.

Everything feels perfect and right, the way it was supposed to on that first gig with Alexandra.

Reaching this feeling fractures something inside me as we line up to bow. Loved by deafening cheers, I stand between Marshall on my right and Alexandra on my left and stare at the ceiling, because if I look anywhere else— Crap. It's no use.

The tears rip me apart. Hot and unstoppable, they burn tracks down my face. It's monstrously hard to breathe, and I don't remember the last time I cried, but I'm not embarrassed. The breakdown feels too liberating for shame. I just give in and let it claim me, sobbing into the crook of my arm, ugly, snot and all.

Someone grabs me and pulls me into a hug. Someone small. Alexandra. I hug her back. The audience hushes down to an amusing mix of *awww*s and claps. The rest of the guys pile on and around me as if we're on a football field.

"Get off me!" I laugh.

"Never." Marshall ruffles my hair.

Whoa, have I been wrong about settling down. Him telling me he'd never leave me floods my eyes with more tears. I find and squeeze his hand as hard as I can. That jerk. Making me wail like a baby for all to see.

Alexandra pounds me with a fist on my chest, and I realize she's in no better condition than I am. Eyes glistening with tears, she shouts into my ear, "Don't make me do anything like this ever again."

All I can do is try to smile and hope she'll see my answer in my eyes. I won't. I promise.

Graham starts patting us all on the backs, urging us to leave the stage and save conversations for later.

I like that plan.

We bow again and wave goodbye, and for the first time in months, I'm happy with where I am.

However.

Stepping into the backstage space, I drive a sharp elbow into Shane's side, making him buckle with pain. Jumping, Alexandra presses both hands to her mouth.

"What's that for?" Shane wheezes.

"You touch my baby again, and I'll hurt you a lot more."

Cackling, he straightens up. "Fair enough."

He swings to punch me in the side, but I dodge it. Or so I think. Zach pushes me toward Shane, who delivers his retribution.

"Hey, guys. Leave some for me." Fiona's voice cuts through the post-show commotion.

I jolt upward and stare at her. Gray jeans, fitting and flirty, white shirt underneath a dark blue blazer, gold eyeliner, dark brown hair swooped to the side. She means business. Not the work kind. Arms crossed on her chest, Fiona stands tall and braced for trouble. She went away, but not because she ran away. I tossed her out, she regrouped, now she's here to shred me.

Men Need to Cry Too

Fiona

There have been two times in my life I've seen guys cry. The first was my brother sniffling at night a few days after I moved in with him and Nia. I was up late drawing and went to get a snack. His bedroom door was cracked open. I almost walked past but opted to reveal I heard him. We ate the snack together, he cussed and mourned his broken heart, and I realized men need to cry too. The second time is CJ on stage.

He rushes toward me and squeezes me in his arms with enough force to leave no doubt at all he's happy to see me.

I lean away enough to be able to wipe his still damp cheeks with my fingers. "Are you okay?"

"I am now." His eyes search my face, then he holds me tight again and sighs.

There's no way he broke down mid-concert because of me, but I can't help myself. "You missed me hard enough to cry?"

He bursts out laughing, sounding bright and thrilled.

Graham pushes us both in the direction of the exit.

"Patience, hi-hat hopper," CJ teases him, intertwining our arms.

After all the motions of winding down, shaking hands, and getting a quick interview for a local music influencer out of the way, we get into the bus and drive to the hotel. This will be the last luxury sleepover of the tour.

In the bus, not the tour one, just a regular small kind meant to ride around the city, I sit at the window while CJ drops next to me and yells at Marshall, "You were flipping late!"

I smile. CJ's caused a lot of disturbance in the past weeks. It's no wonder he jumps onto this opportunity to be on the chastise committee for a change.

"And I made up for that with that second encore," Marshall replies. "What are you, Kiera's agent of vengeance now?"

"That would be me." I look around CJ at the now chill singer. I was there when he stormed onto the stage. There's no sign of the earlier murderous intent in his bright green eyes.

"Don't be mad." Alexandra makes puppy eyes at CJ. At me too. I am, after all, one of the few people who can boss the band around.

CJ shoots her a mild glare. "When did you learn to play dirty?"

Alexandra shrugs. "You're the one who taught me."

Zach laughs from his seat up front.

I shift in my seat and find a more comfortable position. I missed this pile of crazy individuals. Working for Project Viper can be challenging, but these guys, and Alexandra, are a treat. Silly, quirky, unashamed to be themselves.

CJ goes on grouching at Alexandra and Marshall. "You two are terrible together. No, I take that back. You were pretty awful to begin with. Only then you were fighting, and now you are…" He waves his hand in a vague gesture.

She rests her cheek on Marshall's shoulder. He kisses the top of her head. It wasn't hard before to see they were in love, but there's something different between them. Some familiarity they acquired while they were away. Somehow, they seem to be even more comfortable with each other. I'd lie if I said I wasn't at least a little bit jealous of their comfortable relationship.

Half of Zach's face appears over the top of his seat. "Did you propose while you were in Hawaii? Or was it a spontaneous, show-off-for-the-girlfriend trip?" he asks Marshall.

Alexandra hides her face behind her elbow. Marshall laughs and takes out his phone.

Hold on. What is going on here? Because something is definitely afoot.

A couple minutes down the road, CJ and I, and everyone else, jump in our seats from Zach yelling, "You did not! Not without me!" He crosses the bus, and, falling onto Marshall's legs, pretends to weep on Alexandra's lap. "How could you do this? I was going to take you to the altar."

Altar?

"How did you know?" Alexandra pushes him away and looks at Marshall in confusion. "How did he know?"

Graham shows her his phone screen. I ransack my shoulder bag for my phone and check social media outlets while CJ leans on my shoulder.

Posted a minute ago, at the top of my Insta feed, sits Marshall's announcement of him and Alexandra getting married. All with a nonchalant one-liner of *By the way.*

"By the way?" I cry out. "You two got married, and that's all you have to say? What about, well, everything? Dresses, parties, bridal photos, tabloid speculations?" I would've loved to throw Alexandra a bridal shower. I would've loved to see Marshall scowl as I dragged him from one wedding planning appointment to another. Now what?

"Overrated," Graham says.

Shane adds, "Charlie will have a heart attack."

"Yes, she will." Zach cackles.

For a good reason. Charlie will be furious she got left out of that magnificent source of social media post fuel.

CJ's the only one who doesn't react. He sits with his eyes closed.

"CJ," I whisper. What if—

He throws his foot across the narrow bus aisle and kicks Marshall in the hip. "I told you not to get married without me!"

Everyone laughs. I clench my hands together to not punch CJ. Here I thought that maybe he still had secret feelings for Alexandra. Never mind.

At the hotel, CJ tugs on my hand as he weaves between the bus and the hotel building.

"Not again," I laugh, not that I'm against another city excursion with him. His friends probably want to have a chat after what happened at the concert.

"I'm not going in yet." CJ glances at me over his shoulder. "I need to talk to you first."

I cling to his arm and press myself to his side. "To me? First?"

He throws me another glance. "Give me a break, Fiona. I'm scared out of my mind, okay?"

CJ showed his emotions on stage, and he's admitted he's freaking out right now. Both of those things lead me to believe he's not afraid of anything at all.

Arm in arm, we walk for a few minutes and come to a large park. As we cross the street toward the collection of trees and shrubs and lush lawns, the night thickens with moisture and the scent of the approaching rain.

"Well, that's London for you, I suppose," I mutter to myself.

CJ chuckles beside me but doesn't respond. We enter the park aptly named Green Park. It's nearing eleven at night, and there aren't that many people out, but we're not completely alone. CJ veers off the path onto the lawn, then drops in the middle of the grass and throws his arms and legs apart as if he's about to make a snow angel.

I stand next to him. "You must be drained."

"Fiona, no," he groans. "Don't be nice to me."

I nudge his ribs with my foot. "Better? You wanted me to kick you lying down?"

He sits and looks up at me. His hair settles in that irresistible, disheveled swoop I love drawing so much. "I'm sorry."

Hating to tower over him like I'm better somehow, I lower myself to the thick grass beside him. Close, but not touching. I need a bit of distance to keep my head clear. "I know."

"You do? How?"

"You wouldn't be talking to me if you weren't." Now I get what he meant earlier when he said he was scared out of his mind. Making up is miserable. "I'm sorry too."

"You didn't do anything wrong."

I shake my head. "You know I did. I dragged you down when you needed to be lifted up. I was upset. Not that it excuses me, but I thought I was helping—"

"And you felt that I lied to you." He gazes at the cloud-shrouded sky. "I did, didn't I? Not telling the whole truth is not any better than lying."

"I understand, though. It was an uncomfortable truth."

"I think I went about it all wrong. I was waiting for some big change after Alexandra arrived, but I missed the fact that I already had everything I wanted." CJ faces me, his expression… He's not smiling or cringing or pleading with his eyes. He's just watching me in the most calm manner, twisting every nerve in my body into a tight coil.

"You lost your publishing deal," he says at last, eyes still on me.

"Yes, I did." I really don't want to talk about this. The publishing deal feels like a long-forgotten dream, and although I was heartbroken when it was snatched away, it's in the past. CJ's in the present. Judging by how things are going, I may still have a chance with him.

Our phones ring at the same time. We pull them out and chuck them far onto the lawn, then laugh at the way our thoughts and impulses match, then fall silent again.

The air between us rings with all the unspoken emotion. I was so determined to find out how he feels about me, for sure, have him say it out loud—

"Dang it, CJ! I can't take it anymore. I'm really sorry I was so harsh on you, and I still don't understand you all the way, and I don't know if we're compatible or if I love you or if you even like me at all…" I run out of breath and suck in a deep one. "You don't date or fall in love, but—"

CJ throws one arm around my waist, drags me over to him, and scorches my lips with a blazing kiss.

The Last One to Bail

Fiona melts into me. I lower her back onto the grass, savoring the feel of her beautiful, willing lips on mine, but crap, she was trying to make some point.

The phones ring again. Forget them.

Breathing hard, I shake my head to banish the daze her presence and hazel eyes put me in. "Sorry. You were saying?"

Something about maybe loving me.

"Yeah, right. Like you care." She tugs on my sweatshirt collar and connects our lips in another kiss.

I break away. "I do care!" And they say men are oblivious. Doesn't she realize what her earlier words are doing to me? "I care about you. I know I told you a bunch of garbage about how I don't fall in love, but—"

She presses a finger to my mouth. "Don't hurry to say it. If you don't know how you feel, it's okay."

"Don't give me an easy way out, Fiona." I take her chin and coax her to look at me. "I know what you say at The Label. *Don't stress the talent.* I want you to challenge me." She really should. "I won't break."

Not with her by my side. "And I don't want to walk the easy road with you. I want to walk the best one."

She presses her lips to my cheek, then moves to whisper in my ear, "Wow, you're smooth."

I kiss her again.

Fiona doesn't seem to mind, both hands curled over my shoulders. Hand on her neck, I slide my thumb to that tender spot under her jaw and relish every beat of her pulse. Frantic and exhilarated, it matches mine.

The phones keep ringing in psychotic disharmony.

I press my forehead to Fiona's. "Don't they know we don't want to be interrupted?"

She chuckles. "Oh, they do. Who cares?"

Oooh, nice. A glimmer of Fiona's wild side I love so much. I arch an eyebrow, playful, teasing, flirting, and give her my first-rate smolder—everything Fiona usually rolls her eyes at. She doesn't this time. Smiling, she reaches for another kiss.

It starts to rain. To pour.

"Crap!" I scramble to my feet and run for the phones before they soak in too much water.

Fiona's on my heels. We grab the devices, silence the ringing, and hide them in our pockets. Then laugh again.

Fiona pushes my hair off my forehead. "I'm glad you feel better."

"You're still too nice to me." I pull her into my arms once more. It won't help shield her from the relentless rain, but I want her to know I'm here for her all the way. "I'm glad you came back. I'm sorry I tossed you out so—"

"Rudely."

"Yes." I did that. In front of our friends, no less. I can't believe how messed up I was. "And I'm sorry I didn't tell you everything. I will do better. I promise."

Fiona hooks her arm through mine. "I also promise to do better, okay? No more judging."

That did hurt when she chewed me out as if my pain was nothing. "Thank you."

Cold, dumping rain doesn't stop us from taking a casual stroll back to the hotel. It's a short walk anyway, but once we're there, chaos will swallow us up all over again.

"How are you feeling about the publishing deal?" I cover her hand in the crook of my arm with my fingers. I love that I don't have to try too hard to get her to relax with me anymore. "Can we talk about it or would you rather not?"

Fiona pulls her arm away and sticks her hands in the pockets of her jeans. With rain streaming down her face, she looks sadder than sad.

"Sorry, I won't bring it up again."

"No, it's fine. I wasn't sure what to say." She stops on the narrow sidewalk, only a few yards away from the hotel entrance, and leans her shoulder on the building. "I think I'll take a break from trying to reach the stars."

Speechless for a second, I stare at her.

Fearless Fiona is taking a break?

"I'm a hypocrite, right?" She detaches from the wall and swipes water off her face. "I gave you an earful when you said you needed some time and space."

"No, you're not—"

"I understand now, CJ." She takes my hand, threads our fingers together, but looks away, guilt all over her face.

"Well, I don't think I need a break anymore. I might need a therapist, though. Think Connor"—our recording label president—"knows someone who's good at dealing with unhinged musicians?" I quip, but Connor probably has a whole list of contacts in that department.

Fiona chuckles.

"Don't laugh." I bump her with my hip. "I'm the only one of the guys who dodged therapy after the Tangs took custody of us, and it may be coming to collect its debt."

Fiona's eyes pop. "Are you serious? You all had therapy?"

"Everyone but me. And Zach. He said, 'I'm not being dragged in from foster care, so what do I need it for.'"

"Why did you refuse to do it?"

Memories of my not-too-distant teenage years put a smile on my face. "I was sixteen and cool, and therapy was super uncool. Besides, I was learning to play guitar. It was a waste of time to go to therapy."

"That explains a lot." Fiona laughs again even though I reach to flick her nose.

She dodges it, and I let her be, laughing along.

All things have been resolved within one evening? How lucky am I? Oh, I am grateful. I am beyond grateful. I'm also grateful when it stops pouring buckets of water on us.

Fiona looks around then steals an unexpectedly cautious look at me. "Did you... Did Alexandra show you my drawings?"

"Did you want her to show me your drawings?"

She manages to combine a shrug and a nod into one bewildering gesture.

"You're one heck of an artist, Fiona. I haven't come across any comics before that guilt tripped me so hard."

"I didn't want to guilt you. I didn't want you to see them at all. Since you did see them, though, I hope you remembered where you've been."

"And what I stood to lose." A breeze slithers along the street, causing me to shiver in my damp clothes. I can't imagine Fiona feeling any warmer. "Good art, Fiona. Life-changing."

"I also hope Zach didn't see it."

Ummm…

I pull Fiona toward the hotel entrance. "Let's go inside before we catch colds and Kiera flies out here to give us a proper mothering lecture."

"CJ?" Fiona's tone is a big, fat warning.

"I told you before. Not everything is my fault. Blame Alexandra. She's the one who left the binder with Zach before she and Marshall flew to Hawaii." Going through the thing for the first time with Zach in the room, though, was my mistake.

Fiona yanks her hand out of mine and presses her fingers to her eyes. "I'll never hear the end of it now." She really doesn't want us to do anything with those sketches.

Had I known that, I wouldn't have sent them to one of the top honchos in the graphic novel publishing industry.

"I want them back," Fiona declares. "Tonight."

Why is my life one disaster after another?

"I don't have them." I hurry her through the lobby and toward the elevators. I already saw the hotel booking and know exactly where to go. "I sent it all to the United States. Didn't want anything to happen to them."

Fiona nails me with an evaluating look.

She'll kill me when she finds out I'm lying again, but I hope it'll be worth it. I just want her to have one more chance to show her art to someone with deciding power if she doesn't want our help to publish it.

When we get to our common suite, laughter and banter float from behind the door. I brace myself and push the door open.

"Ah! I thought you also eloped," Zach greets from a gold velvet sectional with brown cushions. He's holding a plate with what looks like half a pizza on it. A black coffee table with inlays of colorful birds in front of him is piled with more pizza and cans of soda.

Everyone—Zach, Marshall and Alexandra, Shane and Elise, and Graham—is staring at us. At me. I take a step back, right into Fiona. Gently, she steadies me with her hands before claiming a spot on the crowded sectional.

"Who sanctioned the grease fest?" I joke. Our diets are monitored, especially during tours since there's less opportunity to exercise.

"I told Rick you threw a fit on the stage because they don't let us eat more carbs." Chortling, Alexandra takes a huge bite of what looks like sausage and olives.

My stomach implodes on itself and stabs me with hunger pains. That's totally what it is. Not me crumbling apart under everyone's knowing—

"I'm sorry for everything, okay?" I look at my friends, and even though I feel like I'm going to get a canker on my tongue from apologizing—*sorry* is a sharp word—I must do it.

They wave for me to come over, and Marshall locks my neck in the crook of his arm as soon as I sit next to him.

"You hit some serious burnout at last," he says.

"I guess." I still don't know what to call what happened.

"There's no guessing." Marshall releases me and offers me a plate. "Music and the band have always been the juice to your batteries. It's always been fun for you. But you hit a snag, and the juice ran out because we relied on you too much, and you became exhausted."

"And you haven't learned yet"—Shane tosses me a can of soda, which I catch easily—"to rest properly or recognize when art is work and work is art—"

Elise clamps a hand over his mouth. "Art is work and work is art? That makes no sense!"

He pushes her hand away and glares, for which she kisses him on the cheek. Shane squints at her, then continues, "You're a dumb workaholic who thinks if he doesn't do everything, the world will fall apart even though you have a whole team, all of us, your family to share everything with."

I stuff my mouth with pizza and glance at Fiona. She was right. I am full of fear. I don't share. I don't have to share everything, but I should share more. It's not as if I don't trust these people or hate them. Although, I did hate Marshall a few hours ago.

About that.

I scarf down a pizza slice, set my plate on the coffee table, grab a cushion, and use it to backhand Marshall in the face as hard as I can.

The girls yelp, the guys choke on their food, and Marshall seems to be the only one not surprised.

He rips the cushion out of my hands, slams it against my side, then drives his fist on top of it. "I knew you were holding something back still. You wouldn't let me keep you off the stage and not—"

"Exactly!" I throw the dumb cushion to the floor. Our bandmates watch us with the same level of attention they'd give a TV wrestling match, and the girls choose to sit on the floor on the other side of the coffee table. We're one last show for them tonight. "You don't get to decide whether I'm out there or not. It's my band, you howler monkey—"

"That was for making my wife cry." Marshall manages to land a hefty smack on the back of my head. "Besides, you weren't sure you wanted to be in the band."

"I am now. I'll never leave." I try to punch his jaw, but Marshall intercepts my fist with his hand and twists it aside. Pain flares through my wrist. I respond by ramming his arm into the couch. Plus, I'm not too old to kick him in the kneecaps since there's no asphalt available. "I'll be the last one of you all to bail. And she wasn't your wife then!"

Marshall seizes a handful of my sweatshirt and yanks me toward him. "So it makes it okay?"

"Of course not. I was— I already said I'm sorry, okay?"

"Oh my gosh." Alexandra gets up. "I'm going to my room."

Everyone else echoes her desire to leave me and Marshall alone to finish what we started. They leave, but as soon as they do, we quit and sit there with mostly eaten pizza.

"That worked surprisingly well." Marshall parks his feet on the empty corner of the coffee table.

"You mean getting everyone out of the room so we could talk?"

He nods. "We should do this more often."

"Talk or fight?"

"Your choice."

I adjust my sweatshirt and take a box with two slices. Marshall tries to poach one, but I slap his hand. We both burst out laughing.

"You already stuffed your face," I complain, "and I just barely got here."

He huffs and finds himself more pizza. "I won't apologize for tonight's show, by the way. You needed an awakening."

"Thanks a lot," I grumble through a mouthful of thin crust and too much cheese.

"What did you want me to do? Nothing?"

I open my mouth to say that yes, he should've let me figure it out, but I realize that would've been so much worse. Marshall's done the right thing. A harsh one, also a vengeful one, but he remained a true friend. He chose to take the risk instead of letting me burn on my own.

We eat in silence. After I can't swallow another bite, I tell him, "Like I told Fiona, I'll do better. Whatever it takes."

"Fiona." The way Marshall savors her name instantly makes me feel like I've sprung a trap. "Are you in love or something?"

I rest my head on the back of the couch. "Jerk."

"No. Wait. Are you really in love? Like, seriously in love? Heart stopping, breath catching, hands shaking when you're apart kind of love?"

Is that what love is? Then… "Yeah."

Marshall stares at me, his mouth open.

"Did you write me off as a hopeless case?" I kick his foot one last time.

"No. You always claimed you couldn't actually fall in love, and I believed you."

"So did I."

I was a fool. About everything.

Don't Mock My New Title

CJ

6 weeks later

Portland, Oregon, United States

The phone has been ringing non-stop, and there are more emails every day, people clamoring to get a scoop on the latest Project Viper news. The tour wrapped up without any more insane adventures, but the guys have been all over the media constantly, on every tabloid and every gossip website. Everywhere. Ever since Marshall dropped the bomb about him and Alexandra getting married, everyone needs to know everything. Where, how, why, and did he bring Alexandra into the band because he loved her?

I copy-paste a formulaic response to yet another request for an exclusive interview. Everyone seems to have forgotten Alexandra's talent is undeniable. She says she doesn't mind. It's easier to let them think she had been brought in through her connection to Marshall than to give the world the truth. It's more peaceful to be Marshall's girl than a tragically orphaned young adult who happened to have an influential family friend.

A single knock on our already open office door provides a welcome opportunity to drag my eyes away from the laptop screen.

"Oh, CJ." Kiera sounds surprised to see him. "How can I help you?"

"Hi, Kiera." CJ leans on the doorjamb and nods toward me.

Hands in his shorts pockets, black T-shirt with a V-neck hugging his toned body, and that grin. Too smug. He knows he looks irresistible. There were many times in the past where I wished he'd tone his confidence down. None of his charms were for me. Now that we're together, kind of, I smile back at him and freely enjoy the way his posing sexiness softens into the genuine joy he hides from most people.

"Are you ready to go?" he asks me.

"Sure am."

I've been waiting for tonight all week. Date night, instituted by Mr. Flirty Pants himself with a demand that there be at least one evening every week to spend together outside of work.

"That's right. You two are dating now." Kiera's eyebrows come together. "You listen to me, young man. You break Fiona's heart, and I'll have words with you. More than words. You're going to be in serious trouble."

I laugh. "Don't worry, Kiera. I have an older brother to avenge my sorrows. Besides." I shut my laptop and slide it into my shoulder bag. "CJ can't break my heart."

He did. Oh, he did so badly, but he doesn't need to know that. Not until we're engaged or at least a whole lot more serious than we are now.

"I can't?" CJ pulls a disheartened face. "You don't love me at all?"

"Who said anything about love?" I come to him and plant a light kiss in the corner of his mouth.

"Awww." Kiera's a wonderful woman, but that doesn't stop her from mocking others. "You two are too cute. Get out of here. The rest of us still have work to do. For you."

"It's six o'clock," CJ says to her. "You work too much."

"Then give me a raise."

CJ points a finger at his manager in a good-one gesture. "How about a Labor Day bonus? That's coming up soon."

"I'll take it. Now go."

"Bye." I take CJ by the upper arm and haul him out of the office. "What have you been up to today?"

"Just got out of a therapy session."

I stop in the middle of the orange-carpeted hallway. "You went to therapy?"

Unease all over his features, CJ lifts my shoulder bag and wears it himself, positioning the strap across his chest. "I wasn't joking when I brought it up last time. I really slipped, and I need to learn how to handle life if I wear myself thin again. It's been rather helpful. I feel more grounded already."

"I'm impressed." In London, when he mentioned seeking professional help, I thought he was making light of the situation. But he's serious and taking steps to get his mental health into better shape. "Good for you."

We continue on our way to the elevators, and maybe it's my adjusted perception of CJ, but he seems to stand a little taller.

"How's your day been?" he asks.

"Marshall owes me a bonus too. I'm sick of copy-pasting the same response to the media two thousand times a day." I groan in exaggerated discontent.

CJ laughs. "Let's see if tonight's dinner will cheer you up. Are you done packing? If not, I can come over and help you again."

"All done."

Xavier moved to California last week. It's become weird to be in that apartment all by myself, without Nia leaving a mark of her carefree childhood ways everywhere, so I decided to move out. When Charlie heard about it, she talked me and Elise into renting a snazzy townhouse with her on the outskirts of a college campus. Between the three of us, the rent is nice and manageable.

"Either way, I'd rather do something more fun than sorting through my belongings."

CJ pushes the elevator button and rubs his hands together. "All right. There's this one place I want to check out with you."

"I thought we were going out to dinner. I'm starving."

"Don't worry, my hungry one. There will be food." He wraps one arm around my shoulders and gives me his signature smolder.

My pulse picks up, and I breathe out slowly. "You think that works on me?"

"It does without fail. That's your favorite thing about me."

The elevator doors slide open, and CJ guides me in. And he's almost right. That suave gaze is one of *many* things I like about him.

Half an hour later, we enter one of those places that's a cafe but also a book shop, a bar, and who knows what else. Couples and groups of friends on their nights out fill the open space. The conversations are vivid and animated, but I can still hear casual piano pouring from the speakers. Scents of coffee, pastries, and French fries mix in the velvet, late summer air flowing through the open windows. This refusal to blast air conditioning is refreshing, and I weave my way to a table for two that has freed up next to one of the windows.

"Not this one. Too small." CJ nudges me toward the table nearby that can accommodate six.

"Nah-ah. I don't want to sit between the windows. I want to look out."

"Please?" CJ smiles and immediately presses his lips together.

What's with that? What is he up to? "Okay."

He helps me with the chair upholstered in short, green, faux fur then hangs my shoulder bag on a chair next to me. "I'll order us some food. What are you in the mood for?"

"Anything with an Italian flavor, sparkling water, tarts—"

"Got it." He taps my nose with his finger. "Anything and everything. I'll make it happen. You, though, don't go anywhere."

He saunters off, and I pull out my phone. Stupid habit. I place it on the table, screen down. No phones. I need to unplug. This place is just right to relax and forget about emails, social media, and whether I need to check Project Viper merchandise inventory or triple check that we're not overpaying for something for their next photo shoot.

I watch CJ order our food at the cash register. He's quick, and when he's done, he drops off the order number at our table, exhales hard as though bracing himself for something, then walks away.

"Where are you going?" I call out.

CJ looks over his shoulder and winks at me but doesn't answer. He heads to a small stage at the far wall and picks up the guitar resting on a stand next to a microphone. An older man who looks like he could be the owner, or the manager, comes up to him, they shake hands and exchange a few words, smile and nod to each other, then CJ takes a seat on the barstool.

Okay. I guess he's planning to sing.

CJ taps the microphone, and conversations hush down with great reluctance. Some people scoff at him, annoyed.

"Good evening, everyone." CJ pauses to pluck the guitar's strings to check if they're in tune. They are, and he goes on, "I'm sorry to interrupt. You don't have to listen to me at all, but I'd like to enlist your help tonight to test drive a song. Oh, but allow me to introduce myself first."

His husky voice gets a few girls to whisper to each other, eyes ablaze with recognition. I don't even try to hide a smile when I catch a few guys scowling at CJ because their dates focus all their attention on him.

"I'm CJ Sanchez from Project Viper—"

A chorus of excited gasps ripples through the establishment, and even the guys are starstruck once they connect the face with the name. Many people move closer to the front, some of them sitting down on the floor next to the stage. Phones come out and thumbs mash that camera button non-stop.

CJ and I exchange a look across the room. I shake my head, hoping he knows I think he's crazy. CJ chuckles in return.

"Like I said, I hope to try out a new song with you, if that's okay," he says and is rewarded with a wave of applause and *woo-hoo*s. After another chuckle, he adds, "Please, feel free to film or whatever and post it anywhere you like."

Too late for that permission.

"This song is called *I Should've Known Better*, and, um…" He looks at me again. "I'll just get on with it."

Soft, major chords float through the place, hushing most voices to whispers. As always, CJ's fingers weave a steady, ear-caressing melody that makes it impossible to pay attention to anything else.

Invincible,
Unbreakable,
One step ahead in every game,
I told you,
Promised you,
I had it all together and ignored the pain,

I couldn't show,
I couldn't show

Believe me when I say I saw it coming,
Forgive me for pretending it was nothing,
I should've known,
I should've known,
Better

Even though I've been on the Project Viper team for over two years now, this is the first time I'm witnessing the birth of a song. Are the lyrics about him? I'm certain of it. Could they be about us?

CJ looks at me over everyone else's heads. The somber expression that seems to seek my approval answer all my questions. Yes. This song is about everything that's happened to CJ recently, including me.

I forgot what his voice does to me. Smolders are nothing compared to the light gravel on the lower notes and breathiness on the high ones. The room grows still, along with my heart, but no, I can hear it after all, drumming along with the determined tune. There may be a few yards between us, but I feel inseparable from CJ, tied together through music and a mutual hope that everything will be okay. That we'll each become someone unbreakable, that he'll rediscover himself, and that I'll find strength to carry on with my art despite the naysayers. That we'll…

We. I've been cautious with my expectations for CJ's heart, but I want us to become something more solid. I want to mean the world to him the way he does to me. Over the course of the summer, he has become my everything. That idea of exposure therapy backfired hard. Not that I'm complaining.

The song ends with a few energetic chords, the small crowd cheers, and I kick myself for not recording this performance. The song will be forever embedded into my soul, but it would've been nice to have a reminder of this moment.

"Thank you so much, everyone." CJ gets up to bow and tries to set the guitar back on its stand, but the girls plead for more.

He shoots me a questioning glance. I shrug. It's up to him. I remember he's a musician first, and it's such a relief to see him basking on stage again. He should sing and play guitar and not worry about me.

"Okay. One more," CJ says and gets booed for that.

"How about two then?" He tries to sound reluctant, but the smile is a dead giveaway of how much he loves the haggling.

The audience demands, "Mo-o-re!"

He laughs. "All right. Three. But then I have to get back to my date. Sorry, everyone."

People twist their heads in my direction, and for the first time ever I consider what it's going to be like to be his girlfriend. *If* he asked me to be that.

A young man my age in a crispy black apron delivers three bottles of sparkling water and a long platter of bruschetta. "The rest of the food is coming soon," he promises me.

"Why the three bottles?"

"That was the order." He gives me a courteous smile before leaving.

Fine. Sooner or later I'll figure this out.

I pick up a piece of grilled bread.

"Excuse me. Are you Fiona Knight?" a man asks right as I bite into the tomato-loaded bread.

I hurry to swallow and wince at the lump of food going sideways down my throat. "And you are?" I croak out and freeze in my chair when I face him.

A tall, dark-haired man with warm brown eyes smiles at me. "I'm—"

I'd recognize him anywhere. "Erik Cho."

"All right. You must be Fiona Knight then. Do you mind if I take a seat?" He points at a chair across from me.

"I don't— Not at all, um— And yes, I'm Fiona." It's not often that I turn into a blathering dummy, but here we go. My face burns. "I'm sorry. I'm a huge fan, but what are you doing here?"

"May I?" He points at one of the bottles of water. "The flight left me parched."

"Yes, please. Help yourself." I slide the water closer to him.

Erik twists the bottle open and takes a few sips. "Actually, I am here to meet you. It seems, though, you weren't expecting me." A pleased smile appears on his lips as he glances at the stage. "I like that song."

CJ's switched to *Let's Keep It Complicated*. I also love that song, but oh my gosh! Erik Cho is sitting across from me. He came all the way from New York to see me. What is happening?

He drinks some more water then opens his briefcase—not the kind my grandpa had, but a stylish gray one with a thick black zipper and pockets for a laptop and other day-to-day essentials—and lifts out a black binder.

My heart stops abruptly when I spy a leather cord and a sticky residue on the front of the binder left from a beautiful but cheap sticker of a narwhal I used to have there. "Oh no."

Erik's forehead creases in concern. "Is there a problem?"

"How do you—"

I twist a paper napkin into a tight, shredding knot. That CJ.

He said he sent my sketches to the States because he didn't want anything to happen to them. He did send them back home, all right, only not for safekeeping. He sent them to Erik Cho.

Not knowing what to say or do, I remain silent, and Erik has no choice but to talk.

"So." He opens my binder and spreads out a few sketches. "Tell me about these. I had zero context when I looked through them. Only that, 'Hey man, check 'em out. They're pretty dope. Can you do something to get them out there?'"

The way he quotes the sender would be hilarious on any other day, but I stick the drawings back into the binder and tie the whole thing with as much force as I can. I probably will have to cut the leather cord later. No. No, I won't. I'll burn the whole thing. My most personal observations of my life with the band... My whole body throbs from humiliation. If I ever got to show my work to Erik Cho, this cheesy collection of sappy stories about the band would not be it.

"They're nothing," I mutter when I find my ability to speak again. "Just a bunch of doodles. I'm the band's manager's assistant, so I get to be with them a lot. I love to draw, and I draw what I see, and—" I exhale. "I'm sorry for wasting your time with these."

Erik drums his fingers, slowly, against the tabletop. "You're not proud of them?"

"Well, I don't hate them, but—"

"Would you rather I came across this for your submission?"

He sticks his hand into his briefcase once more and produces a spiral-bound version of *Dimensions of Darkness*.

"I got this from your agent. CJ said you've been passed for a publishing contract in favor of Kat Runn. With my connections, it wasn't hard to find out who got tossed aside for their story to happen," he explains before I even open my mouth to ask anything. "Want to tell me about this project?"

CJ drops on a chair next to me. "Hey, Erik. Glad you made it. Sorry I couldn't introduce you."

Erik smiles. "You didn't need to. She knew who I was the moment she saw me."

I look between the two men, then stomp on CJ's toes under the table. "How do you know each other?"

"Marshall and my younger brother are at the same university doing the same art history degree," Erik says. "I lived in Portland until about two years ago. We used to hang out with Project Viper all the time back in the day."

That must've been before I got hired to help Kiera because I would've known the guys are hanging out with Erik Awesome Cho otherwise.

"That's how you had that early sketch of the banished vampire queen," I say to CJ.

He winks at me. "It's been hanging on my corkboard of cool stuff for ages."

How didn't it occur to me to ask where the sketch came from? I assumed he bought it, and the Vipers had this connection this whole time.

I rotate my shoulders to chase away an odd tension that settles at the thought. It's not anger, not frustration, and not foolishness either. Or maybe it's all three. Had I known they're in cahoots with someone like Erik, I would've used that—

No. I know myself. I wouldn't use that to my advantage. I would've wanted to ask for help but wouldn't.

"How's it going so far?" CJ stuffs his face with bruschetta, unaware of my world tilting off its axis.

"Fiona was about to tell me about her *Dimensions of Darkness.*"

My shock subsides enough to morph into confusion.

"You already saw the blurb and the query and everything. My agent submitted it to your company. You passed, remember?" I exclaim, all of the frustration with the publishing industry exploding on poor Erik, and hide my face behind my hands. "I'm so sorry. It's just that I've—"

Erik finishes my sentence. "Been rejected too many times?"

I nod, fingers still pressed to my eyes.

CJ places his hand, lightly, on top of my thigh, as if saying, *You're okay.*

Erik clears his throat. "I didn't know you submitted to my imprint. I don't see most of the submissions. A couple of my partners oversee all incoming projects because if I took care of those along with everything else I have to do, nothing would get done. I trust them to make the right choice. In your case, unfortunately, it translated to being rejected. I'm sorry."

I lower my hands. "You really have nothing to apologize for."

"The thing is, your *Dimensions of Darkness* was rejected. It's great, but it's not quite baked. We can make it awesome, though. I think it'll work well for our digital-only collection."

Not quite baked. Digital only. We can make it.

Does that mean…?

Erik slides a yellow paper folder toward me.

Holding my breath, I open it. The top line of the first sheet inside reads, *Offer of Contract.* I snap the folder shut, afraid to believe my eyes.

"I won't rescind the offer," Erik says with a slight disgruntled edge to his tone. "What happened to you wasn't cool. I don't do that to my artists."

His artists.

CJ shakes my shoulders. "Fiona, say something!"

I wiggle away and glare at him. "How dare you send my stuff without my permission! And lie to me about it?"

He shrinks back. "That was the last lie. I promise."

"I will kill you," I hiss.

Chuckling, Erik asks me, "Do you want me to get in touch with your agent, then?"

"Yes." I bite my lip, hesitation claiming me all of a sudden. What if— No. He said his word is solid. "Yes. And thank you. It means so much to me."

Erik starts helping himself to the food. "I know. I've been there too. These days, people look at me and think, *That lucky jerk*. They get so surprised when I remind them I started my career drawing high school play posters and designing Christmas cards."

That's right. I forgot about that too.

I allow myself to relax enough to smile. I am going to be a published artist after all.

CJ takes my hand under the table and gives it an encouraging squeeze. I try to come up with something nice to say. He's the one who made this happen after all, but my heart's too full.

He grins. "Go ahead. Hug me like you did last time you got good news. Remember? Squealing and so on?"

First, I smack him on the upper arm, then throw my arms around him and whisper in his ear, "Thank you." He can have a kiss on the cheek, too, for that. For now. When it's just us again, he can have a real one.

When I move away, CJ swipes his hair away from his face. The gesture is rather shy, and he avoids meeting my eyes. I managed to make the incurable flirt CJ Sanchez blush? Today's full of victories.

Erik clears his throat and reminds us about his presence. "What do you want to do with these?" He points at my Project Viper binder.

"I don't know."

He gives me another yellow folder. "Consolidate them, make a coherent narrative, add more, engage a group of fans to get feedback, and I'll print them. You'll get fifty percent royalties and full rights."

My mouth drops. "Full rights with fifty percent royalties? What about the band? What do you get?" Never mind that he, for some unknown reason, wants to publish a graphic novel about a rock band. He deals with sci-fi and fantasy and time travel.

"That's how I'm paying back for the Tangs investing in me. Plus, it'll sell like crazy. My ten percent will be nothing to sneeze at."

I don't know whether to laugh or cry or roll my eyes. The Tangs invested in Erik Cho. There's nothing and no one they're not involved with.

Erik takes out his phone. "Let me set up a meeting between you, me, and your agent. Could you fly out to New York for a couple of days? I'll foot the bill, of course."

My phone dings with an event invite—a meeting at Speech Bubble Publishing in two weeks. Immediately after, Callie sends me a text.

    Call me ASAP. I MEAN IT!

Unblinking, I stare at the text. My publishing deal is happening after all.

"But don't expect me to be easy on you," Erik warns. "You may feel like I'm your genie right now, but I'm strict and expect consistent quality, on time, no excuses. You might have to quit your job. Two projects will leave you very little time to sleep."

I check with CJ.

Erik gets up. "I need to make a phone call, and you two seem to need to talk without me."

As soon as he leaves, I blurt out, "What do I do? I can't quit my job. I still have to pay the bills, and I love to work with you guys. But this is an opportunity I can't pass."

CJ places his hands on my shoulders. "If you quit your job, you won't stop being part of the Viper family. Perhaps we can figure out an advance on Project Viper origin story comics. Or, and don't rip my head off for suggesting this, I could take care of my girlfriend while she settles into her new life."

The rest of our food comes, including the best looking apple tart I've seen in a long time.

"That was a great little show," the waiter says to CJ.

My date beams. "Glad you enjoyed it. Thanks for having me."

Would the waiter go away already? Of course not. They have to take a picture, and the delay winds my nerves up.

Girlfriend.

Here it is—something tangible.

We're officially a couple.

CJ scoots his chair closer after the waiter finally departs. "So. What do you think? Can I be your…investor for a while?"

I cringe. That's what he wants to talk about after sealing our relationship status? "I'd rather not. I don't want you to support me. You don't owe me anything. I'll figure it out."

He purses his lips to the side and gives me a mild glare that warns me he's more than ready to argue. "I spent who knows how much on stupid things like jewelry, cars, and designer handbags. Let me help you. Let me put money to good use. At least part of the way?"

When he puts it like that.

I stack my binder and the contracts in front of me. This can't be real.

It is.

Also, I'm here with the guy I thought could never, would never be mine.

"We'll see how it goes." I relent, a little. "If I have to quit my job, you can assist me. Depending on how desperate I get. I prefer the idea of an advance."

"Fair enough. One more thing." He fishes in his side pocket for a while, then offers me a…

I gape at the ring, heart leaping against my ribs. Is he proposing? We haven't even said I love you to each other yet.

"Are you crazy?" I exclaim at last, unable to look away from the silver band etched with a black pattern.

He frowns at first, then grins. "Relax, Fiona. Just a couple's ring.

Cheap silver at that. I'm practicing commitment here. I like you. I…"
He draws a staggered breath, takes my hand, and slides the ring onto
my finger, then leans in until our noses almost touch. "I think I'm
even in love with you."

I place my hands on the back of his neck and press my lips against
his in a deep kiss, forgetting where I am, the food, the contracts on
the table. Everything. CJ's hands encircle my waist, and he kisses me
back without care for who will see us. We'll probably end up on social
media like this. Whatever.

But I do break off the sweltering kiss before it goes beyond publicly
appropriate levels. CJ slumps back in his chair with relief that could
only be proportional to me sparing him of a death sentence.

I fan my face with my hand a couple of times. "Where's your ring?"

CJ lifts his hand, and there it is. A wide silver band with a black
snake etched around it.

I examine my ring closer. The black pattern I've spotted earlier
is a matching snake. Vipers and their loyalty to serpents will never
fade. Fine with me. It's a cool ring. "I remember someone saying that
cutesy couple's rings were for other people, boyfriend."

"Hey! Don't mock my new title. I've never been a
boyfriend before—"

"Never?"

"Never. I love it." Once again, he wraps an arm around me and
squeezes hard. "I love you."

My heart was already in the Jell-O state, but those three simple
words and him being all cuddly do me in all the way. I lean against
him, pressing my nose to his warm neck and inhaling that CJ scent
of ocean waves and tropical sunsets. "And I love you."

"Thank goodness. I thought you were merely tolerating me
because you work for me."

I make a face at him and get busy with my apple tart.

"Are you ready to take over the world with your imminently illustrious publishing career?" He shakes my shoulders again, acting a whole lot more excited than I am.

"Yes! So ready." I take a huge bite.

"Good." He pulls over the contracts. "May I?"

I swallow. "Knock yourself out." I have a feast to eat in honor of, well, everything.

"I have more songs," CJ says quietly. "We've been recording all week like insane."

A different kind of happiness surfaces from the joyful cocktail of emotions inside me. "Not garbage?"

"Not garbage. Chart-topping stuff." He gives me a sly, sideways glance.

"Who's ready to take over the world now?" Resting my elbow on the table, I offer him my hand.

CJ laughs and clasps it tight. "You're the best, you know that?"

"You're not too bad either."

He glares, but the smile is still there, so it's no use. I laugh again.

Who's ready to take over the world?

We are.

The End

Thank you for reading!

Enjoyed this book? If you have a minute, please leave a review on Amazon, Goodreads, BookBub, or a reader's platform of your choice. Other than buying a book, reviews are the next best thing to help authors support their careers.

You can also post a review on social media and tag #projectviper to spread the word.

RELUCTANT HEARTBREAKERS *& SWEET* TROUBLEMAKERS

   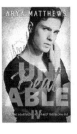 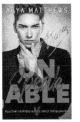

unREASONable (vol. 1 - Marshall - vocals)

unBREAKable (vol. 2 - CJ - lead guitar)

unSUSTAINable (vol. 3 - Shane - rhythm guitar)

unBEATable (vol. 4 - Graham - drums)

unSPEAKable (vol. 5 - Zach - keyboard)

Acknowledgments

As you probably already know, we couldn't have done this alone. Frankly speaking, we are so very happy we didn't have to.

Our biggest thank you goes to our families. Always. We're sure you understand why. They see the best, the worst, and everything in between. And they make us cookies.

The rest of our acknowledgments don't go in any particular order. Everyone's important, even essential in our writing process, and we feel truly blessed to share this journey with so many amazing, kind, helpful, generous people.

Our writing buddies and a whole lot of friends who encourage us through reading, critiquing, and texting late in the evening when our brains melt from creative anxiety. Tanya, Sarah, Briana, Jessica, Paige, Jennifer, Peyton, F.C., Sara, Tasha, Francesca, and so many, many others.

Our encouraging editor, Lynda D, who doesn't cringe at all the insanity we cram into our stories and helps us polish our beasts of imagination into readable words.

The readers. You wonderful, wonderful believers in gems hidden between the lines of copious text, behind obscure covers, and vague titles. Thank you for flipping to that first page. Thank you for your time. Thank you for making all of this possible with your purchases, library loans, social media shares, telling your friends, and everything else you do for us. When we say we couldn't have done this without you, we promise you, it's true.

Thank you.

~ Arya

About the Author

Arya Matthews is a husband-and-wife creative duo that codes web applications by day and molds their snippets of imagination into stories by night.

We chase two kids, play guitars, can't pass up a bag of Sweet Chili and Sour Cream chips at the supermarket, and dream of Tokyo ever since we went on a vacation there three years ago.

Website and newsletter: www.aryamatthews.com
Instagram: @arya_matthews_author
Facebook: www.facebook.com/amatthewsrockstarromance
Say "hello" or questions: hello@aryamatthews.com

Playlist

DREAMERS "Painkiller"

Relient K "Devastation and Reform"

Shinedown "THE HUMAN RADIO"

Art Of Dying "Best I Can"

VIA Gra "Сумасшедший"

Vicci Martinez "Come Along"

Take That "Shine"

Saint Motel "A Good Song Never Dies"

Churchill "Change"

Daughtry "Heavy Is The Crown"

The All-American Rejects "Can't Take It"

Franz Ferdinand "Take Me Out"

Plan Three "When Everything Comes To An End"

Poets of the Fall "Moonlight Kissed"

Jay Smith "White Wedding"

Post Malone "Take What You Want (feat. Ozzy Osbourne & Travis Scott)"

5 Seconds of Summer "Castaway"

AFI "Death of the Party"

Collective Soul "AYTA (Are You The Answer)"

Relient K "Which to Bury; Us or the Hatchet?"

Andy Black "We Don't Have To Dance"

Godsmack "Under Your Scars"

Barenaked Ladies "Did I Say That Out Loud?"

Young Rising Sons "Undefeatable"

Walk Off The Earth "Fire In My Soul"
My Chemical Romance "Famous Last Words"
Shinedown "State of My Head"
TheFatRat & RIELL "Hiding In The Blue"
Shakira "Empire"
The Amazons "Fuzzy Tree"

Printed in Great Britain
by Amazon

87684785R00157